D0521999

COMHAIRLE CHONTAE ÁTHA CLIATH THEAS
SOUTH DUBLIN COUNTY LIBRARIES

CLONDALKIN BRANCH LIBRARY
TO RENEW ANY ITEM TEL: 459 3315
OR ONLINE AT www.southdublinlibraries.ie

Items should be returned on or before the last date below. Fines, as displayed in the Library, will be charged on overdue items.

HAPPY LITTLE BLUEBIRDS

Happy Little Bluebirds

Louise Levene

BLOOMSBURY PUBLISHING
LONDON · OXFORD · NEW YORK · NEW DELHI · SYDNEY

BLOOMSBURY PUBLISHING
Bloomsbury Publishing Plc
50 Bedford Square, London, WC1B 3DP, UK

BLOOMSBURY, BLOOMSBURY PUBLISHING and the Diana logo
are trademarks of Bloomsbury Publishing Plc

First published in Great Britain 2018

"Somewhere Over the Rainbow" Words and Music by E Harburg
and Harold Arlen © 1938, Reproduced by permission of EMI Feist
Catalogue, London W1F 9LD

A catalogue record for this book is available from the British Library

ISBN: HB: 978-1-4088-7877-4; TPB: 978-1-4088-9647-1
eBook: 978-1-4088-7878-1

2 4 6 8 10 9 7 5 3 1

Typeset by Integra Software Services Pvt. Ltd.
Printed and bound in Great Britain by CPI Group (UK) Ltd, Croydon CR0 4YY

To find out more about our authors and books visit www.bloomsbury.com
and sign up for our newsletters

For Clement Crisp

Chapter 1

Monday 30 September 1940

'I'D NO IDEA *anyone* actually spoke Polish,' the girl was saying. 'Apart from Poles, obviously. The customs chap looked awfully surprised. Whatever on earth made you learn?'

She didn't stay for an answer but began shoving her bags alongside Evelyn in the back of the waiting car.

'Budge up.'

Evelyn edged along the wide seat and the girl closed the door and leaned forward to instruct the uniformed driver who was wiping his mouth on his handkerchief as he wedged the pungent remains of a sandwich into the glove compartment.

'No mad hurry, Carson, the Chicago train doesn't leave until five so we may as well let Mrs Murdoch enjoy the scenic route: head north along Broadway, through the Park and down Fifth. Jolly good.' She turned to Evelyn with a stillborn smile then gripped her fingers in a well-practised handshake.

'Genista Broome. HQ have detailed me to shepherd you across town and generally get you up to speed.'

Genista Broome was a lot younger than Evelyn had anticipated and affected the kind of flashy glamour she had noticed among the Americans on the ship: a showy brooch on her lapel, glossy nut-brown hair rolled in

1

permanent curls beneath her hat and enough scent to fumigate a church jumble sale – hardly businesslike.

The smell of perfume combined unpleasantly with the prevailing fog of Swiss cheese and German sausage in the limousine's interior. Still queasy from her voyage, Evelyn felt for the folded paper bag in her pocket as she sniffed the air: Jicky. Her late mother had worn it. Evelyn's father, a Methodist minister, had disapproved of scent but he had liked the smell of flowers and so his wife had filled the vases with violets or jasmine or nicotiana and then sprinkled a matching fragrance on her handkerchiefs depending on the season, hiding the bottles behind her underthings. Jicky was what she wore at lavender time. Evelyn's husband Silas had had the same Wesleyan horror of adornment and had not liked women to wear scent, or earrings, or eye-black ('You would not be at such pains were none to see you but God and His holy angels', as John Wesley was so fond of saying). Nine months since his death Evelyn still could not break the habit of imagining Silas beside her, seeing all she saw.

Genista Broome was what Silas would have called 'light-minded'. She seemed to have used her exeat from the office as an excuse for a shopping trip and was now fretting over the bags and parcels while dispensing a steady stream of pleasantries with the girlish spontaneity of a speak-your-weight machine: *nice day … surprisingly warm for the time of year … had it been an enjoyable voyage?*

Enjoyable? As if Evelyn had braved the torpedo-infested Atlantic merely for a change of air.

'Well, you got here safe and sound which is the main thing. Unlike the poor *City of Benares* – but I don't suppose they told you about any of that … Said to be rather smart, the *Mouzinho*, as that class of boat goes … And Portuguese is one of yours, isn't it? So quite social?'

'My spoken Portuguese is pretty rudimentary, I'm afraid, but hardly any of the passengers actually hailed from Lisbon itself. In any case, I spent most of the passage in my cabin.'

'Oh dear, what a shame.' The girl lit a cigarette, adding petrol fumes to the fug. '*Mal du mer.*'

'*De* mer, not *du* mer,' corrected Evelyn before she could stop herself. 'The memo said to keep a low profile and the public rooms were extremely crowded. Refugees, I think. Jews mostly –' Genista Broome's nose wrinkled in sympathy '– most of them were ferried off to the island place before the rest of us could disembark. It took forever but luckily – as you saw – I was fished out of the crush in the customs shed by some chap in uniform or I'd be there still. Wasn't even searched –' Evelyn nodded in the direction of her suitcase on the front seat. 'I might have had anything in there.'

'What happened to your trunk? Carson here looked everywhere but it appears to have gone AWOL.'

'They said to keep personal effects to a minimum. There was talk of a berth on a submarine at one point …'

'Golly. What have you got in there, anyway? Two nighties, a Hungarian phrasebook and a pound of finest Ceylon? It can't hold much more, surely? Ah well, not to worry. Lots to get through –' She looked at her wristwatch. 'The original plan was to debrief you over at HQ but we reckoned without the huddled masses slowing everything down and queering the timetable.'

She opened her pocketbook and produced a slim deck of buff-coloured index cards.

'Now, while I remember: you will need to fill in one of these.' She handed Evelyn an official-looking form. 'New thing: you need to register as an alien with a post office within the next thirty days: height, weight, fingerprints, all that. Purely a formality, we've all had to do it. There's a bit asking whether you've had anything to do with "organisations devoted to furthering the political activities of foreign governments", which you haven't, so you can tick "have not" with a clear conscience. And you have signed the you-know-what, haven't you? London said you had.'

Evelyn nodded and the other woman lowered her voice to a mutter barely audible above the thunder of Eighth Avenue traffic.

'You'll have to leave the address bit blank for the moment, I'm afraid. The thing is …' she looked embarrassed '… there's been a bit of a mix-up. A few months ago our Colonel Peyton from HQ chummed up with this Anglo-Hungarian film chap and spent quite a bit of time over in Hollywood in hopes of getting him to help out on the propaganda front. You didn't hear me say that, obviously: they take their neutrality very seriously over here; one whiff of any of this and Saucy and his film-producer friend would be back in Blighty before you could say Un-American Activities.'

'Saucy?'

'Colonel Peyton. Henry Percival Peyton.'

Evelyn looked blank.

'HP? Like the sauce? Anyway, the chap said he'd play ball and so Saucy took to whizzing back and forth to Los Angeles seeing how the land lay. This was all well and good up to a point but Saucy soon spotted that those studio men won't give you the time of day if you drive your own car or answer your own telephone and said he would need some sort of aide-de-camp, preferably a linguist. Practically everyone in Hollywood hails from foreign parts and they all tend to talk amongst themselves rather, which left Saucy at something of a disadvantage. Anyhow, Kiss was all in favour – he's frightfully keen on *presteesh* as he calls it – and volunteered to hire someone at his own expense.'

'Kiss?'

'Kiss. Did London not brief you? He's a film producer, Hungarian Jew by the name of *Zan-dor Kiss*.' Each syllable handled like a caterpillar being tweezed from a salad.

'Kiss would have gone ahead and hired someone locally but Saucy wanted to be certain of their loyalty so he arranged – unofficially – to have London muck in and scan the files for a suitable polyglot – all madly unorthodox. After the usual delays, a wire was received saying that they had selected "E. Murdoch" of Postal Censorship for the task: meticulous bureaucrat; no family ties; *nine* languages. Might have known you were too good to be true but it was only when one of our Lisbon friends got in touch that we realised you weren't actually a man and by that time the *Mouzinho* was halfway to the Azores. Red faces all round.'

'I was interviewed in person by a Major Bannister,' protested Evelyn. '*Twice.*'

She smiled at the memory. After a few paper preliminaries – a German prose; translate 'Jabberwocky' into Italian; usual pedagogic larks – she had been wheeled in for personal assessment.

'However did you come by so many languages?' marvelled the Major, whose own skills were taxed by the menu at Prunier's.

'I had a knack for it,' said Evelyn. 'It became a sort of habit after a while.'

'You seem to have spent quite a bit of time *abroad*.' He looked up from her file. 'Rather unusual.'

Evelyn's unusual facility had been revealed quite by chance at the age of three when she had regaled the lunch table with all eight verses of 'Alouette'. Her late father soon discovered that a child he had hitherto found uninteresting combined a swotty willingness to memorise irregular verbs with a parrot-like ability to repeat whatever was said to her. The Reverend Charles Dent had always taken the Parable of the Talents very much to heart and felt it was incumbent on all of them to make the very most of his daughter's surprising gift. He set about teaching her Latin with the aid of a handwritten textbook of his own devising. Any mistakes and she would be made to begin at the top: '*non amatus sum, non amatus es, non amatus est*' (the romance languages were a piece of cake in comparison). Once she had outstripped his own limited mastery of French and German, he had dug out his old university address book and begun a campaign of letter-writing and for three summers in a row the young Evelyn had been packed off to the Continent to lodge with a string of Nonconformist clerics.

'I see you have a smattering of Hungarian,' said the Major. 'They're particularly keen on the Magyar angle. Spend much time in Buda?'

'Not as such. My school had a Hungarian singing teacher for a bit ...'

It was important not to overstate one's competence, Evelyn felt: Postal Censorship's recruitment officer had been plagued by optimistic applicants who assumed that their various smatterings – restaurant French; railway German – would qualify them to monitor the idiomatic scribblings of potential fifth columnists.

'I could catch a train or order a meal, I suppose.'

'We'll put you down as "conversational",' Major Bannister decided, 'though I'm sure you're being unduly modest.'

'Poor old Lefty Bannister,' sighed Genista Broome, ducking her head to check her reflection in the rear-view mirror. 'I dare say he got his wires crossed but everything's up in the air at the moment, particularly now that Saucy has had to toddle off to Bermuda.'

'Doing what?'

'Classified – or at least I *assume* it's classified: nobody told *me*.'

'And when will the Colonel be back?'

'Search me. You'll have to play it by ear until we have a clearer idea of his movements, but he should be joining you once he's got things up and running. The powers that be this end were all for sending you straight back when they found out you weren't a man but Kiss persuaded them that a female linguist might actually be a better bet *vis-à-vis* lurking on the sidelines at a film studio asking stupid questions. Flirtation can be a lot more effective than the third degree ...'

The girl ran an appraising eye over Evelyn's mannish, pavement-grey suit and Evelyn caught her suppressing a small smile before turning to gaze out at the theatre-lined street, the names of plays and players twinkling bright in the deepening dusk. The streetlights gave a jaundiced cast to Genista Broome's prettified face: cheeks thickly powdered, eyebrows pencilled into permanent parabolas of astonishment. The girl had slathered colour over the natural edges of her mouth to make it appear fuller than it was – the way film actresses did. The effect was intended to be voluptuous but the impressionistic brushwork simply made it look as though she'd painted her face in the dark.

Evelyn's sister-in-law Deborah back in Woking kept her make-up next to her siren suit on her night table and would smear on lipstick as they dashed out to the air-raid shelter whenever the warning sounded, blotting her mouth with one hand and wrenching off her hairnet and clips with the other as she, Evelyn and their elderly mother-in-law ('the Outlaw', Deborah always called her) scurried down the garden path. 'I'm *damned* if I'll be found dead with curlers in.' Woking had so far survived unscathed, although there had been a major raid on an aircraft factory in Weybridge which, as old Mrs Murdoch was quick to point out, was only a bus ride away.

'The original plan,' the Broome female was saying, 'was for *Mister* Evelyn Murdoch to bunk up with HP in the bachelor bolthole Kiss leased for him near the studio. That's obviously no go now but Kiss's people are on the case. You'll get further gen on all that between trains tomorrow afternoon.'

The girl rummaged once again in her pocketbook and extracted a cardboard wallet containing two sets of train tickets.

'You reach La Salle station at around eight tomorrow morning, if memory serves. The Super Chief won't leave until gone seven so you've a room booked for the day at a nearby hotel where you will be met at eleven hundred hours by our man in Chicago who will complete your induction: fair hair; English tailor; contact word: "dandelion" – Lord alone knows why.

'You'll have a couple of hours before our chap joins you so you might as well take the opportunity for a few running repairs. There's a beauty parlour in the hotel; Alphonse is the top man – if you can get him. There probably won't be time for a wave ...' She frowned doubtfully at the bale of hair beneath Evelyn's hat. 'And you'll want a manicure –' she gave a complacent glance at her own scarlet fingertips '– although there's usually a woman on the train. Your steward will know.

'It's good form to keep all your receipts but it's all Kiss cash so you won't have to answer in triplicate to the accounts bods. If anyone gives you any trouble about anything on the trains or at the hotel just *keep tipping* until they sort it out. Demented system but you will be *a-mazed* at the difference a well-placed gratuity can make in the

Land of the Free: service with a *lick*. Don't forget about the manicure: they really mind about that kind of thing. And get them to do something with the eyebrows.'

Evelyn opened her mouth to protest but the girl had barely paused for breath. Evelyn might prefer to take her meals in the privacy of her compartment (the club sandwiches were very good) but if she were to head off to the dining car – Evelyn *mustn't* take this the wrong way – she might want to make use of the built-in shower thingy beforehand.

'Americans are frightfully hot on personal freshness.' She wrinkled her nose. 'One becomes rather sensitised oneself after a bit.'

Evelyn, half-suffocated by the car's excessive heat, pressed her thick woollen sleeves to her sides.

'If by any ghastly chance you get buttonholed by fellow passengers – they are the nosiest people on God's earth, *constantly* inviting one to things – crank up the accent and say that you are taking up a position in voice culture – brown cows, you know the stuff – but only divulge if *seriously* pressed. Never, *ever*, volunteer information and for God's sake, keep the old parley-voo under your hat.'

A street-corner hoarding with a gaily coloured daub of sunbeams and palm trees shouted 'See America First! Visit California: The Land of Winter Sunshine'. A road sign up ahead read 'Grand Central Station 1 ½ miles' and Evelyn realised with a surge of panic that in all this talk of taxis and manicures she had been given no inkling of what her duties were to be. It could hardly be a translation job; America must be teeming with suitably qualified *émigrés*.

'But what do I actually *do* once I get there if Colonel Peyton is still in Bermuda? How can I be an assistant if there's no one there to assist?'

The girl became still more evasive – perhaps she too had been kept in the dark?

'He's due back any day now … probably. And if he isn't I should just lie back and enjoy it, if I were you. Smile and wave, as my mama always says. I'm sure the studio can find something to keep you occupied in the meantime …'

She took refuge in her index cards.

'Now then –' a tape measure and a stub of pencil were produced from her pocket '– I don't know what you've managed to cram into that toy suitcase of yours but Mr Kiss doesn't want you letting the side down. Sit up straight.'

It seemed that an operative from Kiss's Hollywood office was going to be sent on a mercy dash to a Los Angeles department store the instant HQ rang through with Evelyn's weights and measures.

'Thirty-eight, call it thirty-four to allow for the tweed. Shoe size? Brassieres? Stockings? Gloves? Hat size? Hats aren't *de rigueur* in California as a rule but older women still wear them.' The insult was all the more wounding for being entirely unintentional.

'Take your lead from the other women in the studio but when in doubt think Côte d'Azur rather than Café Royal … if that helps at all' – another pitying smirk at Evelyn's ensemble. 'The studio's little shopping spree will be waiting at whatever billet they've found for you; in the meantime, Kiss's New York office have supplied some light camouflage – the man's grasp of detail is remarkable.' She yanked a shiny lavender-coloured carrier bag on to her box-pleated lap. 'There's a rather lovely lucky dip in here: a pair of dark glasses, some jolly smart gloves, various bits and bobs you might find useful …' She began to go rather red in the face. 'You'll see that they've – er – tried to anticipate all eventualities … and I've slipped in a couple of last week's newspapers to get you up to speed.'

She snapped a gold watch on to Evelyn's wrist then pulled out a red kid pocketbook and, unasked, began decanting the contents of Evelyn's handbag. 'You'll find plenty of ready money in the wallet.'

The other, larger carrier bag contained a matched pair of silver foxes which she draped around Evelyn's neck and secured by getting one of the animals to bite hard on the hip of its twin. Evelyn jerked her chin away as a diamond pin was attached to her lapel.

'The jewels aren't for keeps, obviously, but the furs will make a nice souvenir when it all ends in tears.'

'Surely it would be better to blend into the background in my own things? I do *have* clothes, Miss Broome,' said Evelyn. 'I've brought a smart frock – two frocks.'

Genista Broome ignored her protests and sat back in her seat to admire the effect of her handiwork.

'Look –' She gestured towards the women dashing along the rainy avenue with their gay umbrellas, dodging puddles in their high-heeled shoes. A fashionably dressed matron, clearly visible beneath a brightly lit awning, was waiting for the doorman to whistle up a taxi. A collar of white fur framed her face like the ruff on a surplice, a sky-blue felt hat shaped like a child's paper boat breasted yellow waves of hair. Evelyn watched as a tall man standing behind her leaned down to plant a fond kiss on the side of her neck, nuzzling at the fur as he did so.

'Think of all this as *uniform*, Mrs Murdoch; you can't wear civvies here. We're talking Wilshire Boulevard, not Woking. You could wear Albanian national dress and sport a lizard on a lead and no one would bat an eyelid once a major studio like Miracle had put you on the payroll. What they don't do is *dowdy* – not on a woman, anyway. Men, *Englishmen*, can get away with anything: holey socks; elbow patches; *beards* even. The Yanks are always

11

a pushover for donnish disarray, Evelyn Murdoch *Esquire*, however dishevelled, would have had a certain bohemian allure, but on an untidy woman it just looks downtrodden, neurotic even. Believe me, you would stop traffic in Beverly Hills dressed the way you are with an unpainted face. You would look like a mad person, or a communist, foreign; in short: *noticeable, a spy*. Precisely what HQ don't want. Do you understand? Jolly good. By the way, do you have any training in self-defence? Pity. Talking of which, can you dance at all?'

'I've waltzed ...' said Evelyn.

'Ah. Not to worry.' She scribbled 'Rumba?' on the back of a card.

Evelyn slipped her new gloves from their cellophane bag. Red. Not a colour Silas would have chosen ('Wear nothing which is of a glaring colour, or which is gay, glistening or showy; nothing apt to attract the eyes of bystanders'). She began pinching the unstretched leather over her knuckles. The surface was astonishingly smooth and she delayed tackling the second glove while her fingertips caressed the back of the first ('Let your dress be cheap as well as plain; otherwise you do but trifle with God').

The driver had pulled up outside the limestone arches of the railway station.

Genista Broome wore a special puzzled face while she frisked her pockets to see if she had forgotten anything – a pumpkin? Half a dozen white mice? – and eventually produced a small cream-coloured envelope – 'Mrs Silas Murdoch. Box No. 541, London WC' – which she tucked into Evelyn's jacket pocket.

'As Lefty doubtless explained, Kiss's personal mail comes from London by air courier and anything addressed to you at his box number will be sent along with it – uncensored, obviously. Lucky you.'

Her final trick was to whisk off Evelyn's cloche and flip the lid from the hatbox where a wigwam of crimson felt was nesting in a drift of snowy tissue paper.

'Get your hat on, Mrs Murdoch. It's showtime.'

Evelyn pinned the stupid thing to her head then got out of the car and peered dubiously at what she could see of her reflection in the wing mirror. She poked at the tilt of the hat.

'It's ridiculous.'

'It's back to front.'

They had fewer than thirty minutes to spare but Genista Broome showed no sense of urgency and steered Evelyn over to one of the news-stands and began whisking titles from the racks.

'Magazines are a great deterrent.'

When they finally reached the tunnel leading to their platform they found the orderly flow of passengers for the 20th Century Limited had been dammed by a large party of young girls who were clustered around the polished wooden desks, yapping at the ticket inspectors. Genista Broome's beady eyes scanned the small crowd and spotted two men: one bald, the other young and flaxen-haired. The bald one raised his hat.

'Damn!'

She seized Evelyn's arm and began talking very loudly in a peculiar, faintly Bostonised accent.

'Be sure and enjoy Chicago, darling!'

'Is something the matter?'

'Krauts at six o'clock,' she hissed, turning up her coat collar.

A fourth-form Evelyn had once been thrown on as understudy for the manservant in *The Importance of Being Earnest* and her companion's keen amateur manner and her own complete failure to respond correctly to a

13

single cue brought the cucumber sandwiches flooding back.

The girl leaned in for a goodbye peck on the cheek.

'Act natural, for heaven's sake!'

Evelyn ducked her head and tried to get a look at the men from beneath her new red hat. Was she being followed? Should there be a change of plan? Was there a Plan B to change to? And what was HQ's telephone number? But before she could ask a single question the smiling girl had planted another powdery farewell on her cheek and with a parting shot – 'Enjoy it while it lasts!' – she was gone.

Chapter 2

B ACK AT THE OFFICE, Genista Broome drew a cup of
tea from the fast-cooling urn, reached for one of
her telephones and put in a request for a trunk call
to Los Angeles. Her colleague, Gregory Fenn, was still at
his desk but the other tables were deserted.

'Where is everybody?'

'I expect they probably have homes to go to. I've still
got the last post to sort. Besides, this way I avoid the crush
on the subway – always a bit of a bind with a gammy leg.
How was your Mrs Murdoch?'

'She isn't *my* Mrs Murdoch.'

'Afraid she is, old girl. We all drew lots and you lost.'

'Well that doesn't make her *mine*. It would have been so
much better if you'd gone to fetch her.'

'Why? You're the one who knows the ropes. You've
been out there, after all.'

'Only for five minutes.' Genista Broome frowned and
changed the subject. 'I wish you could have seen her.
This is never *ever* going to work. I don't care how many
languages she speaks. Postal censorship? By all means.
Code-breaking? Very possibly. Malibu Mata Hari? Never
in a million years. She'll be back in New York before you
can say "sensible shoes". And she'll *never* pass muster with
those Hollywood snobs – called me "*Miss* Broome", if you
can believe it.'

Gregory Fenn palmed a smile.

'Oh dear. How galling for you. No sense having a title if people don't use it. We must get you a lapel pin – or a dog collar. Such a jolly name, too. And yours for life, of course, unless you marry a royal duke or take the veil. I mean, even if you married the dustman you'd still be *Lady* Genista Bloggs, wouldn't you? If you went into parliament would you be "the Honourable Lady Lady"? What do they call Nancy Astor?'

'All sorts of things.'

'Anyway, was that your only objection to our polyglot pal? Not everyone has *Debrett's* as their bedtime reading, you know. Was she nice to know? What was she wearing?'

Lady Genista had never learned to spot when she was being taken for a ride and Gregory Fenn chewed on another smile as she began a gleeful commentary on the new signing's toilette.

'Stood out like a nun at Newmarket: sixteen-ounce herringbone tweed: tan Oxfords; home-cut hair and a dead hat – at least I *think* it was a hat – and a suitcase the size of a shoe box. She claims to have two frocks in it. Probably both brown.'

'Oh dear. But nice and discreet at least?'

'Not especially. She was showing off at the pier until I shut her up – actually thanked the customs-shed man in Polish.'

'Didn't know you knew any Polish.'

'Only "thank you". Our governess made us: Russian, Slovene, Armenian, Bulgarian. Manners cost nothing, apparently.'

'Any of the chums about when you saw her off?'

Lady Genista bit her lip.

'That chap from the German legation was at the barrier seeing off one of his catamites.'

'Oh dear. Were you seen, do you think?'

'I spotted him in time,' she lied, 'and my hair's quite different now.'

'But if he *did* see you then the Murdoch woman's cover is blown before she even starts.'

'I'm sure he didn't. We did a whole flowers and chocolates act on the platform and I changed my voice. Besides they wouldn't be expecting a woman – always supposing they were expecting anybody – and Langer's people have never been especially efficient. It did actually say "Esquire" on the *Mouzinho*'s manifest, which was a help.'

A courier arrived with the evening's dispatches and, as Fenn turned away to sign for them, Lady Genista slid a biscuit from the box concealed in her desk drawer – offer them round and you got through a packet a day.

Fenn picked up the mailbag and limped across the office to the wall of pigeonholes behind his colleague's desk.

'Has Colonel Peyton been given the glad tidings?'

'HP doesn't know a blind thing about it,' she snapped, 'because HP, typically, has far bigger fish to fry and buzzed off to Bermuda before London's cable had even been decoded. He's setting up that new mail-interception unit.'

Fenn rested his walking stick against the side of her desk and took the relevant flimsy from its folder: SUBJECT DOUBLEPLUS ABLE LINGUIST STOP WIDOW DENTIST STOP NO FAMILY TIES STOP DISCREET RELIABLE HIGHLY INTELLIGENT ZERO NONSENSE STOP.

'Zero nonsense,' sighed Fenn. 'Oh dear. What fun it all sounds. You ought to put in a report about spotting Langer just now, cover your tracks, or you might find yourself getting blamed for the whole fiasco. Whose fault is it, in actual fact?'

'Do you remember HP getting cosy with that film-producer person at the Fourth of July beano we all had to go to? Zandor Kiss.'

'Is that a name you made up?'

'Oh do keep up. Kiss: large white moustache; Hungarian; did that Florence Nightingale thing Churchill liked so much?' Her colleague still looked blank. 'You *do* remember.'

Fenn shook his head. 'Probably when I was away at the vet's having the knee mended.'

'Well anyway, he and HP got chatting about the need to win over the Yanks and the next thing you know the Colonel decided they should join forces. He spent a week or so out West spreading the good word (this was all before Bermuda) and next thing you know Mr Kiss – who appears to have friends in *extraordinarily* high places – persuaded the chaps upstairs to post Colonel Peyton to Los Angeles on a more permanent footing so that he could hover on the fringes and generally run his eye down the fifth column. It then dawns on Kiss that Saucy doesn't speak a word of German so he sets about supplying him with a multilingual sidekick.

'HP said we had to humour him but I think he secretly hoped that red tape in London would strangle the whole thing at birth, and we all thought we'd heard the last of it when up pops old Lefty Bannister who had been buttonholed by Kiss over drinks at Claridge's and told to jolly well get a move on. Lefty then insists on taking the entire matter in hand, conducting the interviews himself and generally riding roughshod. Within *forty-eight hours* the post had been filled and "Evelyn Murdoch" was tucked up on a ten-day boat from Lisbon all arranged at top speed at the Very Highest Level, money no object. When I suggested they might like to save a few dollars by sending him out steerage, Kiss said it would be "bad for studio *presteesh*" and insisted on a first-class cabin and deluxe drawing rooms for both trains. I thought Kiss might cut up rough when he eventually found out that "E. J. Murdoch" was a she-Evelyn rather than a he-Evelyn, but when I rang Los Angeles last Friday to break the news all he said was, "Ah yes! I remember! Fluent Hungarian."'

She glanced again at Evelyn's paperwork. '*Conversational* Hungarian, it says here – not that she has any conversation: "Leave me alone. We have not been introduced" is probably about the size of it. You'd think a linguist would at least be talkative – hardly any point otherwise.'

'What do Hungarians talk about, I wonder?' mused Fenn '"My goulash has been struck by lightning"? Are there a lot of Hungarians in California?'

'Not really. Just sentiment on Kiss's part, I reckon.' Genista Broome squinted crossly at the application form. '"Schools attended" gave nothing away sex-wise – some Nonconformist dump – but you'd have thought "Marital status: war widow" would have been some kind of clue. We fired off a rocket to London last week as soon as we realised a monumental blunder had been made, but they stuck to their guns – as you can see from that snooty cable – and Lefty said he couldn't see the difficulty, silly old fool.'

'*Is* there a difficulty?'

'Of course there's a ruddy difficulty. Our lucky linguist was due to rough it with Henry in that lovely Hollywood flat – chaps mucking in together.'

Gregory Fenn manoeuvred painfully into a chair, interest rekindled by Her Ladyship's obvious annoyance. *Henry*, eh? *Lovely flat*, was it? How did she know it was lovely? Was the departmental gossip true?

'Oh dear. Oh yes, a shared bedroom. I think I saw that movie,' he said. 'Clark Gable. Perhaps they can hang a sheet down the middle? Has Mr Kiss made suitable provision?'

'Didn't turn a hair. Said his secretary will sort something out and it *vazzn't* a problem. Nothing ever *is* a problem for those film people. They'd get a herd of buffalo if we asked nicely.' The lipsticked lips pouted. 'I wouldn't have minded if they'd sorted out someone with proper *experience.*'

'Cheer up, she'll probably be out on her ear in a fortnight if HP doesn't get back from Bermuda pretty sharpish – there's not much point her being there with nobody to translate for. She'll be completely surplus to requirements.'

'Oh I daresay Kiss could find her something to do. Overmanning is rife out there. Chap I know got a cushy little job with one of the studios just telling them what kind of armour to put on. I suppose if all else fails we can always drag her back east. The Library bods might take her: they're not particularly particular.'

'Oh I say, have a heart. I wouldn't wish the British Library of Information on my worst enemy. "Cruel and unusual punishment", I should call it. HP always says it's an elephants' graveyard for academic deadbeats and incompetents. They do nothing whatsoever except write memoranda and make tea. No one in the outside world even knows they exist. Do you know how many telephone calls they received the day war broke out? Zero.'

'Perhaps they'll just send her home.'

'They can hardly send her across the pond a second time,' reasoned Fenn. 'She only made it by the skin of her teeth as it was. Perhaps they'll take her on here? All those languages would come in very handy and there's careless talk of a reshuffle. Jolly well hope it's true. I'm hoping for promotion to Deputy Press Liaison in the FO's news department. The cove in charge can't manage the whole show alone, his liver won't stand it. *Liaison*. Doesn't it sound marvellous?'

Gregory Fenn drained his teacup and smiled at his colleague in happy anticipation of this glamorous new role.

'I do feel a bit sorry for her in a way.' Lady Genista's tone did not convince. 'There she was, minding her own business in Postal Censorship, merrily scissoring out anything *verboten*, and then this happens – but it serves her right for learning all those languages. *Eight!* Including *Yiddish*, of all things.' Lady Genista's overpainted lower lip stretched unpleasantly tight and the tendons of her neck fanned out above her collar as she exaggerated the capital 'Y'. 'You'd have thought Special Ops might have shown an interest? Perhaps her accents aren't up to snuff?'

'Ticklish blighters, accents,' agreed Fenn, 'although the real giveaway is no accent at all. Especially in Germany, apparently: Swabians, Saxons, Bavarians. They can hardly understand each other half the time.'

He took another look at the file on the desktop. '*Japanese?* Nobody, *nobody*, speaks Japanese. I even wonder if *they* do really – the Japanese, I mean. Have you tried? I was sent on a course last winter, depths of Cornwall. Hopeless.' He turned the page. 'French, German, Italian …'

'Mother half Swiss – which can't have hurt. Father was very eager (according to Lefty's notes). Quite a lot of it was done by correspondence but school hols frequently spent on the Continent.'

'Mis-spent?'

'Doubt it.'

'Still … "on the Continent" …' a wistful smile'… doesn't *sound* especially Nonconformist.'

'Methodist.' Genista Broome indicated the relevant box on the form. 'I say, you don't suppose Lefty Bannister's a Methodist, do you?'

'God no. Drinks like a fish. Why do you ask?'

'Oh I don't know. Some sort of Wesleyan old-boy network? It's the only thing that makes any sense.'

'Methodists? Don't be absurd,' said Fenn. He removed his spectacles and pinched the bridge of his nose. Like all of his gestures, it had the deliberate, artificial look of a Shavian stage direction or Humphrey Bogart registering deep thought. 'It may all be for the best, you know. The trouble with giving a man that kind of job is that chaps create difficulties, much harder to work a cover story. These America First types can get very white-feathery – "Why aren't you fighting for your King and country, young man?". A man on the loose in Hollywood might have made matters very awkward unless he had a glass eye or a club foot – or a smashed knee.' He looked ruefully down at his flannels. 'I've caught one of our esteemed colleagues aping my limp before now in unusually hawkish company – Christian Matrons for War Relief, all that malarkey.'

The telephone trilled into life as the trunk call finally came through. 'Hello? Is that Mr Kiss's secretary? Oh hello again, Genista Broome here. We spoke yesterday about getting a few bits and pieces for HP's new assistant? The one Mr Kiss organised? That's right. Just waved her off at Grand Central.' A brief squawk from the Los Angeles end. 'Her *type*? Hard to say ... Rosalind Russell with a sick headache? Dark hair, dark eyes, fair skin, height five seven, 34-24-35, shoes an American seven, hats six and seven-eighths, gloves six and a half, scanties 34, stockings nine. Passport says twenty-seven but she looks nearer forty-seven, so nothing too *jeune fille*.' Another pause. 'Just fill a few suitcases with whatever the well-dressed junior matron is wearing out West. We rely entirely on your taste and discretion. Cheerio – and thanks again.'

Fenn had been rummaging through the Murdoch file and unearthed a fading photostat.

'Oh Lord. I do see what you mean.'

'The studio are going to die laughing when they see those tweeds. Can you picture her entrance?'

'I can, actually. Indeed I almost feel I've seen it already – that Garbo thing.' He lowered his voice to a Swedish growl. '"You are the unfortunate product of a doomed culture."'

'The snapshot doesn't tell the half of it. And *body odour*. Although to be fair –' Lady Genista took a pencil and doodled a fluff of fur around Evelyn's black-and-white shoulders and a pointy hat on her head '– there have been a few minor improvements since that was taken. I'd hardly put the phone down last Friday after breaking the news when Mr Kiss rang back to say that his New York office was sending round a few luxury trimmings from Bergdorf Goodman to make sure she didn't excite comment on the train. Wouldn't fool London or Paris but a fox stole and a diamond brooch will get you a long way over here.'

Fenn took a final look at the defaced photograph.

'Still looks like Himmler in a dress.'

'Yes. Although the red hat did liven things up considerably,' conceded Lady Genista. 'Himmler in party mood.'

Chapter 3

A GIGGLING GAGGLE of young women were gathered around the ticket inspector, their braying mid-Atlantic voices begging for access to the platform reserved exlusively for the 20th Century Chicago express. One stood apart from her friends, a few feet from Evelyn and close to where the two Germans were still standing. She was engaged in a one-sided, whispery tiff with a disgruntled young man clutching a lady's slipper orchid in a small cellophane coffin: *Why* was she going? *Who* would she dance with? *Why* couldn't she spend the weekend with him here in New York? He had tickets for *Johnny Belinda* at the Belasco. Yes, of course he liked her to have a good time but his sister Betsy always said those military dances weren't *nice*. The girl actually laughed in his face.

None of her friends was especially pretty but, like the Broome woman, they had tried so very hard to appear that way with their vulgarly bright hats and topcoats and painted faces that it would have been churlish to argue the point. A passing troop of naval cadets certainly seemed willing to play along, tooting and whistling in automatic appreciation of anything in heels that had gone to the trouble of having its hair marcelled.

The girls' porters stood waiting for them a few yards away in their natty red-topped caps, trolleys piled with trunks and dress boxes. Some of the swankier luggage had fitted canvas cosies and cunning felt covers that buttoned over the handles, Evelyn noticed, even though the darkies wore gloves.

Her own bag looked very shabby alongside all that pigskin and alligator. At home, her battered suitcase, with its faded collage of continental railway labels, was a badge of cosmopolitanism; in America it merely meant that you couldn't afford a new one. Her porter had taken charge of it with a very dubious air.

The log-jam persisted until a bolder pair of redcaps, piloted by a uniformed lady's maid holding a French poodle, surged forward and parted the chatty throng like a spoon drawn through sauce. Evelyn's man slipped into their wake and Evelyn was immediately surrounded by a fragrant fog of new clothes and face powder. The girls made no attempt to move permanently aside, blocking the way to other passengers with the heedless assurance of the very young – and very rich.

A minky matron, forehead furrowed at the prospect of sharing a carriage with a herd of noisy débutantes, had buttonholed one of the train officials.

'The company should have a separate car for this kind of thing, a separate *train*. There must be nearly thirty of them. I'm a very light sleeper. I'll pay a surcharge if I have to.'

The man mumbled something about a yearling prom at West Point and explained that the young ladies had been about to board an entirely different train – the 5.20 to Peekskill – when one of them thought she had spotted Gary Cooper, which had resulted in the whole gang rushing down the access tunnel and trying to talk its way on to the Chicago platform to get a closer look.

Evelyn's porter left her at the train side and dashed back to deal with her reservation. The lady's maid was now taking charge of her mistress's caravan of luggage, giving the porters instructions about what went where. Evelyn marvelled at the baffling variety of cases that seemed to have been custom-built around their contents, like morocco-bound Christmas presents: typewriter, tennis racket, guitar, gramophone. One – a writing desk? – had a set of legs that folded underneath.

The desk's owner, an eccentrically hatted woman in a sable stole, swept past the débutantes moments later followed by an entourage of raincoated men with press accreditation tucked into their mad hatbands. Genista Broome's Germans, still in deep discussion, turned to look as the mysterious celebrity sailed by and the older man muttered something in the young one's ear. It made him laugh: teeth lint-white against his nut-brown face.

The woman stopped a few yards from Evelyn and perched matily on the corner of a crate. Elbow on knee, she settled her furs, cupped a gloved hand beneath her chin and arranged her head at a calculated angle for the waiting lenses. The pose was one that flattered her sagging face – or would have done had the bleached fluff on her upper lip not caught the light so prettily.

'Be sure and book me a stenographer, Lucette,' she called after the maid. 'I need to send some cables.'

She turned confidingly to the pressmen and went to work on them with a smile that offered the frosty cheer of a Wesleyan wedding.

'Lucette is a *godsend*. Only girl I've ever had who really *understands* my hair.' She patted the back of her greying coiffure.

It seemed that the woman's attractions were more than skin deep because the journalists began calling out their questions with the Gatling-gun delivery that made Yankee cinema dialogue so very difficult to follow. Their demeanour – trench coats unbuttoned, hats on backs of heads, an instinctive lack of deference – was certainly very well copied by the film-makers or perhaps it was simply that the press pack were modelling their manners on their celluloid counterparts? It was hard to get any proper sense of reality. Even Genista Broome, with her rolled hair and painted fingernails, might have been straight from Central Casting. Evelyn's glimpses of the New York cityscape, her arrival at the pier, the drive along Broadway and through the Park, had also looked absurdly synthetic, like a postcard – or a cartoon. The porter, 'George', was only the second Negro she had ever spoken to but even he felt strangely familiar. A kind of *déjà vu*. A New World that wasn't new at all.

How did Miss Harper find Europe? Had Mr Hitler forgiven her yet? Had Miss Harper spoken to the President today? Why was she going to Albuquerque?

Miss Harper was of the opinion that theirs was a grand and glorious country and that the women of America were a force to be reckoned with, none of which was likely to have been news to any of them but they pencilled it all into their notebooks just the same. Editors short of copy had found that Miss Harper uttered her bromides in such rolling paragraphs that most of it was pretty much ready to print (in the more serious-minded journals at any rate). Those pressmen less excited by her tea with Mr Winston Churchill stood at the back making notes on her wardrobe for the society pages ('Miss Harper, 43, wore a sage-green tailor-made with matching hat and a collar of Russian sable') while keeping a lookout for more splashable prey.

Their interviewee was about to explain why the Nazis lived in fear of a Roosevelt third term when one of the more eagle-eyed photographers slipped away from the pack, raced along the red carpet and fell to one knee at the feet of a young redhead in a leopard-skin coat. He snatched his first picture in a smoky flash of magnesium oxide.

'Heading back home, Miss Del Ray?'

The actress paused mid-stride, gave a warm smile and grabbed a hatbox from the teetering pile beside her, swinging it carelessly by its braid handle, as if she travelled with nothing more than a toothbrush and a change of toque. More flashes now as the other journalists, despairing of the international situation, readjusted their news values.

Evelyn, still anxiously waiting for her porter to collect the relevant dockets, was forced further along the platform by an overalled man gliding down to the restaurant car on a motorised crate arrangement laden with fruit veiled in cellophane. He pulled up alongside an open window and began passing the baskets to a platoon of liveried delivery boys.

As she looked up from checking her watch for the dozenth time, Evelyn saw a woman reflected in one of the train's plate-glass windows: tall and rather imposing with her killingly fashionable hat and the luxurious glint of precious stones at her throat. It was a long moment before she recognised herself. She turned her head to get a better look at the set of her red felt brim and noticed the younger German – Sepp, his friend called him – looking her up and down. An unfamiliar sensation. Not altogether pleasant.

Evelyn's porter had hardly pocketed his tip when his place was taken by a black, white-coated steward who bustled into her train compartment with towels and a vacuum jug of iced water. Was there anything he could get for her? Tea, please. *Hot* tea? Yes, of course hot tea.

The luxury and newness of a 20th Century drawing room were a far cry from the frayed and faded gentility of a European sleeping car and Evelyn was entranced by the ingenuity of its fittings. A schoolfriend's family had once taken her swimming in the Thames at Runnymede and they had all eaten lunch from a wicker basket kitted out with square cups and plates and beakers – finer china and glass than anything in the dresser at home – and instead of her father's smelly old Thermos they had made tea from scratch with a spirit lamp that had its own leather suitcase. The whole of America seemed to be like that: the train; the newspaper stand; Miss Harper and her folding desk: everything slotting together like a box of puzzle bricks.

As Evelyn hung up the coat of her suit she slipped a silver and enamel St Christopher's medal from the breast pocket and let it dangle from one of the compartment's canny little coat hooks. The tiny papist trinket had been a parting gift from Deborah, her sister-in-law, which shared its chain with a lucky rabbit's foot – 'Don't tell the Outlaw, for heaven's sake; she saw me touch wood once, thought I'd never hear the end of it.' Evelyn picked up the tiny paw and rubbed the fluffy white fur against her upper lip.

When she emptied the remaining contents of her jacket pockets on to the dressing table she discovered the cream-coloured envelope with the twopenny-halfpenny stamp that had been sent to Major Bannister's mysterious box number. She had been gone less than a fortnight but her sister-in-law's letter had beaten her across the ocean and ran to three quarto sheets of italic scrawl.

Evelyn had originally met Deborah a year before the war at a girls' school in County Durham where Deborah washed test tubes as a laboratory assistant and Evelyn was teaching French and German conversation. In the early 'Alouette' days there had been talk of Girton or even the Sorbonne but her mother's death had prompted her father to resign his living and pursue an itinerant career, gypsying around the country covering for sick or absent ministers.

When Evelyn left boarding school it was suggested (only her father had such steely powers of suggestion) that she take part-time teaching posts while simultaneously keeping house for him in a succession of featureless rented rooms.

Evelyn had been obliged to leave the Durham school mid-term and follow her father to a new posting in Surrey. The Reverend's constant removals made it almost impossible to form new friendships. Although addresses would occasionally be exchanged with school colleagues, the correspondences usually fizzled out. Deborah had been far more persistent, determined not to lose touch with her clever new friend. She had carried on working at the Durham school but was laying plans for her escape via the appointment columns of the London *Times*. A bank clerk's daughter, she could keep accounts (a trained baboon could keep accounts, in Deborah's opinion) and had taught herself to use a typewriter.

The Reverend Charles Dent's Surrey posting turned out to be his last. After his death Evelyn had remained at the same address, a cabbage-scented flat above a stationer's in Byfleet, but she had resigned from her latest teaching post and found work with a Fleet Street translation bureau. Her father's final batch of parishioners had all been very kind to her after the funeral but this kindness generally took the form of weak tea and strong hints that she might join them sorting jumble or ladling soup. She had kept up her church-going for a month or two but she gained little comfort from begging forgiveness for uncommitted sins or giving thanks for non-existent blessings. She took to spending her Sundays at the National Gallery and her weekday evenings were passed working up her Hungarian and Portuguese (which were paid a premium rate by the bureau) with only her newly acquired kitten, Kowtow, for company.

Two months after the funeral, a letter arrived informing her that Deborah had successfully applied for the post of receptionist-cum-bookkeeper to a general practitioner in Woking, and had Evelyn seen *Idiots' Delight?*

Their first outing went very well. Deborah was rather 'soft' on Clark Gable (and Tyrone Power and Errol Flynn). She had snapshots of all of them but didn't bother with autographs which she said were all forged by a team of elderly ladies in the studio's publicity department. The very next evening after *Idiots' Delight* they had both cried over Bette Davis in *Dark Victory* in the front row of the Woking Ritz and soon the two friends were spending three evenings a week together. Not every trip was a success (a second feature about Russian spies knifing people in alleyways and identifying one another with torn banknotes was not Deborah's cup of tea) but they saw *The Hound of the Baskervilles* twice and Deborah began a new Basil Rathbone section in her scrapbook.

Their cinema-going was interrupted when Deborah began courting Gilbert Murdoch, a young local dentist. 'They say Gilbert's big brother Silas is very nice,' said Deborah out of the blue one day. 'He's a dentist too …' Evelyn knew by the tone of her voice that Deborah was once again laying plans, mapping out their futures like the plot of a four-reeler. Within a matter of months Gilbert and Silas married Deborah and Evelyn. Three months later war was declared. Three months after that Silas was dead.

Deborah was impressed, if slightly unnerved, by Evelyn's unorthodox postal arrangements.

If a courier collects my letters from the PO Box does that mean they bypass your old friends in Holborn?

Probably just as well. They would probably cut out
most of it – 'alarm and despondency', all that. It
said in the paper that Stalin was shooting people for
defeatism – Woking would be decimated on that basis.

Evelyn's reading was interrupted by the return of the
steward who began reciting a list of the onboard facilities:
restaurant, barber shop, manicurist, stenographer, cocktail bar, nurse, florist, shoeshine. One of his front teeth
was very slightly chipped (Silas always noted things like
that) and she could see every pore on his shiny black face,
smell the starch on his white mess jacket.

'And is there a chapel?'

The dark face suddenly crestfallen.

'No, ma'am. No, ma'am, there ain't.'

'And is the famous Mr Cooper on the train?'

'No, ma'am' – another apologetic duck of the head as
he pocketed his tip.

If she hadn't chummed up with Deborah, Evelyn
might never even have heard of Gary Cooper. As a child,
the cinema, like scent and music halls, had been catego-
rised as 'light-mindedness' by her father. The Reverend
had, grudgingly, licensed a handful of outings to films
with Sunday-serious subjects but even these treats ceased
after he had happened upon a screening of *The Sign of the
Cross* and realised that the American film industry – 'run
by Jews and renegades' – viewed the ancient world as a
convenient pretext for depravity and undress. While he
would not have deigned to forbid his nineteen-year-old
daughter any commonplace diversion, he frowned upon
things with a heavy, dampening force that sapped all pleasure from them.

Deborah and Evelyn had resumed their movie-going the
moment the Murdoch brothers were mobilised – 'better

than moping around at home' – and even Evelyn's widow-hood was to be no excuse. The War Office telegram confirming Silas's death had arrived the same week as *The Wizard of Oz* and Deborah had insisted that it was what he would have wanted (people were always saying that: Silas would have wanted the most extraordinary things).

Evelyn had cried a great deal when the news first came. She carried on – everyone always carried on – and her life quickly resumed an appearance of normality but she felt peculiarly detached, as if she were watching herself from the stalls, the same strange, suspended state of mind that descended upon her when she ironed sheets or revised verbs. There was a dreamlike unreality to her widowhood: days spent in Holborn blue-pencilling other people's love letters, evenings spent in Hollywood watching lives of thrilling excess: motor cars, marabou slippers, refrigeration, constant kisses and regular breakfasts in bed. Did every woman in America wear satin pyjamas? (What Silas would have wanted?)

The hours passed in the darkness of the Regal or the Odeon or the Plaza had paid unexpected dividends during her interview with Major Bannister when he asked her whether she spent much time at the *cinema* (he'd pronounced it with a K and one had the sense that for two pins – and in older, more county company – he'd have gone the whole hog and said 'kinematograph'). Was she a 'fan' (slang always wore a very stiff collar when Major Bannister used it). A trick question, surely? Some sort of test of light-mindedness? But she had answered truthfully that, while not a fanatic, she attended her local picture houses two, sometimes three, evenings a week.

'I go quite often with my sister-in-law,' she confessed. 'Her husband – my late husband's brother – is away and it takes her mind off it.'

The Major had squeezed another illegible word into one of the boxes in the printed form on his blotter.

'Jolly good. No dependants? And an Irish grandmother, I think you said? Excellent.'

Before the week was out she was aboard the *Mouzinho* on her way to New York.

Sixty-two cargo and passenger ships were sunk in the Atlantic in September. Her own ten-day crossing had been blessedly uneventful, but although there were still a few passengers dressing for dinner and playing quoits on the chilly promenade deck, you could almost smell the mounting sense of panic in the public rooms. The ship's course had not been exactly as advertised in the window of the steamship office and a small boy with a map had had his compass confiscated by his increasingly tetchy mama. Morning prayers of various kinds were unusually well attended but Evelyn, a poor sailor, had spent half the voyage in her cabin sipping bouillon, watched over by St Christopher.

She was very tempted to adopt the same strategy on the Chicago train but the steward reappeared to make up her bed and she decided to take refuge in the club car. As she turned to put on her jacket, she caught her reflection in the oval looking glass. Her face wasn't mirror-ready and her mouth and forehead still had the unfriendly, exasperated look she had been wearing for the steward.

She plumped her features back into a faint smile but the improvement was only marginal. The woman in the mirror looked bad-tempered and underfed. The grey suit muffled her shape like a herringbone loose cover. 'You'll fatten up soon enough over there,' Silas's mother had prophesied nastily during one of her less confused moments. '"A land that floweth with milk and honey"? All right for some.'

Evelyn looked doubtfully at the red hat on the shelf: 'older women still wear them' … but did they wear them at dinner or only at lunch? And what was the form for furs? The dark wool looked drab suddenly without its foxy garnish. She heard female voices outside and opened the door the merest crack. A large, blonde woman and her daughter were swaying unsteadily down the corridor. Both had marcelled hair and both wore identical pale green dresses (same colour, at least: different sizes). No furs, no hats, although the mother had a scribble of frilly green veiling perched on the top of her head like butcher's parsley.

As she closed the compartment door, Evelyn remembered the collection of lucky-dip packages in the carrier bag Genista Broome had given her and found two lace handkerchiefs, a pair of sunglasses, a flagon of Odorono and, right at the bottom, a tin of prophylactics. The brand was Merry Widows – some sort of sick joke? No wonder the girl had blushed. Evelyn was about to put the tin into the waste-paper basket when it occurred to her that the steward might find it so she slipped it into the inside pocket of her suitcase.

The last remaining parcel in the carrier bag was a roll of violet-coloured tissue paper containing a length of pleated white organza. Evelyn wound the collar around her neck, tucked the edges inside her lapels then pinned it in place with the diamond brooch. She looked back at her reflection: white features highlit and dramatised by the ruff of snowy silk: a portrait of an unknown woman. She snatched some magazines and newspapers from the bedside shelf and followed the sound of laughter.

Two men on high stools were telling the barman how best to make a dry martini.

'Easy on the ice, Jefferson baby, we don't wanna *bruise* it.'

Their shoulders were wider, their ties gaudier, than any she had ever seen but there was, again, that nagging sense of familiarity. Back at the Woking Ritz or the Weybridge Odeon, Evelyn had assumed that Hollywood substituted a bigger, brighter, version of American reality but here they all were sitting on a train: large as life; twice as unnatural.

The waiter found Evelyn a window seat. The railway track hugged the path of the Hudson River and the sunset burned like a bushfire beyond the trees on the far bank.

She stared uncomprehendingly at the cocktail menu until the waiter took pity and suggested 'punch'. The tall, frosted glass looked refreshing with its long ringlet of lemon peel but there was a sour aftertaste beneath the first fizz of sweetness and she had to swallow hard not to choke on the medicinal blast of liquor.

She pulled a cigarette from her jaunty new pocketbook. A man with a sixth sense for such things reached across from the neighbouring table and lit it for her, scanning her face and figure for points of interest before turning back to his friends.

Evelyn inhaled deeply and half closed her eyes. The buzz of voices created a queer kind of calm. It wasn't that the Pullman car was quiet – far from it – but Evelyn had always found that, provided the people around her – in a railway carriage, in the lunch bar, in the queue at the cinema – were all speaking the same language, she could block out their conversations: *I'll say, Don't mind if I do, Didn't he just, Can't say I blame him.* The 20th Century's passengers spoke only English and it was as soothing as silence to have her thoughts unmolested by the random anxieties and endearments that had midged about her head on board the *Mouzinho.* Newly uprooted from their homelands, her fellow shipmates had assumed that their

36

mother tongue would be an impenetrable private code and that nothing they said would ever be understood.

The library on the ship had been colonised by a large, very argumentative group of Austrian Jews and it was easy enough to screen out their tirades, but in the other public rooms where the signals switched constantly back and forth – Polish, Portuguese, a full set of German regional dialects – Evelyn's super-sensitive ear had scarcely a moment's peace: *Heinrich will meet the boat*; *Mitzi will be with us very soon*; *All the girls wear high heels in America, Mutti*; *We should have stayed in Amsterdam*; *There was room in the trunks for his books but he lets his wife dress like a cleaning woman*. It was like being able to read people's thoughts – and every bit as unsettling. It was all Evelyn could do not to blush at the enforced intimacy. The customs shed at Pier 94 had been another such Babel, with anxious first-class passengers muttering to each other about who had hidden what where or bickering about the most suitable demeanour when lying to an official: '*Shout? What do you mean, I shouldn't shout? Sure I shout. Shout and they think you're a bigshot [Gantseh Macher].*'

It had been the same at home in Woking with the wireless. Tracking between the pre-war choice of Home and Light and Third, she would sometimes stop in the wrong place, her well-filled head automatically translating – did she even translate any more? Only realising she had tuned it wrongly when Silas's mother complained.

Mrs Murdoch had seen no need for Abroad and nor for that matter had her son. Whenever Evelyn had spoken to Silas of her travels he would lose no time in changing the subject. Her knowledge of other languages was, likewise, something he'd rather she didn't talk about. She had tried explaining her father's views on Talents but old Mrs Murdoch was unimpressed by Evelyn's skill,

viewing it much as she would any other freakish afflic-
tion – double-jointedness, webbed toes: as something that
couldn't be helped but needn't be mentioned. Talents?
Scant excuse for spending so much time away from her
family and friends. While one might, in Christian charity,
'remember all the people who live in far-off lands' when
the occasion required, there was no need to fraternise with
them to that extent. And as for her reading matter … the
very titles were suggestive: *La Bête Humaine*; *L'Éducation
Sentimentale*; *Au Bonheur des Dames*: highly unsuitable.

In peacetime the *Mouzinho* would have printed off a daily
newspaper summarising world events but the Captain had
made some excuse about the copying apparatus. Evelyn
soon realised why when she settled into her seat in the
20th Century's Pullman car and made a start on one of
the newspapers that had been stuffed into her bag. Of the
113 children being posted off to safety in Canada aboard
the *City of Benares* only thirteen survived, six of them found
frozen and starving in a lifeboat a week after the ship was
torpedoed. 'The children behaved magnificently,' said a
woman adrift with them. 'Never at any time did the boys
complain.' Surgeon Lieutenant Silas Murdoch had not
complained when *Exeter* caught fire (or so the Captain said
in the letter), but when his personal effects were returned
two months later there wasn't so much as a charred scrap
of uniform, not even his wristwatch.

   The front pages of both New York newspapers
carried prose poems on the continued 'super-bombing'
of London: 'Germans Claim Secret Ray', 'Ambulances
screeched through debris-piled streets, collecting the dead
and injured. The horizon was lighted by great angry red
splashes of flame.' There were uncensored pictures of
blazing buildings and craters but it didn't take much to

push European news down the front page. A very small, very rich child had been kidnapped by 'a hook-nosed man' demanding $100,000 ransom but had been safely returned: 'His joyous mother, the Countess, dry-eyed, audibly whispered "My angel!" as she clasped him in her arms.' 'Dry-eyed'? Oh dear. The Countess was obviously not sticking to the script. Evelyn found herself warming to the woman.

The cover story of *Nation* was an article by Sybil Harper, the lady journalist from the station platform, on the menace of the German Bund, which she claimed was using its beer and bockwurst parties as a front for Nazi sympathisers. The article ran to over a dozen pages: eight, perhaps ten thousand words. Evelyn sighed. Perhaps not.

'May we?'

The only free chairs left in the train's club car were at Evelyn's table and these were now taken by the yellow-haired woman she had spotted in the corridor together with her matching daughter and a small, pop-eyed dog. The girl – who could hardly have been of drinking age – wanted a Horse's Neck and her mama ordered a martini with a cocktail onion in it at which point her daughter told her that no, Mother, that was a Gibson, after which their dialogue dried up rather.

'May I take a look at your magazine?' The woman jabbed a manicured finger at the cover of *Nation*. 'She's on the train, you know, holding court down there in the observation car. They say she'll be Woman of the Year. *Such* a command of language– ' she leaned over confidingly '– and such *large* helpings …'

The woman drained her cocktail, ordered a second and turned to Evelyn with a sunny, gin-washed smile.

'I should introduce myself: Ida Van Clark and this is my little girl Wanda.'

'How do you do?' muttered Wanda.

'And this is my other little girl, Delilah,' simpered Mrs Van Clark, pushing her lapdog's ratty pink snout towards Evelyn for a kiss. Its collar was the same bilious shade as the women's clothes. Did it travel with its own doggy suitcase?

'Van Clark ... Is that a *Dutch* name?' asked Evelyn, who had once spent a week with a family of Calvinists in Utrecht.

Wanda sniggered into her powder compact while Mrs Van Clark swallowed half of her second Gibson. 'You're *English*, aren't you? We were in Europe a couple of years back. Shopping mostly, but we saw everything: Buckingham Palace; the Changing of the Guard; Saint Paul's Cathedral: the full set. Which reminds me, Wanda, I meant to say: it said in the paper that arcade place where we bought the damask dinner napkins was bombed the other day.' Mrs Van Clark looked pointedly at Evelyn, brow furrowed, meaning obvious. 'It must be *such* a relief to be here in the States out of harm's way.'

Not a word one could say, of course. Several of Evelyn's work colleagues had said much the same and her mother-in-law had been very scathing but her sister-in-law's reaction to her posting had been uncharacteristically good-natured: 'Jammy old you. The dear knows I'd jump at it, war or no war.'

Mrs Van Clark and her little girls were going to be staying with her sister in Palm Beach until Thanksgiving.

'Or *Thanksgivings*, I should say. It always used to be the last Thursday in November but there are five Thursdays this year and Mr Roosevelt says it oughta be the 23rd and there's been quite a fight about it. My sister's husband is a Republican but a lot of his clients are voting for a third term so she's going to make some turkey farmer very happy. Her cook isn't too pleased.'

Ida, Wanda and Delilah had spent most of the summer at a lake resort and Mrs Van Clark had been intending to take Wanda back to Paris in the spring but that plan had been put on hold thanks to what she called the International Unpleasantness. Buenos Aires was said to be very lovely in the spring and of course they all spoke English there.

Evelyn took another sip of punch but made no reply. She could make conversation in nine languages – more if one merely wanted to find the way to the bathroom or ask for one's meat well done – but 'small talk' had always eluded her. What small things was one supposed to talk about?

Mrs Van Clark appeared nonplussed by Evelyn's failure to contribute. She tried her usual gambits – children; health; servants; dietary regimes; travel plans – but the Englishwoman didn't seem to know how to keep the ball in play and poor Ida found herself rambling on and on. She had met Oscar on a train, she said; she'd been on her way to a dance at West Point – just like those girls at Grand Central this evening. She'd worn the palest green *mousseline de soie* (green was always her colour).

Evelyn had worn darkest chocolate brown on the evening she first met Silas. Deborah had introduced them at a church hall dance and then left them to it. It had been a very awkward ten minutes with the silent Silas staring glumly at the other couples Lambeth Walking across the dance floor. His brother, Gilbert, Deborah's new fiancé, was rather nice-looking but Silas did not resemble him. He had a curiously narrow face – the hinges of his spectacles had to be bulked out with tightly wound black button thread to help them grip his head – but when viewed in profile his aquiline nose and chiselled cheekbones made him very nearly handsome. He hadn't asked her to dance. Dancing, she later learned, had numbered among Wesley's original list of Questionable Amusements, a list that old Mrs Murdoch was forever adding to: lipstick, icing on cakes, brilliantine, hair ribbon, earrings, fires in bedrooms. As a last resort in all matters of leisure and any borderline social vices, the Murdoch boys were to ask themselves: What Would Jesus Do? It seemed that Jesus, given the choice, would opt to sit mumchance on the sidelines slurping watery orange squash.

Silas hadn't had much to say for himself and eventually Evelyn could stand the silence no longer. Asking people what they did was a bore's question (or so her father had always insisted) but she asked it anyway (even though she knew the answer). Was he a dentist too?

It was as if someone had put a penny in a slot. He gave a sudden grateful smile and began to speak. Evelyn had very nice teeth, very nice, very nice indeed. And then, quite unexpectedly, he had taken her hand and squeezed it and said in a low, mad, urgent voice that everything, *everything* about her was nice. Nice as could possibly be. Every bit as nice as his brother's fiancée had promised. He had hoped to meet someone nice at the dance but he couldn't have talked to any of the other girls, he said, because they were too flighty for him. Not like Evelyn. Evelyn was nice. Would she please come to the cinema with him? A patient had said that *Gunga Din* would be 'suitable'.

Many films were not, Evelyn discovered, and Hollywood's output that summer – *Next Time I Marry*, *A Royal Divorce* and *Bachelor Mother* – meant that their brief courtship included only half a dozen cinema outings. *Gunga Din* was a rare exception but their evening in the dress circle had not been a success: you could see the strings on the snakes, Silas had hissed, and they were using quite the wrong sort of bayonet. He would have walked out, he said later, but they were in the middle of a row.

Evelyn soon learned that Silas's chief cinematic pleasure lay in spotting the inaccuracies in costume pictures. He was always exasperated when Ancient Romans spoke with American accents (as if Caesar and Mark Antony and Brutus would all have been to Radley or RADA) and he was constantly deploring the actors' bridgework (C. Aubrey Smith's dentures were a regular source of professional amusement). Like Evelyn's father, he frowned upon the constant love scenes and the cheap, tarty appearance of the actresses (although he was always decidedly more ardent afterwards).

The remainder of their dates were spent driving into the Surrey lanes in his glossy black motor car past pretty pubs and on to balding grass verges where Silas would assemble the folding table and chairs and Evelyn would unpack the sandwiches he had asked her to bring. Once he'd finished holding her hand and pronouncing on her niceness he would turn away from her to admire the view and she would be struck afresh by how much better looking he appeared sideways on.

His proposal came at midsummer during a picnic on Horsell Common.

'I shall be sorry to go if there is a war,' he had said, staring across at the sunset. 'It's been nice.' And, turning his other face towards her, he asked her to marry him.

She thanked him and promised to think about it and he had squeezed her hand some more. He had very soft skin.

He had driven her home to her lodgings and she had sat with Kowtow on her lap and looked around her at the cheerless oddments of furniture and thought of all the long, solitary evenings she had spent and would spend there. Her eye was caught by the gilt lettering on the spine of her father's Bible. The Reverend had disapproved of bibliomancy but John Wesley himself had practised it. It fell open at the Book of Psalms: 'My days are like a shadow that declineth and I am withered like grass.'

The next Saturday afternoon when she met Silas at his favourite tea shop Evelyn had nodded her head and he had grabbed her hand uncomfortably hard and pushed a ring on to her third finger. It had been his grandmother's, he said, and the seven stones spelled 'dearest'.

'Evelyn Murdoch ...' he had said, testing the name on his tongue like a foreign phrase. 'It'll be nice, won't it?'

They were married in early August. Deborah had wanted a double wedding but, while Mrs Murdoch was tempted by the economies of scale to be made, she had eventually ruled that double weddings were 'showy' and that Jesus would make do with garden flowers and fish-paste sandwiches.

During the last war, Silas's father, a Methodist lay preacher, had gathered enough white feathers to stuff a sofa cushion but, after much prayer, his widow had decided that Jesus would definitely have joined the Dental Corps. A more militant pacifist might have argued that stopping teeth and fitting dentures and wiring jaws was aiding the war effort but Mrs Murdoch, surprisingly Jesuitical for a Methodist, had convinced herself that a dentist's duties to his fellow man transcended such petty, temporal considerations. Men died from their teeth! she had shouted one teatime. Ask Silas. Or Gilbert. Blood poisoning. Septuagesima. Happened often.

Silas and Gilbert had signed up at once and when Silas set off for his basic training his pack contained a framed photograph of Evelyn standing outside the ugly new Methodist church in Knaphill in a nice navy suit, nice hat, nice posy of white violets (no earrings, no icing).

Evelyn saw Silas every weekend during his training but after four short weeks Deborah's Gilbert had been sent up to North Wales to minister to new recruits and Silas was on his way to join HMS *Exeter* somewhere off the South American coast.

When Evelyn had imagined married life she had assumed that she and Silas and Kowtow would have a home of their own but Mrs Murdoch had had other plans. Evelyn and Deborah soon discovered that they were expected to move into the large, chilly redbrick villa that the brothers had grown up in and take care of their seventy-two-year-old mother-in-law.

Mrs Murdoch's mental faculties had been lightly scrambled by a minor stroke. She did have occasional sunny spells of rational thought (most often when meals were being planned) but the current hostilities remained a mystery to her. She could never quite understand how Britain had managed to be at war with Germany for more than a matter of weeks, convinced that the other country had been drastically reduced in size after their crushing defeat in the last war – 'I tried showing her on the map,' said Deborah, 'but she's got them confused with Denmark.' Most troubling of all for Mrs Murdoch was the shameful failure of diplomacy. Either way, it had all been Chamberlain's fault ('neither use nor ornament') and 'that blackguard' Churchill ('as much use as a choco-late teapot').

Evelyn and Deborah were to become very familiar with their mother-in-law's turns of phrase. Mrs Murdoch had argued that one if not both of her daughters-in-law should remain at home with her in the daytime but was unable to find a medic who would testify to her need for round-the-clock care by two childless, able-bodied young women. Deborah continued with her job at the doctor's surgery and Evelyn left the translation agency for a desk in the Postal Censorship office (Uncommon Languages had practically bitten her hand off).

Mrs Van Clark had just ordered a third cocktail.

'So what part of England are you from? And what brings you to the States?'

Mrs Van Clark had the kind of voice that rose easily above the drawling murmur of her fellow passengers. A man seated at the counter with his back to the room swivelled round to look at the three of them, as if he too wanted to know what had brought Evelyn across the Atlantic. He was in his mid-twenties and wore a dark suit, a soft-collared shirt and a blue silk tie that matched his eyes: the younger German on the station platform. Delilah the lapdog's ears pricked up at the man's sudden movement. Young Wanda Van Clark's ears did not but her spine arched very slightly and her chin tilted with the self-conscious, mirror-minded manner of Dolores del Ray in close-up.

'Your dog is very well behaved,' said Evelyn and she saw the watching man smile and swivel back as she said it, as if aware that she was ducking Mrs Van Clark's question.

Mrs Van Clark went off to the ladies' room, leaving Delilah on the lap of Wanda who immediately grabbed hold of the dog quite sharply with her tangerine talons and flumped it on to her mother's empty seat. She made no attempt to talk to Evelyn but took a pad of writing paper from her clutch bag and resumed work on a long letter. She wrote in a florid and not particularly legible hand (although the M of mother was very distinct).

'Will you make my excuses for me?' said Evelyn, gathering her belongings. 'I have a very long day tomorrow.'

She had planned to finish reading Deborah's letter when she got back to her compartment but she caught the words 'poor dear Silas' at the top of the third sheet and stuffed it back into her skirt pocket. It was funny to see an envelope with no censor's stamp on it.

Her work in Postal Censorship had generally been a simple matter of marking up any indiscreet references to addresses, numbers, troop movements, bombing raids and anything likely to spread alarm and despondency (the actual cutting-out was done by the section leader). The workload had hotted up considerably since the Blitz began, as careless writers hastened to tell foreign friends (who could easily turn out to be enemies) where bombs had fallen, how close they came, how well or badly the rescue services had coped. The naiveté was staggering.

They were usually far cagier when it came to more personal matters, with most correspondents sensing the censor's eye upon them, but one letter in a hundred opened a window on to a dark and unsettling world ('I wear them under my uniform and pretend the straps are your teeth tearing at my skin'). They must surely have known that some stranger would be reading it all but they didn't appear to care. Evelyn's colleagues had grown inured to these glimpses of private life but Evelyn never really got used to the sense of guilt she felt while eaves-dropping on who had done what to whom.

For Mrs Murdoch the scandal was that so many letters were written in the first place – 'Making all that *work* for people! What can they all find to say, for heaven's sake?'

Evelyn herself became so conscious of the censor's prying eyes that she struggled to fill a sheet of paper and found that her handwriting increased in size whenever she wrote to her husband. The parcel sent back to her by Silas's commanding officer included all the letters she had sent to him and she was depressed to see how dry they were, how repetitive, how dull: 'Deborah sends warmest regards, Mother keeps well' – 'keeps well' like a heavy pre-war fruitcake. Among the correspondence was his own last unposted note. Like every one of his five letters home it had been addressed 'To all at Number 9' and ended, kissless, with a request to forward him the article on focal infection he had written for *The Mouth Mirror*. The CO hoped the unsent letter would 'be of some comfort' to his widow but Evelyn had not found it especially comforting.

Chapter 4

THE STEWARD BROUGHT breakfast to her compartment: big yellow eggs, ringlets of smoked bacon and a golden pile of fried potatoes. A waxy, purple and white corsage was nestling alongside the cream jug. There was no note with it. Who could possibly be sending her flowers? She remembered the look the young German had given her on the platform, how he had affected not to listen to her conversation with the Van Clarks. She felt rather foolish when she gazed out of the compartment window at the disembarking passengers and realised that every man now had a buttonhole and every woman a crunchy new purple and white orchid: like a Harvest Festival on the move as they streamed along the platform to the waiting taxis and limousines, clutching their half-eaten baskets of fruit.

Evelyn pinned the flower to her lapel and angled her new hat into place. Her old one looked ill at ease in the Fifth Avenue hatbox. She had gone into town to buy it when she first got the Holborn job and Silas, home on leave, had insisted on joining her, an unconvinced face behind her in the mirror. She had never worn it without remembering the grudging shrug he had given as she paid the cashier: 'You've got hats.'

She looked down at the old hat. There was a chromium-plated rubbish bin under the sink in her compartment. Plenty of room once she'd folded the felt into four.

Sybil Harper disembarked the moment the train stopped and was one of the first to the gate where the latest edition of pressmen was waiting for the low-down on her busy day: a flying visit to the Governor of Illinois, lunch with the Mayor and a pep talk for the Chicago branch of the Anti-Nazi League.

'Can Wanda and I drop you anywhere?'

Mrs Van Clark (entirely against daughterly advice) had wedged her breakfast orchid beneath the brim of her hat where the glaucous petals lurked like bracket fungus under the eaves. She had two porters in tow and looked askance at Evelyn's hatbox and bag.

'Travelling light?'

'It's very convenient: sending your luggage on ahead.' Evelyn was surprised at how easily the lie flowed. 'Such a bore fussing with it all.'

'The train companies always try to sell you that idea,' tutted Mrs Van Clark as they climbed into their taxi, 'but I like my luggage where I can *see* it. I remember one time on the Orange Blossom Special I lost my trunk key and do you know the conductor had a bunch as big as a man's fist? Opened that case easy as pie.' Mrs Van Clark's kid-gloved claws tightened their grip on the handle of her vanity case. 'You never did say what it was brought you to the States,' she persisted, instinctively registering Evelyn's third finger. 'What does your husband say about it?'

'He was killed.'

For a split second Mrs Van Clark looked shocked – and a tiny bit excited. The short sentence, so normal now to English ears, sounded utterly outlandish: Silas Murdoch gunned down in a bank raid or poisoned by a jealous lover or otherwise seen off in some dastardly crime. She rearranged her face into a look of stricken sympathy as she gave Evelyn's arm a vague squeeze like a faulty blood-pressure cuff. 'How *offal!* You poor dear. How long has it been? I see you don't wear black' (a faint nod towards the scarlet hat).

'One tends not to: *morale*, you know.'

A prim sigh from Mrs Van Clark as she rubbled her cheek against Delilah's muzzle. 'So many young lives. Where did it happen?'

A lot of questions … *'the nosiest people on God's earth'*. Or was this ageing, blondined matron actually an enemy agent? In a film she would have been.

Mercifully, Evelyn's hotel was barely ten blocks from the railway station and they had pulled up outside the entrance while Mrs Van Clark was still pawing vaguely at the back of her hand. They must have a good long chinwag about it on the Super Chief tonight. The three Van Clark females were spending the nine hours between trains with a cousin on Lake Shore Drive and Evelyn mentally rehearsed a refusal ready for when she was asked to join them (*'constantly* inviting one to things') but the offer never came.

Evelyn climbed out of the taxi and was all but swept under the metal awning and through the main doors by the stiff, lakeward breeze. The hotel's vast entrance lobby was over two storeys high and the coffered ceiling and gilded columns were an orgy of Egyptian pastiche – one half-expected Claudette Colbert to be carried down one of the staircases and unrolled from a precious carpet on to the spotless marble pavement. No music – too early in the day perhaps? – but there ought to have been: something with lots of strings spiced with oriental woodwind. The air smelled of lavender and cigar smoke and floor wax.

A very black boy in a very white uniform stood guard with the neatest of brooms, his cartoonishly wide eyes scanning the floor from behind a parlour palm. A passing guest lit a cigarette, then tossed the match aside and the young lad darted out from his cover and swept the sliver of wood into a chromium-plated dustpan before returning to his hide. Rotten manners, thought Evelyn, throwing rubbish about like that, but then if the guests behaved better the boy would be out of a job.

She strode through the lobby past the clubby clumps of armchairs and occasional tables to the sepulchral mahogany reception desk where a bevy of smartly dressed operatives were hard at work answering telephones, filling out telegraph forms and sharpening pencils. One of them peeled away from the pack and breasted the desk with a smile of greeting so wide and warm that Evelyn wondered if they had met before somewhere.

The receptionist's white blouse had a frothy fichu in front – as if her whole bosom was being served *à la mode*. She was wearing a dark-blue tailor-made. It was actually rather a shoddy piece of work but the crisp pretence of the padded shoulders and exaggerated waistline made the brash ensemble pretty and eye-catching in a way that Evelyn's suit would never be. The short skirt showed slim, honey-coloured nylon calves. One never saw stockings like that in England. Not in Woking anyway.

'My name is Murdoch. I believe I have a room reserved for the day? I'm taking tonight's train to Los Angeles. Perhaps you could arrange a taxi at the appropriate time?'

The girl gave a doubtful frown while her fingers bourréed across the card-index box at her elbow. Evelyn stifled the habitual pang of front-desk fear. Fear that they might not know anything about her or not have anywhere to put her or demand more currency than she had brought. The girl found the booking and unhooked a bronze key fob the size of a life preserver from the wall of pigeonholes behind her.

Evelyn instinctively spoke more softly. 'I'm expecting to meet someone.'

An immediate beam of recognition.

'Ah yes, Mr Fitzmorton. He sends his apologies,' explained the girl. 'He did get your company's wire but he's all tied up until eleven forty-five. He'll be right with you just as soon as he can.' She might have been the man's private secretary – his wife even – so familiar and confiding was her tone.

Evelyn's eighth-floor room was reached via half a mile of closely carpeted corridor. She felt a thrill of anticipation as the porter's gloved fingers fumbled the key into the lock, but the polished rosewood door swung open to reveal a gloomy cabin barely wider than the bed it contained and when Evelyn asked the man to draw the floor-length curtain she found that it had been hung against a blank wall and that the only ventilation was a small grille near the ceiling.

She was ready to cry with disappointment but, like a princess in a folk tale recalling the three wishes the goblin had given her, she remembered Genista Broome's advice and handed over a dollar bill and demanded that something be done about it, hinting that Mr Kiss – Mr *Zandor* Kiss (there might be other Kisses) – would not be pleased.

A fervent 'Yez *ma'am*' from the porter and the two of them retraced their steps to the front desk. He would fix everything, he promised. Evelyn looked at her new wristwatch.

'I think I might visit the beauty parlour. Whereabouts is it?'

'Straight down the stairs, ma'am,' said the boy, 'on the left side.'

The basement was a cathedral to human vanity and its central nave was flanked by chapels dedicated to separate articles of faith. Evelyn hovered on the grand staircase. Just below her, a bespectacled man was seeking a good home for the coin glinting in his fingers. A brass-buttoned boy dashed across – 'Right this way, sir! Yessir! We'll find you a nice chair momentarily, sir!' – and ushered the man into a barber shop lit by crystal chandeliers and part-paved with hundreds of real silver dollars.

The morning rush had subsided and only a few of the three dozen stalls were occupied by unhurried men being mummified in hot white towels while young Negroes buffed at the uppers of their bench-made Oxfords till they gleamed like rainy slugs. Pin-curled girls in chiffon shirt-waists clipped and poked at the fingers of one hand while the other five soaked in the craters of porphyry that dimpled the stands moored beside them.

There was a Turkish bath next door to the barber shop and its double doors yawned wide as Evelyn passed. A man, his prawn-pink face clammy with perspiration above his astrakhan collar, swerved out between the swinging jaws. She made to look away, afraid that a hot and hairy harem of moist male flesh would reveal itself behind him, but a perforated copper screen had been erected the width of the entrance to spare the modesty (or thwart the curiosity) of passing females.

'May I help you, ma'am?'

Another pantomime soldier.

'I wanted to spend a penny, er …' Evelyn blushed brighter than the Turkish bather. 'Your *smallest room*?' (Odd how much easier it was in a foreign language.)

In the ladies' room two women, freshly coiffed and dressed for a hard morning's shopping, were repairing their faces. They turned to look at Evelyn – pricing her hat, deploring her goofy English shoes, coveting her unlikely diamonds – but they didn't say good morning. As she checked her own reflection she took a sidelong peek at theirs. Their hair had been worked over in identical auburn waves like something piped out of a forcing bag.

Two attendants sat behind a painted screen yacking away in German about a Bund beer festival that weekend and Evelyn had to make a conscious effort not to react when their *Besprechung* turned to the ageing redhead touching up her lipstick in the glass. '*Die Hässliche Juedin hat Haar wie ein gelber Scheißhaufen*' (the ugly Jewess's hair looks like a yellow turd). Evelyn left no tip on the tray.

There was a vile smell of violets and ammonia in the beauty parlour. Lesser hairdressers were available but there were, as foreseen, no appointments to be had with Monsieur Alphonse until, with another sprinkling of green fairy dust, there jolly well *was* an appointment with Monsieur Alphonse, who magically materialised from behind a curtain, resplendent in sponge-bag trousers and a weirdly dental-looking white coat that reminded her, inevitably, of Silas.

The chemical stench intensified as he guided her into the salon's interior and past one of the private cubicles where an anxious-looking woman sat with her thin silver hair rolled around countless tiny steel bolts, each wired to the Frankenstein-like gadget that was frying her curls into place.

Monsieur Alphonse installed his new client on a red velvet throne in her own little room then smarmed away to bow his goodbyes to a previous customer. Meanwhile, one assistant took Evelyn's hat, coat and furs and draped her in a pink rayon cape while another swabbed the maestro's scissors and combs with a rag dipped in surgical spirit and eau de cologne.

Alphonse quick-stepped through the door, pulled the hairpins from Evelyn's head and teased out the fuzzy

mass of dark hair, complaining Gallically and extravagantly about the state of *la coiffure de Madame*. *Who*, pray,
had cut it last? His accent was more Marseilles than
Rue de la Paix (the e at the end of *Madame* was very
characteristic).

'I'm afraid I can't remember ...' stammered Evelyn –
her second lie that day ('my sister-in-law' would have been
the correct answer). 'Why do you ask?'

The twitch of his lips was as slight as he could make
it but the *moue* was magnified by his music-hall moustaches. He pulled her hair this way and that and said that
Miss Jones must do *sum-sing* about Madame's *sourcils* (the
eyebrows were the architraves to the windows of the soul,
n'est ce pas?).

Evelyn surrendered herself to being combed and
tweezed and poked. She tried to avoid her reflection but
if she looked down she saw the tiled floor furring over
with alarming quantities of hair and if she closed her eyes
she became aware of a strong, open-wide whiff of surgical
spirit that conjured Silas back into being.

One of the pink girls handed her a magazine called
House Beautiful whose 'Hollywood Special Issue' featured
a ten-page glimpse of 'Raymond Games's lovely Bel Air
home' which had just been remodelled by Wally Grendon,
'decorator to the stars'. A journalist called Myra Manning
had spent the day with Mr and Mrs Games 'and their pedigree Sealyhams Whisky and Soda'. Games, who would be
playing King Arthur in the forthcoming *Knights of Love*,
was pictured with his charming wife Cynthia in a variety
of gaudy sports clothes playing croquet or pretending to
weed the fern dell or mixing brightly coloured cocktails
in his smoked-oak saloon bar ('"Cynthia has a shocking
weakness for orange curaçao," laughs the Englishman
in his booming baritone'). Elsewhere in the magazine,

a man called Kramer was showing off the paintings in his 'famous blue salon'. A golden-haired child star called Rindy McGee was swallow diving into a heart-shaped swimming pool and a woman called Magda Malo was explaining that she maintained her figure by adhering to a strict no-solids regime every weekend.

'*Et voilà!*' cried a delighted Alphonse. '*Très belle!*'

After ninety minutes of snipping and teasing, the little Frenchman finally handed scissors and comb to his assistant and stepped back to admire his work.

'And wizz a leetle twist *comme ça –*' he skewered the whole thing into a sort of cottage-loaf arrangement with some species of tortoiseshell toasting fork '*– Madame est en grande toilette. Très simple, très elegante, n'est ce pas?*'

'*Oui.*' ('Keep the old parley-voo under your hat.')

'*Et du maquillage, non?*' A wag of the finger. '*Très important.*'

Her face did look pasty and undercooked after Monsieur had finished and so when Evelyn had tipped her way out of his salon she paid a visit to the hotel's 'beauty booth' where she bought a box of face powder and the lipstick (hat-red) that the young woman recommended. Silas would have frowned upon the whole transaction.

Luncheon was about to be served in the Maple Room where waiters waltzed between tables to the glockenspiel chink of Bohemian crystal, balancing domed silver trays on the palms of their raised hands. The maître d' checked his reservations.

'Is Madame joining anyone?'

'That's all right, François, the lady's with me!' The voice, as English as brown soup, rang out through the marbled hall as a slim young man loped towards her. 'Mrs Murdoch? Mrs *Dandelion* Murdoch? Allow me to introduce myself: Fitzmorton, Jeremy Fitzmorton.'

Jeremy Fitzmorton would have been invisible at the Savoy but here passers-by turned to look at him, social antennae alerted by the alien tailoring, his swaggerless, un-American walk.

'Can you face lunch this early? Perhaps François will stretch a point and let us have elevenses? The pastry chef here is a definite force for good. Viennese, they tell me ... Tea? Tea for two, François.'

'I was told to look out for the hat,' he said as they sat down, 'or I doubt I'd have spotted you from HQ's description.'

Evelyn looked over at one of the swagged and cherubed mirrors that lined the room and poked uncertainly at Alphonse's handiwork, wondering what HQ had said about her. Her new eyebrows made her look much younger suddenly and very slightly surprised (pleasantly so).

Jeremy Fitzmorton took a cigarette from the Turkish side of his case and screwed it into a holder (seaweed amber, no less).

'Now then. As was doubtless explained, you shouldn't really be here at all – you're what we call an "illegal" and this is hardly the place for amateurs. If that wasn't bad enough, it seems the whole thing is turning into a sort of ghastly *sex* comedy.'

Hat feathers quivered at nearby tables and he dropped his voice to an almost ventriloqual murmur: 'As you probably know by now, HQ were hoping for a boy but I suppose it may all turn out to be for the best. Selecting operatives for this sort of task has never been what you'd call an exact science – my opposite number back in London spends a fair amount of time steaming open enemy communications and sealing them up again and he picks *his* girls according to the slenderness of their ankles. More likely to be neat, d'you see?'

He sat back in his chair and frowned down at Evelyn's feet but perked up as the waiter materialised with a double-decker tray of fancy cakes.

'What were you actually up to back home? Or was it all something so-secret-you-can't-possibly-say? If I had half a crown for every little gin and French who told me she was doing something hush-hush in Hertfordshire, I could ...' He drifted off, thinking of all those half crowns, and helped them both to a large éclair. Silas had never been keen on cream cake.

'Nine languages, eh? I only managed three – unless you count Esperanto which none of us does. Esperanto is a serious waste of time. I should know: six months of my life completely wasted. Do you speak Esperanto? Of course you do ...'

Mr Fitzmorton forked up the last bite of éclair and pushed his plate away.

'Right then: to business. Mr Zandor Kiss divides his time between his own studio in West London and the Miracle men in Hollywood, and his aim in life – entirely unofficially – is to get the Yanks on side by showing the old country in the best possible light – you saw the Florence Nightingale thing? Quite. Now this is all well and good provided Kiss is kept on a short leash – as he was while Colonel Peyton was there to keep an eye on him – but he's been sailing pretty close to the wind lately – the villains in his latest film all have little black moustaches. This did not escape the notice of our friends at the Los Angeles German legation whose days are spent sniffing out that kind of thing and reporting back to their pet isolationists – money men, senators, newspaper columnists and so forth – and generally doing what they can to get Kiss and his ilk in the bad books of the Senate Committee who take a very dim view of all that. They will eat him for breakfast and his influential friends aren't likely to come to his rescue – not with the election six weeks away. The very last thing we needed was the addition of a rogue operative.'

He paused for a moment and tonged a slice of mille-feuille on to a clean plate. 'You mustn't take offence, Mrs Murdoch, but if anybody had asked my opinion (which they never do) I should have said that placing anyone, male or female, in California-of-all-places was an extremely stupid, potentially dangerous idea. Los Angeles is teeming with Kraut diplomats and fifth columnists – even the waiters, sometimes.' He gave a weary smile. 'Still, it can't be helped. You're here now and we can't very well post you back again. New York will have to take you if the worst comes to the worst – Lady Genista could probably find something for you to do.'

'*Lady* Genista?'

Evelyn scraped her pastry fork across the plate to salvage every delicious scrap of cream.

'Your guide in New York. Lady Genista Broome. Earl of Tring's youngest – first earl of course, but you can't have everything.'

'I had no idea. She didn't specify.'

'Her type never do, then grouch about you afterwards. No matter. Between you, me and the gatepost she's not long for HQ: being transferred to Library Services – and lucky to get it. She's pretty enough – if you like that sort of thing – but if she ever bets anyone she can spell "manoeuvre" she's going to lose her shirt.'

Evelyn was to keep her head down, nose clean, eyes peeled and ears to the ground. HQ were to be kept informed – informally informed – should anything of genuine interest arise but she wasn't to go looking for it and under no circumstances should she draw attention to herself or attempt any sort of heroics (she hadn't the training). Her mail (as she was probably by now aware) would be bypassing the usual channels and would be paged across to her in a sealed studio document wallet. She was to reply by the same route.

'On the whole we'd rather you destroyed anything you're sent but I expect your work in postal censorship should alert you to what's what.'

There was a tiny blob of *crème Chantilly* on his upper lip.

'The studio are sending a car to meet the train at Pasadena station at eight thirty-five ack emma the day after tomorrow. They've arranged a desk for you in the writers' wing. *This* is the key to the Colonel's office which will ensure a modicum of privacy. There's a designated external line – the *red* telephone, I think he said – so you could book a trunk call *in extremis* but the calls still have to go via the city exchange. If you do have to make contact, be as circumspect as it is possible for you to be: no names, no addresses, no details. The mere fact you've phoned will put HQ on the alert.

'You were given some pocket money? Kiss will be paying you $1,200 in cash via studio messenger on the seventh of each month – keeps you off the books, I suppose, but best to keep it quiet. You've been written into the plot as some sort of expert assistant. *These* will probably have their uses.'

He handed over a tortoiseshell case filled with a selection of business cards: Evelyn J. Murdoch: Voice Culture; Evelyn J. Murdoch: Special Projects; Evelyn J. Murdoch: Consultant.

'But consultant *what*?'

'Whatever your little heart desires. Fencing? Knot gardens? Harpsichord tuning? Stained glass? Deportment?' He looked at her shoes again and sighed heavily. 'Or something. It's an absolute madhouse, Saucy says. Voice culture is as good a front as any – so don't be afraid to talk up that angle. And *always assume*, as Lord Curzon used to say: no one ever questions a *fait accompli*. It's Colonel Peyton's motto and it's damned good advice.

'Saucy won't actually be there when you arrive – if at all. He volunteered to head up a new department – anything to get away from La Broome, I suspect – so he'll be in Bermuda for the foreseeable.'

'Doing what?' wondered Evelyn.

'None of your business. Sorry, I don't mean to be rude but we like to operate on a strict need-to-know basis and you really don't need to know.'

'Yes, but what if someone asks about him at the studio?'

'Lie. And don't whatever you do refer to him as "Colonel". *Mister* Peyton will suffice, or HP if you feel up to it – they're awfully keen on initials.

'Now then. There's been no word from the studio on your billet but you'll find them all terribly *hospitable*.' Fitzmorton, already a veteran of eight months of hands-across-the-sea hospitality, uttered the word in an almost disapproving undertone. 'But I expect you will be spoiled for choice: guest wings, pool houses or possibly some species of *bungalow* – their back gardens are infested with the things. If I hear anything I'll wire the train but if not the driver who meets you should have all the gen and someone at the Miracle office is sorting you out a motor …'

'And will Mr Kiss be at the studio?'

'He's away on location all this week but will make himself known at a party on Sunday evening – venue to be advised. Then you're due to attend a special meeting on Monday morning where Mr K plans to discuss proposals for new films that present an opportunity to generally wave the flag, so you'll need to familiarise yourself with these.'

Fitzmorton reached down for his briefcase and extracted a small book bound in plain brown paper and two red folders: *Duchess in the Dirt* and *The Boy in the Iron Mask*.

'Basically you're to run your eye over those and blue-pencil anything that isn't quite like Mother makes: Anne of Austria chewing gum, Louis XIII on a Western saddle, that kind of thing. They like to show due diligence on the historical front but chances are they will carry on regardless, Saucy says.'

Silas would have relished pointing out all the wrong bayonets.

The book in the brown wrapper was a pocket edition of *The War of the Worlds*.

'Everyone at HQ was struggling to think of a suitable property that didn't involve goose-stepping Normans or Philip of Spain in jackboots and then Saucy had a brain-wave, genius really. Haven't read it since prep school but I seem to remember Woking getting razed to the ground by the Martian blitzkrieg. You're from that part of the world, aren't you? California should make an extremely pleasant change: very clement weather and vast quantities of fruit. Ask nicely and they air-freight it back to Blighty for you in little crates.'

Jeremy Fitzmorton gave a last look at his checklist, folded it lengthways and lit his next cigarette with it while Evelyn gazed about her. The lunchtime clientèle in the Maple Room was mostly female but there were two men in deep discussion at a corner table and one of them had a lean, tanned face she recognised. The young German from the New York train platform was seated with his back to the room but had taken care to position himself beneath one of the immense gilt looking glasses. He was watching the door but Evelyn was firmly in his line of sight. He would surely have seen her – he'd have remembered the hat if nothing else. What did one do? How best to alert Fitzmorton without arousing suspicion? She thought of silent film stars who mimed one thing but said another: Ronald Colman reciting cricket scores to Vilma Bánky while kissing his way up her arm.

She flashed Fitzmorton an uncertain smile, edged forward and grasped his hand. He flinched in alarm.

'A man in the corner.' She dropped her eyes. 'Your Lady Whatsit pointed him out at the station in New York. He and another man were on the platform and I got the impression that they recognised her. He was in the train lounge yesterday evening and he seemed to be watching me.' Evelyn ducked her head further. 'Seemed odd.'

'Ah,' murmured Fitzmorton. 'Recognised her ladyship, you say? Awkward. They must have run across her in Los Angeles during the summer. Her visit was very ill-advised.'

Fitzmorton toyed absently with Evelyn's fingers while she rechecked the mirror from beneath her hat brim.

'He can definitely see us.'

Fitzmorton pressed her hand to his lips.

'Describe. I can't turn round.'

'Tanned, fair, tall, early twenties. The man with him is wearing a bow tie in a blue and white lozenge pattern.'

He brushed his cheek against her knuckles.

'Sounds absolutely ghastly.'

'It's the Bavarian flag.'

'Well spotted.' He played for time, kissing each fingertip in turn. 'Not the fool you look.'

'And there is a long scar down his left cheek.'

'Is there, by Jove?'

Evelyn had always thought it a strange coincidence that all duelling scars should be the same – like the slashes in the top of a baguette – until it was explained to her that cadets did it to one another at *Kriegsschule*. Like sailors having tattoos or a gang of shop girls all having their ears pierced.

Fitzmorton caught sight of the electric wall clock.

'Crikey. Nearly half one: I ought to be getting back. Your train's not until seven fifteen; you should probably keep to your room.'

He picked up Evelyn's cigarette packet and tumbled it thoughtfully in his long fingers.

'Used to smoke those at school. Filthy things. And a frightful giveaway.' He dropped them into his pocket. 'We'll get you fixed up at the kiosk.'

He took her hand and guided her past the desk and a battery of gleaming fire extinguishers partially concealed by a glade of potted ferns.

'Taking no chances. The previous building burned to a crisp about a week after the grand opening: three hundred dead all told – even their own dentists didn't know them.'

Odd, thought Evelyn, how often people mentioned dentistry. Like everyone banging on about cancer when her father died.

He kept hold of her hand while he bought her some American cigarettes and made her choose a smart enamel case to put them in. He then walked with her to the reception desk to retrieve the key to her new room.

'You'll find that California can get quite chilly at times, darling,' said Mr Fitzmorton, patting at Evelyn's fox stole and still very much in matinée-idol mode. 'Especially near the coast.' He slid an arm about her waist, pulled her towards him and kissed her cheek while he looked back into the Maple Room behind her.

'Yes, I see the chap now,' he muttered. 'Sure it's the same one?'

'Yes. Your colleague was quite agitated.'

65

'Mmm ... not a face I recognise. Try not to fret. It may be nothing – her ladyship can be somewhat excitable. They get that way at HQ sometimes. They forget that nearly thirty per cent of the population here has its roots in the Fatherland – more than half in some states. Doesn't do to get too worked up about it but keep your guard up and remember to keep cavey on the *plume de ma tante* front.' A final absent-minded kiss on the cheek. 'We must have a proper lunch on your way back.' He made it sound days away.

*

Evelyn took the next few meals in her Super Chief compartment. The train was not due to stop for passengers until it reached California so she was surprised when they slowed down to a halt at the town of Albuquerque, New Mexico just after four o'clock the next day. Even when the train hadn't stopped, there were always people lining the platforms of the stations they passed through, watching the famous locomotive glide by like disappointed passengers who had misread the timetable. There were far more of them than usual in Albuquerque. A group of Red Indians gathered around the train windows hawking moccasins and primitive pots but were bundled off the platform by a brass band and a regiment of women wearing gardenias as big as football rosettes who were massed beneath a banner informing anyone passing that 'Albuquerque Women's Club welcomes Sybil Harper'. A very small child in Shirley Temple ringlets and an obscenely short frock was waiting to present the guest of honour with a bouquet of yucca flowers.

The steward had come to replace Evelyn's water jug. 'We only stop here for supplies in the regular way,' he explained, clearly expecting her to be impressed, 'but Miss Harper's a VIP.'

In the corridor outside Evelyn's compartment heavy male feet were marching in time to the band. She opened her door a few inches and saw a dozen or more men heading off to reclaim the observation car where Sybil Harper had apparently been in the habit of regaling the smokers with all ten thousand words of her next article.

'Look on the bright side, Jim,' laughed one of the men. 'It's saved us a dollar on next week's *Nation*.'

'My wife says they named a sweet pea after her,' said his friend.

'Was it red?'

Evelyn yearned to stretch her legs and explore. Dare she risk a visit to the bar? She had not thought to pack a Bible in her suitcase – the Hungarian dictionary seemed far more to the purpose and space was limited. When Silas's posting was announced she had bought him a tiny, India paper Bible to take with him but he hadn't been especially pleased. There must be six, seven copies of the Good Book in the house already, he said ('You've got Bibles'). She had tucked it into his kit bag without telling him but it hadn't been among the personal effects that had been sent back to her.

To her surprise, there was a copy of the King James Version in one of the cubbyholes in her compartment. Its American cloth cover and gilt lettering glinted alluringly in the light of the bedside lamp. Evelyn slipped the book from its place, looked up at the ceiling and let the leaves fall open: the Book of Joshua: 'Be strong and of a good courage; be not afraid, neither be thou dismayed.' What would Jesus do? Jesus would pick up *The War of the Worlds*, rub on some lipstick and head for the cocktail lounge.

Mrs Van Clark was seated in the corner enjoying a preprandial Gibson.

'Why there you are! Come and join us.'

Mrs Van Clark was very impressed indeed by Sybil Harper's unscheduled stop but, from habit, recast the event to reflect on her own life, reminding Wanda that they always used to stop the trains for Great-Grandpa Hopkins. Great-Grandpa Hopkins practically *owned* the old New England Railroad. Wanda appeared unmoved but then Wanda had probably heard this boast before.

'Mimi Hendriks took the clipper last time she went to Palm Beach,' said Wanda, winding her wristwatch. 'Only takes fifteen hours. I *hate* trains.'

'Do you have children, Mrs Murdoch?' said her mother suddenly.

'No.' Evelyn lowered her head.

Mrs Van Clark tipped her mad little topknot to one side. Blue today, like an ailing budgerigar (Delilah had been collared accordingly). She pulled a sad face the way people always did when Evelyn admitted her childlessness then began fondling her little girl's hand.

'They can be such a comfort ...'

Wanda ordered a second cocktail and took her hand away.

Evelyn was only six when her mother died and she found it hard not to covet the easy friendliness of mothers and daughters she saw shopping or lunching together. She had once found her father sitting in their wirelessless parlour with his wife's photograph on his lap (she realised afterwards that it must have been the anniversary of her death) and, emboldened by the growing darkness, had asked him if she was like her. Not in the least. He had not even looked up.

She gathered up her things and smiled her apologies at the Van Clarks.

'Excuse me, won't you. My dinner reservation is for six thirty.'

'You sure you won't have another drink?' coaxed the older woman as Evelyn rose to leave. 'There's so much I want to ask you.'

'I want to get an early night.'

Evelyn was shown to the only free table and presented with a glass of iced water and a folded card. A life of irregular verbs and vocabulary lists had not prepared her for the Super Chief's bill of fare: *meunière* and *à la minute* were simple enough but 'Harvard beets'? 'Devilled squab'? Did one eat it, drink it or pray for its sins?

'Can I help at all?'

Evelyn looked up in alarm as the blond young man from the Maple Room reversed unasked into the seat opposite and signalled to the waiter to bring him a menu.

The suit was blue now, a pale, almost girlish shade, and his club stripes had been replaced by a foulard tie like a strip cut from a headscarf.

She watched a look of surprise – and mild interest – flambé across his face as he registered Alphonse's work with the tongs. She scowled back at the bill of fare. Grits?

'Kind of mean the way these bozos print such a lot of it in French, isn't it? *Parfait, julienne, charcuterie*, all that baloney.'

Evelyn couldn't very well explain that it was not the French that required translation without blowing her 'cover'. Besides, it obviously pleased him to patronise her. She was about to make some reply when a small, many-buttoned boy marched in bearing a chromium-plated tray.

'Telegram for Mrs Murdoch?'

Evelyn took care to keep Jeremy Fitzmorton's cable out of view but realised too late that the man had already seen the address on the envelope: 'Mrs Silas Murdoch, Miracle Studios'.

'FELIX KAY MEETING PASADENA,' read the telegram. 'WILL ADVISE HOUSEWISE STOP WALLS STOP EARS STOP.'

The boy produced a printed form and Evelyn quickly pencilled a reply: 'WILLCO STOP ALL SERENE MURDOCH.'

She handed over the slip but the boy remained beside her, waiters cursing wordlessly as they shimmied around him bearing huge trays of squab and grits. It was only when her unwanted dinner companion produced a magic coin from his pocket that the child finally disappeared.

Evelyn pocketed her telegram.

'Thank you. I owe you a dime.'

He shook his head and turned to the waiter, his small bronzed ear a relief carving against the close-cropped side of his skull. There was something disturbingly *anatomical* about the tendons that built the column of that tanned hairless throat, like the curved and turgid shaft of a hyacinth stem.

He began ordering before she could protest.

'We would like a bottle of the Margaux and we will both have *consommé*, *antipasto*, a *truite aux amandes* and a *filet mignon* – medium rare, with *pommes alumettes*.' He turned to Evelyn with a well-rehearsed twinkle. 'A hundred and thirty years since the Louisiana Purchase but we still have to dine *à la carte*.' *We* not *they*. 'Why we can't call a clear soup a clear soup I will never understand.'

She knitted him a tiny, grateful smile, to mask her irritation.

'Thank you for ordering; I was miles away.'

'Not *bat* news in your cable, I hope?'

'No. No. Not at all.'

'There is no one to introduce us,' he said. 'My name is Weiss –' he pronounced it with a W '– Joseph Weiss but please call me Joe. And you are …'

'Evelyn Murdoch.'

The handshake was carpus-crushingly Teutonic but it was hard to be completely sure of his origins. Weiss was not an English name but then so few American surnames were. Even the grand ones were Dutch (or tried to be). His pronunciation of individual words – *nooze* for news, '*coll* me Joe'– was irreproachably transatlantic but his Yankee twang was very faint – it took more than a flat 'a' to make an American accent. He had ordered her steak and potatoes in flawless French – a far cry from Mrs Van Clark's struggles with *mousseline de soie* – but his speech in general had the clipped fluency found only among those who had learned another language first. Swiss, perhaps? But he'd been 'Sepp' to the man seeing him off in New York – nothing Swiss about that. Evelyn thought again of his Chicago friend's blue and white bow tie.

She tried to rebuff further sallies by turning to *War of the Worlds* ('The Heat-Ray in the Chobham Road') but Mr Weiss was unsquashable. He refilled her glass. Was she joining her husband? (The faintest nod in the direction of that telltale ring finger.)

There had been moments during her *Mouzinho* voyage when she thought she might very well be joining Silas. The purser had talked airily of 'target practice' – *alvo prática* – when they heard sounds of artillery but none of the passengers was convinced and Evelyn had lain terrified in her bunk anticipating the imminent heavenly reunion. Her mother-in-law was fond of savouring the joys in store: 'Dear Silas has gone to a Better Place.' 'I think she may mean Walton-on-Thames,' said Deborah.

'Is he based in LA?'

Evelyn gave a guilty start.

'Is who based in LA?'

'Your husband.'

'No. He was killed …'

Joseph Weiss's well-kept hand flew to his face.

'I'm terribly sorry. So many *tratchedies* …'

Silas would not have approved of those polished fingernails or that hand-painted necktie. The train, with its cunning modern fittings, would have appealed to his tidy mind but the excesses of the menu would have been Frowned Upon.

Evelyn's *antipasto* had been served and she looked up to see that during her reverie her dinner companion had balanced his water glass on the top of his head. Evelyn laughed in spite of herself and a man sitting across the aisle clapped his hands. Silas would not have been laughing.

'What's wrong, Mrs Murdoch? You were *away with the fairies.*'

Another hard-won idiom on parade. She chased the last olive across her plate.

'I keep wondering what my husband would have made of all this …'

'Did he like Italian food?'

'Not particularly.'

The shilling lunch at the hotel where Evelyn and Silas had spent their three-night honeymoon had been *spaghettis à la sauce Bolognaise.* Silas hadn't cared for it and said so repeatedly while he cleared his plate. Mr Weiss changed tack.

'So, where are you headed, Mrs Murdoch?'

She was suddenly very conscious of Jeremy Fitzmorton's telegraphic warning in her pocket and it struck her that this handsome young man was showing an unnatural amount of interest in her affairs, but his questions were so insistent – and so *normal*, after all, in this nosy new world – that she had little choice but to answer them. Stonewalling would only arouse further suspicion.

'Pasadena.' No sense fudging, he'd be sure to see her get off the train.

'*Hollywoot?*' Another appraising glance as he tried to decode her contradictory wardrobe. 'No! Don't tell me!' Roguish suddenly. 'Let me guess … They'd have put you on the Union Pacific if you were just a script girl and you aren't exactly the starlet type …'

Hard to say why this remark should irritate and her face evidently betrayed her because she could sense him easing into reverse.

'And far too pretty for a writer … I haff it! Voice culture?'

'How clever of you.' Far too clever. She could have been a thousand things.

'I *thought* so.' The tip of his tongue came a fraction too far forward as he made absolutely certain of the *th*.

'And a mistress of the art, yes? To warrant a drawing room on the Super Chief?'

'The studio want me to start straight away,' murmured Evelyn. *How did he know she had a drawing room?*

'Who's your boss? I probably know him. It's a big town but it's a small world –' a preening pause '– for anybody who *iss* anybody.'

He was every bit as nosy as Mrs Van Clark. Mrs Van Clark seemed the lesser of two evils – unless of course the script had made the Connecticut housewife the spy and Joseph ('call me Joe') Weiss the knight in shining armour. Melvyn Douglas, possibly, or nice Michael Redgrave.

Joseph Weiss leaned forward to bone his trout, releasing a blast of cologne: vanilla; lavender ('the smell of thy garments is like the smell of Lebanon'). Nothing about Silas had smelled of vanilla or lavender (he had been trained by his mother to take his shoes off in the house). The sweet scent intensified in the heat of the dining car. Evelyn's *filet mignon* had been garnished with fried onions.

She felt a qualm of nausea as Joseph Weiss placed his hand on hers. A much smaller, softer hand than Jeremy Fitzmorton's. It took real physical effort not to twitch her arm away. Pretty young men did not make passes at women like her, Alphonse or no Alphonse.

She grabbed her bag and her book with her free hand.

'You must forgive me but I'm not quite the thing. Please let me give you some money for dinner.'

'I wouldn't hear of it. I'll walk you back to your compartment.'

He paid with a note from a crocodile billfold. As he was doing so, the train swerved into a bend and a passing martini fiend tottered towards them in high patent-leather heels. Joseph Weiss put an arm out to steady the woman, letting the open wallet fall on to the tablecloth between them: two pockets, a tidy wad of dollar bills in the first and, just visible behind them, the torn half of a million-mark note.

Chapter 5

WHEN EVELYN woke the next morning the New Mexico moonscape had cut to a backdrop of citrus groves with tidy trees that stretched out to a vanishing point like a perfectly plotted perspective drawing: gay as a child's colouring book, neat as a Swiss orchard.

Oranges and tangerines were a Christmas food in the Murdoch kitchen which had offered pretty short rations even before Lord Woolton took a hand. Mid-morning and afternoon tea came with one very plain, very yellow biscuit. 'They don't grow on trees, you know' – but maybe they did, smiled Evelyn to herself as she looked out of the train window, maybe they did *here*, in this strange, Oz-like world.

Evelyn's summer dress hung dispiritedly from her thin shoulders. Its wash-weary fabric looked quite different in American sunlight and after a few minutes spent sighing at her reflection on the back of the compartment door she had retrieved her grey coat and skirt – it was October now, after all – but the sun was far too bright for the foxes. As she stepped from the refrigerated atmosphere of the Super Chief the early-morning heat of Pasadena was like opening an airing cupboard.

The way to the station exit was blocked by a group of pressmen that had gathered around the starlet from

Grand Central who was posing for a photograph beneath the 'Pasadena' sign, a bunch of salmon-pink roses against her gleaming-white dress, lips wide and red beneath big black fly's-eye sunglasses. A well-corseted woman in a large organza hat stood at the back of the pack, scribbling in a notebook. An anklet glinted beneath the sheer fabric of her stocking, digging into the plump flesh of her shin.

The rest of the platform was crowded with waiting friends and relations all in the gayest pastels. Albanian national dress would have been the mildest mufti in comparison with Evelyn's sober subfusc which made her as conspicuous as a barmaid in Bible class. The chap from Miracle spotted her at once.

'Mrs Murdoch?' The tall, dark-haired man raised his hat, shook her hand and introduced himself as Felix Kay then led her to an open-topped car parked in pride of place in front of the main entrance. A large printed card was tucked behind the windscreen wiper: 'Waiting for Miracle'. A camera flashed as Felix Kay helped Evelyn into the front passenger seat and when he walked round to the driver's side the lady journalist in the hat caught him by the sleeve.

'Anyone the *Hollywood Examiner* should know about?'

'Good morning, Miss Manning. Felix Kay from Miracle. That's Evelyn Murdoch, we just signed her from England.' Miss Manning's rapid mental cross-referencing drew a blank: a woman of absolutely no importance. She gave a slight shake of her head but Felix Kay wasn't giving up that easily. 'And that's Fox Meredith over there.' He jerked his chin in the direction of a lissom young man waiting by the station entrance. 'Foxton Meredith? Plays Galahad in the new Miracle movie. Gonna be big. Want me to introduce you?'

Felix Kay turned back to Evelyn apologetically.

'This won't take a minute.'

He took the columnist's arm and led her and her cameraman across to the young star then stood clear as the photographer went to work. Foxton Meredith had dressed for California in white trousers and a short-sleeved shirt with an initial on the front. A lime-green sports coat was slung over one shoulder in the hook of his forefinger. He looked faintly unreal; too smart, too handsome for every-day use. Like an advertisement for Virginia cigarettes or a tennis professional in a country club. Evelyn had never actually seen one of these in the flesh but they lurked on the edges of love stories and murder mysteries: clean, pressed, bronzed and faintly untrustworthy.

When the snapshots had been taken Evelyn saw Felix Kay whisper something in the actor's ear before darting back to the long, white car and vaulting into the driving seat without opening the door.

'All set?'

'This is terribly kind of Mr Kiss but I was thinking that it might be nice to stretch my legs and see something of the city. Is it awfully far?'

'Fourteen miles but it's a pleasant drive.'

Felix Kay pulled out of the parking space and eased into the morning traffic. His fingernails were as shiny as the wheel, with smoothly curved whites of a crisp and even length. Either he spent time doing it or he paid a girl to do it for him on a little marble table. Both possibilities were unnerving. Silas's nails, jaundiced by disinfectant soap, were always pared with a penknife.

What was the Kay for? she wondered. Kravitz? Kellner? Katzenellenbogen?

Almost every street on the route was an avenue. Hothouse plants were growing abundantly in the front gardens. After fifteen minutes of driving through a never-ending suburb of hedge-ringed villas there was a sudden bend in the road and the city opened out beneath them, feather-duster palm trees pin-sharp against the dusty haze beyond.

The sun was still quite low behind them but the sky's brightness appeared to emanate from all directions at once, as if someone had just taken the lid off the world. Evelyn blotted her cheeks with her handkerchief and took her new dark glasses from her pocketbook.

'It was eighty-six degrees yesterday but they forecast some rain later. You should have been here in August. The desert made a hundred and forty in the shade. I should imagine your place will be air-conditioned – you definitely seem to be getting the VIP treatment. Did the great big Kiss hire you himself?'

'No –' Evelyn had been mentally rehearsing her answers to this one '– it was all done through the London office.' She realised that she had better change the subject before he probed more closely. She fought with the urge to ask the bore's question but, rather like Mrs Van Clark, he supplied information without any prompting.

'A couple of us Miracle writers are on part-time second-ment to the Kiss outfit – kind of like a sub-let. It doesn't exactly say "driver" in my contract but the Kiss office said he wanted someone to come and get you and it never hurts to be nice.'

Nice. Highest praise from Silas but it meant something else when Felix Kay said it and it was clear that, just now anyway, this young man needed to be very nice indeed to a *gantseh macher* like Zandor Kiss. Mr Kay had looked dapper enough in long shot but close-up you could see the furry fray of his shirt cuffs, the baggy knees of his flannels, the pulled threads on the blazer. These were not the clothes of a successful person, Evelyn knew that now.

Only a European could get away with that kind of dishevelment. Anyone important would have been better dressed and anyone important would have been far too busy to pick up stray Englishwomen from the railway station.

'How long have you been a film writer?'

'Too long, my mom says. My mother would be glad to see me out of here, back at my desk job in the publisher's office. My kid brother's an accountant and I was supposed to be a dentist. Every time she gets a cavity she reminds me how much it shouldn't be costing. And she can never understand why films don't have my name on them. In the end I told her I worked on *Gone With the Wind*. Come to think of it, who *didn't* work on *Gone With the Wind*? Maybe it wasn't Scott Fitzgerald who did those rewrites? Maybe it was me. That's the great part about being a writer – no one has ever heard of you.'

Their progress across the city was slowed somewhat by the downtown traffic. No pepper trees here but office buildings and apartment blocks that loomed high and strange against the cobalt sky: Mexican; Moorish; Egyptian – as if the Pharaohs had branched out into banking and life insurance – and the empty lots in between were filled with parked cars and fronted by giant advertising hoardings: 'Fireproof Your Home: No Job Too Small; Wafer-thin Bespoke Hairpieces: They're Undetectable!' A boy on roller skates was gliding between the vehicles in order to pass a newspaper ('Hitler Warns US on British Aid') through the window of an ancient black motor car, its right-hand passenger door held shut with string. Not everyone in Los Angeles drove a large white convertible and not everyone drove especially well but the mood on the street was oddly forgiving and the tooting minimal – which Evelyn found reassuring ('someone at the Miracle office is sorting you out a motor').

Evelyn had been taught to drive abroad when still a schoolgirl but Silas had refused to put her name on the policy for his glossy black Austin. She could have her turn 'when the war was over'. How would they ever have found time for all the things that had been postponed until then?

Silas had always driven in complete silence, constantly checking the mirrors and making an absurd parade of every gear change. Felix Kay's relaxed grip on the steering wheel was like a man holding the reins of a canny old horse that knew the way home and he treated Evelyn to a running commentary on the city, the studio and any landmarks they passed.

Evelyn was going to like her new Bel Air address. Her lodgings were in the grounds of a house belonging to one of Kiss's movie-producer friends: Manny Silverman. Silverman had been one of the founders of Miracle Studios but he was more of a sleeping partner these days. A guy called Kramer was the money man and all the real movie-making work was done by Silverman's son-in-law: PZ Homberg.

'PZ used to be Silverman's golden boy back in the Twenties. Silverman would have maybe a dozen turkeys written off and in the vault and PZ would stay up all night in one of the screening rooms with the head cutter and make whole new pictures out of them. Three new scenes: new poster, new tunes for the piano player, a new set of titles and he could turn a silent weepie into a screwball comedy and Silverman had a string of low-budget hits on his hands.'

'What does the P stand for?'

'*Eberhardt*, but that would have made it Ee Zee – not exactly ideal – so he changed it.'

'And the Zed? The zee, I mean.'

'There is no zee. It's like the O in David O. Selznick. Purely ornamental.'

'And the B in Louis B. Mayer?'

'Don't tempt me.'

He smiled.

'Anyhow, Manny Silverman used to live in the Bel Air house when he was married to his first wife so naturally it was never going to be good enough for Mamie – wife number two – but Mr Silverman never liked to let go of a house – and neither did Mamie. Her old man made a fortune in the movie business but he sold up just before the crash in '29 and made a killing in real estate. They must have a dozen houses between them because they can't seem to settle on one they both like. You know that story about the fisherman and his wife? The one where she keeps pestering him for more bathrooms? That's Mamie Silverman.

'Mamie and Kiss go way back. I think it was her idea to loan you the house. She's away upstate till the weekend but she's ordered in a bunch of emergency groceries and she'll be dropping by Saturday and you're to tell Mr Hashimoto if you need anything – he's kind of the gardener. Those Japs can grow anything.' He gestured to a man at the road-side who was deadheading the flowering shrubs planted down the middle of the untrodden pavement.

'It's very tony to have a Jap gardener but the snobs prefer to have English servants in the house if they can afford them – and if they can hang on to them. Practically every English butler I've ever met has been an actor-in-waiting – some of them hand out photos. I may even have a crack at it myself. Your man HP gave us all a master-class: *Anyone fency a snifter?*'

The houses grew larger and smarter as the car turned under a huge white archway reading 'Bel Air'. It was a public highway but there was a strong sense of trespass as they wound up through the hills. Some of the mansions were hidden behind ironwork and high hedging with only turrets and gables visible from the road but many were less coy: Colonial, French provincial, Italianate, Hispanic villas, houses so grand and ivied they seemed to cry out for velvet ropes, sixpenny tours and shilling teas in the old tithe barn afterwards.

Finally the car cruised into an open driveway and slowed to a halt. Felix Kay took off his sunglasses. Nice, soft brown eyes.

'Welcome to Cedar Point.'

A well-swept sweep of gravel led to a curious-looking wooden house built in the shade of a pair of cedar trees. It had a log-cabin look and appeared single storey from the driveway but its rambling structure clung to the curves of the canyon behind, descending in a series of verandahs and sleeping porches sheltered by overhanging pitched roofs.

The garden had been laid out in the Japanese manner, with bamboo alleys and lily ponds and several tons of stone chippings, but whoever commissioned it all had evidently wearied of this orientalist restraint and had the borders replanted with seed-packet blossoms of phloxes and begonias. Evelyn pulled at a low hedge of Jicky-scented lavender and thought of her mother's dressing table.

Silas had never cared for flower gardening and the garden at No. 9 had been a tidy arrangement of lawn and shrubs until half of it was ploughed up to make way for the air-raid shelter.

'Pretty, isn't it?' Felix Kay tugged at a stray thread on his cuff to mask yet another sneaky peek at his watch. 'The guesthouse is just down thataway, you'll find the key under the mat. A studio driver is gonna meet you with the car they got for you tomorrow at eight thirty right *here*.' He pointed to the love seat under the porch. He took all her things from the boot and climbed back into the Miracle motor.

'I'd love to stay and show you around but I have to run: I have a meeting at ten. You gonna be OK? The gardener guy should be around somewhere but here's my number if you need anything.' He handed her a business card printed in the same style as the ones Jeremy Fitzmorton had given her. This one said 'Felix S. Kay, Script Department'.

It was only as the big white car crunched away over the stones and off down the hill that Evelyn realised she didn't even know her own address.

It had begun to rain. Picking up her bags and hatbox she set off 'thataway', pausing on the hump of the Japanese bridge that spanned the ornamental pond to look back at the house and its stone garden, then noticed with a start that expert hands had raked Mrs Silverman's tidy square of gravel into a maze of interlocking swastikas.

The expert hands had not had time for the rest of the garden. Once over the bridge and through the arch in the hedge, Evelyn had to fight her way through a fairy-tale forest of oleander and bamboo. A grapevine had scrambled across a sagging pergola overhead, each stem thickly clustered with mildewed raisins. Down the hill, at the far end of the weed-choked path, Evelyn could just make out an empty swimming pool. Rotting hibiscus blossoms like discarded cigars filled the puddle at what had been the deep end. The bungalow alongside had unwashed windows, and a broken gutter had created a permanent mudbath alongside the front porch where someone had dumped two brown paper sacks against one of the empty terracotta urns. Next to them a florist's basket of long-stemmed roses had been blown into the mire by the stiffening breeze.

The crunch of her feet on the cinder path disturbed a large Bengal cat. It stood, back arched, all four paws poised, left-right left-right, on a fencing rail in front of a honeycomb of clay drainage pipes. Each little tunnel had been stuffed with straw and leaves to furnish ready-built homes for something. Something quite small – smaller than a Bengal cat anyway. Not a twitch or rustle from the man-made nests but the cat gave a swift lick to its whiskers as Evelyn passed, betraying a recent visit to this catty automat. Just as she reached out to pet the animal, a wiry man in grey overalls holding a curved pruning saw sprang on to the path behind her, brandishing the blade above his head.

'No come today! Lady no come today! Lady come Monday!'

Terrified, Evelyn took a fierce grip on her case and stumbled down the hill towards the bungalow. The man lowered his weapon and followed in her wake, alternately bowing and shaking his head.

'Lady no go little house!' His voice rose to a squeal of panic. 'No go today! House not shipshape!'

He remained screaming on the edge of the swimming pool as Evelyn fumbled under the mat for the key, wrenched open the lock and bundled in the suitcase, flowers and groceries, bolting the door behind her and feeling for the light switch.

House not shipshape. The bungalow had been laid out on *House Beautiful* lines – three bathrooms, glass doors on to a pool patio and a whole saleroom of French furniture – but the gilded fauteuils in the drawing room had been stacked on top of one another to make room for a set of stepladders.

The master bedroom had a bergère bed watched over by a trio of Degas prints showing dancing girls scratching themselves or tying their ballet shoelaces, but when Evelyn walked into the walk-in closet she found a large collection of rakes, hoes and some sort of telescopic mop arrangement which was used – only not used, obviously – to clean the swimming pool. The bathroom had become a kind of ensuite potting shed. The rose-coloured bathtub was littered with tins of house paint and there were flowerpots on all the glass shelves and a dank, outdoors-y smell of wet earth and weedkiller. The water from both taps was ice cold.

Someone had left two dress boxes and a pair of large carrier bags on the only bare patch of bedroom floor. One of them had a handy little manifest taped to the handle: 'sweaters (cashmere) x 6; *faille* (blue), duchesse satin (white), crêpe (navy), grosgrain (cinnamon), knife-pleated chiffon (beige); kimono (yellow); bathing suit x 1'. Miracle had thriftily sourced most of the clothes from the studio's wardrobe department but there was a price tag on the white frock: $180. Evelyn thought again of Silas in the hat shop: 'Every shilling which you needlessly spend on your apparel is in effect stolen from the poor.' She shivered and pulled one of the sweaters from its cellophane (fully fashioned especially for her in 'Bonny Wee Scotland', if the label was to be believed) and buttoned it on over her blouse.

Whoever wasn't looking after the house had made their home in the kitchen which was in relatively good order and boasted a refrigerator as big as her Super Chief bathroom. Evelyn unpacked the sacks of 'emergency' groceries that Mrs Silverman had ordered: eggs, sliced bread, cheese, half a gallon of milk, some tins of fish, a net of oranges, a can of olives, a packet of smoked almonds

85

and two quarts of vodka – what kind of emergency had she had in mind? Evelyn made herself a toasted cheese sandwich and settled herself in an armchair by the sitting-room windows listening to the thunder and stroking her kitten-soft Scottish sleeves. She read another chapter of *War of the Worlds* – 'the Martians have completely wrecked Woking station and massacred an entire battalion' – then made a start on the script of *Duchess in the Dirt*: '"Oh Bill, this is so sudden!" He takes her in his arms, bends her head back and kisses her hard on the mouth again and again, till she struggles for breath.'

As Evelyn sank deeper into the armchair there was a crinkle of paper in her skirt pocket: Deborah's unfinished letter.

It turned much colder the day you left and Mother has made me hang the winter curtains. She continues the same (more's the pity). I'd like to say she sends her regards but she refused to do any such thing. I suggested she might and she said 'Evelyn who?' – she has days like that. Mrs F has finally said she will do for us Mondays *and* Thursdays, which is a great help although Mother I know has never approved and why can't I keep my own house – you know the drill.

Mrs F and I don't normally coincide but I found her still swabbing the scullery floor with a wet rag when I got in from work on Thursday so I asked how she was managing. Turns out Mrs F's Arfur was called up back in August what with the conscription age going up to thirty-six (having argued without success that 'bookie's runner' was a reserved occupation or bleeding well ought to be – her words not mine). She was very tight-lipped at first but then I made her a cup of Oxo and she broke down and said that Private F hadn't liked basic training in Shoeburyness one little bit, that the food was something chronic and the beds left a great deal to be desired and that Private F had gone absent without leave at his old uncle's place on the Isle of Sheppey or similar.

He'd gone to ground for the best part of a month before he finally paid a call on Mrs F and the two little Fs last Sunday teatime shortly followed by two military policemen (you can tell it's them apparently because they wear red hats though you'd think mufti would be more to the purpose). They had a dog of some kind with them but had left it in their car or tank or whatever they drove up in which was something of a blessing because Mr F had by this time got under the tea table which had a long plush under-cloth with a kind of giant doily on top – I could practically draw it for you Mrs F was so particular.

Anyway. He dives under as soon as he spies the MPs through the net curtains at which point F minor and little Rubella or Scarlatina or Salmonella or Eczema or whatever the child's name is decide what larks and do let's join Daddy playing bears under the table. Lucky he didn't slit their throats, I reckon, but he must have sat on them or something because his beloved wife was able to remain seated at a table set for four – red salmon, boiled bacon and a nice tinned Dundee cake to follow according to Mrs F (all black market, obviously) – and swear blind that no, she ain't seen hide nor hair of him straight up and wossy done now and wipe her eyes on a drawn-thread serviette her old mum had made and all that twaddle. But it must have been a cracking performance just the same because the nasty men went away and daddy bear and baby bears emerged from hibernation and tucked back into their tinned salmon (not too much vinegar but you've got to have a bit because it can be very dry, salmon, thank you Mrs F).

He's now back on the Isle of Sheppey (or so he said in his last postcard). They have a code and the uncle posts them. Uncle Sid, should anyone ever ask, though you'd better not tell anyone any of this. Poor Mrs F, I say. Poor Mr F really. I've been to Shoeburyness. Rained every day. Ghastly hole.

I dare say it is very nice for you to be out of it all and away from all the memories of poor dear Silas but it is funny not having you here to talk to. Mother would probably appreciate some chocolate (two small rather than one large as she will eat the lot otherwise). I now hide everything in the mending basket. Last place she'd look. Lazy old so-and-so.

Hoping this finds you (as they say). Literally in your case of course. We both remember you and poor dear Silas in our prayers.

Yours truly

Deborah

PS. Is Errol Flynn as tall as he looks? I do so envy you.

Evelyn must have been asleep for several hours because it was dark outside when she woke. It was still raining hard and the splashes fell heavily on the bamboo that crowded against the glass doors but there was something larger and louder than raindrops rootling around the front porch and something else howling like a big, sick spaniel in the canyon below. She grilled herself another sandwich then tried the kitchen wireless but it made a noise like cellophane whichever way she turned the dial. There was a distant rumbling sound and a faraway dring of burglar alarms. Glasses tinkled in the kitchen cabinet. She realised with a tearful feeling of panic that not only did she not know her actual address, she hadn't even the vaguest idea of where the house was located except that it was fourteen miles from Pasadena. Was that still Los Angeles even? There was a letter rack by the kitchen telephone but it contained nothing but a stack of tourist leaflets urging her to visit Santa Monica pier or an ostrich farm and the only map showed the best ski runs at Lake Arrowhead. She found the business card that Felix Kay had given her and picked up the telephone receiver. The line was dead.

Chapter 6

THE SWASTIKAS were much harder to see by the time Evelyn had mastered the gears on her borrowed car the next morning and she and the studio driver headed down the hill and into the traffic on Sunset Boulevard. She could imagine Silas nagging as she drove ('keep left; check the mirror'), sense him wincing in anticipation whenever her foot pressed the accelerator, but her test drive went smoothly enough and the man in the peaked cap and brass buttons had been surprised by the ease with which she reeled off the route he showed her – 'My old lady can get lost in her own driveway.'

The noticeboard next to the second-floor office at Miracle Studios had four names slotted into it: T. V. Monroe, F. S. Kay, C. M. McAllister and H. P. Peyton (this last sign written in a slightly different hand). The door was held open by a small stack of scripts. A female voice, very angry, rather shrill, could be heard from the stairwell. How come this dame was getting her own office? How come Peyton got his own goddamned office? Mr HP fancy-pants Peyton had only shown up for a week or three at a time and yet there was a corner office with his name on it. And now this English dame was going to waltz right in? Not if she had anything to do with it. No key: no office. There was the sound of a door being locked.

Evelyn took a silent step back and watched the scene play out through the hinge of the open door. The long room was lined with Venetian-blinded windows and filled with large steel desks. There was a (now locked) door in one corner and the prime space in the other was taken up by a writing table heaped high with unopened post. The shelves behind it were untidily filled with scripts and reference volumes bookended by a tennis racket and a set of gaily painted Indian clubs. On the wall beside it was a dartboard with a pockmarked photograph of Hitler pinned over the bull's eye.

The complaining voice belonged to a smart-looking typist type in a tight-fitting dress with a detachable pilgrim collar. She wore very high heels on very large feet and enough cosmetics to grease a Bren gun. Her hair had been elaborately arranged so that two brown Chelsea buns were perched on either side of her head like mouse ears. Evelyn thought of Alphonse and his little steel styling comb and wondered what time she got up in the morning.

The girl's remarks were addressed to Felix Kay who was lounging in a captain's chair with his feet on the desk blotter, a long, brown cigarette in the corner of his smile. He was wearing the previous day's blazer and flannels but his soft felt hat had been replaced by a pink chiffon wimple. The matching bodice and kirtle had been tucked into the open neck of his shirt and flowed down to the chequered linoleum floor. The girl brandished a plywood broadsword and poked him in the chest with it.

'And what's with the fancy dress?'

He flicked the ash from his cigarette, pulled a wisp of chiffon across his face and simpered from behind it. 'I told them I was only doing the rewrites for *Knights of Love* if I could get into character. They're sending a roast ox and some wenches over this afternoon.'

He opened a red-bound copy of the script and began acting out a scene to himself from a sheet of typed foolscap tucked inside, a fruity English baritone alternating with a maidenly falsetto.

'My queen!'

'Lancelot! Lancelot, my prince!'

'Tell me you didn't write that.'

'You wound me, fair maiden. PeeZee wrote it. "Felix baby," he says, "could you lemme see a rewrite on that bedroom scene?" Sure, I say, exactly how would he like it rewritten? "I don't know," says PZ. "I haven't read it yet." Can you believe that? I sweat a pint of O negative redoing the love scenes, rush them over to his office in record time and the guy doesn't even turn the page. Then he dictates this junk to his stenographer, fires off a memo or three, gets them to shoot it and then wonders why the scene is lousy. And the worst part is I can't change a word of Lancelot's dialogue because Lancelot is up in the desert making *Rodeo Romeo* and is unavailable for further shooting.'

'You should be flattered he asked you at all – especially after the job Ted Monroe did on that jungle picture. Didn't have to reshoot a single scene: did the whole thing in the cutting room just the way PZ used to. Guy's a magician.'

'Meaning I'm not?'

Felix swivelled his chair and spotted Evelyn in the doorway.

'Mrs Murdoch! Good morrow!'

The girl was all smiles suddenly. The kind of smile you might give a dentist. There was lipstick on her teeth and one of her maxillary premolars had a gold inlay.

'Why hello! You must be Mr Kiss's little friend: Mrs Murdoch from Woking. He says we're to take extra special care of you. What a *darling* dress. It's English, isn't it? I can *always* tell.' Her accent was inching east as she spoke; she even dropped the 'r' from 'darling'.

'We had *heaps* of fun when HP was here. Did you ever see him do the double rumba samba? He's a knockout. Come right in, make yourself at home.'

'Do you think I might have a cup of tea?'

It was clear from the other woman's face that Evelyn had dropped a brick of some kind. Evelyn gave an uncertain smile. 'Or coffee? If that would be easier.'

'Yes ma'am –' the sneeriest hint of a curtsey '– coming right up.'

The typist vanished into the kitchenette on the landing and began slamming cupboard doors. Felix Kay looked at Evelyn and slowly shook his head.

'Oh dear oh dear oh dear. Connie won't have liked that.'

Not a typist at all, as it turned out, but the C. M. McAllister on the noticeboard. A writer, rather a good writer (or so Felix Kay said), and now rather a cross one.

'Oh dear.'

The telephone on his desk rang. Yes she had arrived. Yes, he would pass on the message.

'Mr Kiss left word that you were to have the full studio tour,' said Felix, pulling off his costume. 'Connie's taking you – we tossed a coin. You'll watch a bit of filming, see all the sights, grab some lunch, then you're to head back to Bel Air and get ready for the big Kramer birthday party this evening. Kiss will see you there if his flights all connect. Gotta go. I'm due at Stage Eight. Kiss wanted the second unit to add some food close-ups to the banqueting scene in *Knights of Love* and rumour has it they're roasting a swan. Cheerio!'

He grabbed his hat from the stand, blew Evelyn a kiss and charged off down the stairs.

Big Kramer party? Evelyn thought of the still-unexplored shopping bags on the bedroom floor and sipped nervously at the coffee Miss McAllister had given her.

'What sort of party is it? Formal?'

Miss McAllister hesitated.

'More black tie than white, I should say, but pretty swanky. Did you come prepared or do you want I should ring Wardrobe?'

Evelyn shook her head, struggling to recall the studio's shopping list. '*Faille* (blue)' could well be a frock of some kind …

'All ready for the grand tour? We'll take your car. It's sure to be nicer than mine. Your man Peyton had a Cadillac.'

The studio chauffeur had told Evelyn to leave her car directly in front of the Writers' Block, a three-storey building got up to look like a New York tenement, complete with fire-escape ladders and neon signs at each end. One read 'Acme Steam Laundry' and the Chinese characters running down the opposite corner actually said 'Cheap funerals' but the Chinese extras hired for *Rickshaw Romance* and its sequel *Mandarin By Moonlight* had been much too amused to point this out to anyone.

'The whole thing's thatched and half-timbered on the other side,' said Miss McAllister. 'Did you see *Young Elizabeth*? Saves on set-building.'

A wall of cypress trees screened this multipurpose structure from the rest of the complex, which had been built in the Moderne style and then royal iced with shimmering vanilla stucco. The sound stages and office buildings had the tidy unreality of an architect's model but in the far corner of the lot behind another line of trees a standing set offered a whole fake city of house and shop fronts. The plate-glass facades of the lawyer's office and drugstore would all look solid enough on screen but when Evelyn peeped inside she saw that the whole block was hollow, roughly criss-crossed with supporting beams like the makeshift innards of a helter-skelter. Huge cables snaked across the road, feeding the massive lights that perched above the cornices. On Main Street a pair of sign-writers were at work rebranding the painless dentist as a hat shop ready for *Duchess in the Dirt*.

There was a real dentist (or a sign pointing to one) and a florist, a gymnasium, a laundry, a foundry – even a private fire station watched over by a 100,000-gallon three-legged water tank which hovered above the two scarlet engines like a Martian waiting to strike.

The rest of the 60-acre site was dominated by the sound stages, their featureless walls like the windowless back ends of an English cinema. Here and there a stair-case could be seen tiptoeing up the side. The doors at the top were there so that the lighting men could access the higher levels within, said Miss McAllister, but there was something oddly surreal about those little doors to nowhere, like a gateway in a dream.

A dozen warpainted and feathered Red Indian tribes-men sailed by in a pedal-powered yellow charabanc which was saving them the long, hot walk from Wardrobe to Wounded Knee. In a shady corner, a wigless Cavalier from a Civil War epic lounged against a fire hydrant chew-ing gum and reading a comic book. Down a side alley, half-hidden by a lean-to, the town sheriff and a knight in armour were sharing an unscripted kiss.

Showing Evelyn something in production was easier said than done, Miss McAllister explained, because the bigger stars tended to throw a tantrum if 'civilians' were smuggled on set.

'But we can go see the pulled scenes from *Knights of Love* – anyone asks, tell them Kiss sent you.'

In the warm dark of the screening room a dozen technicians and rewrite men were watching Magda Malo's next movie. After a batch of takes showing Sir Mordred going through his close-ups, the projectionist loaded the love scene that Felix and PZ Homberg were having so much trouble with. The camera panned silently across Queen Guinevere's Technicolor chamber, lingering lovingly on the stained glass, the blazing torchères, the bearskin rug, the four-poster bed, before swimming in for a close-up of the main attraction.

Queen Guinevere was discovered in a bower of rayon roses wearing an emerald gown so closely upholstered to her shape that Evelyn expected to see bullion fringing round the hem, a line of brass-headed tacks down the back seam, antimacassars over her knees. The actress greeted the advancing camera like a long-lost lover, lips parting an all-important fraction of an inch, lustrous green eyes growing wide and wet.

Evelyn had learned from Deborah's *Photoplay* that the 'Budapest Bombshell' had made quite a sensation in Otto Von Blick's *Cairo Boulevard* and had been signed by Miracle in the belief that she would be a cinch for Guinevere.

The blonde on the screen was not happy. The dewy-eyed queen vanished the moment the actress had delivered her line, her own personality coming down over her face like a safety curtain. She had been made to shoot her scenes out of sequence ('Von Blick he is *neffer* doing this') and all of her lines were fed to her piecemeal by her dialogue coach. Being unfamiliar with Arthurian legend, she remained completely in the dark about the impending plot twists. 'I don't get it. Do I *luff* Arthur or the other guy?'

Guinevere's confusion was not helped by the fact that Lancelot was twenty miles away at the studio's ranch in San Fernando valley making a new Western so her cues had to be fed to her by the director, off-camera, in a dead-pan Mitteleuropean accent.

'My Kveen!'

You could hear the technicians on the set laughing at his delivery but Guinevere's madonna-like maquillage didn't move a muscle.

'Lancy-lot,' she purred. 'Lancylot, my pwince. You came.'

'She *can* speak English,' conceded the man working the projector, 'good mimic anyway but Vivien Leigh won't be losing any sleep.'

In the far corner of the room a shirtsleeved Felix Kay was jotting down fresh dialogue on to a yellow foolscap notepad.

'Is there much more of this schlock? My banquet awaits.'

On the screen the director's voice was saying, 'That was first-rate. Eppsolutely first-rate, Magda my love. But we go for one more take to be safe, yes?'

At the stroke of twelve the screening-room technician shut down the projector and switched on the lights. Felix Kay had already dashed away to his roast swan and Miss McAllister had what she called a working lunch to go to and abandoned Evelyn at the entrance to the commissary.

By the time Evelyn had negotiated a sandwich (White? Brown? Rye? Pumpernickel?) and driven back to Writers' Block, Felix Kay was once again seated at his desk, spreading that morning's paper ('Chamberlain Resigns but Plaints Go On') across his blotter and carefully unwrapping the two half lobsters he had liberated from Stage Eight.

'The swan turned out to be plaster of Paris but everything else was real. Most of the time those big banquets you see on screen are just a lot of piped potato and a pig's head from the props department but your Mr Kiss always likes "authentic". It's like a Jewish wedding over there. Is lobster kosher? I guess I could ring my mother but then what if it isn't? Bang goes my lunch.'

Evelyn pulled out a chair and began nibbling on her sandwich.

'We should fix you up a desk.'

Felix Kay had begun clearing a pile of scripts and dictionaries from an unused table when Evelyn strolled across to the locked inner office. Its key was in her bag but instead of using it she reached a hand up to the door jamb and retrieved the duplicate from where the unimaginative McAllister female had hidden it. Always assume.

The sunlit room was smoothly panelled with bird's-eye maple. The matching desk, a tone poem of caramel curves, was roughly four times the size of those in the outer office and was importantly bare except for three gleaming telephones (one black, one white, one red) and a Rotadex filled with HP's Hollywood contacts. A card in the XYZ section contained a nameless number with a Plaza exchange. Under the blotter Evelyn found a hand-coloured photograph of Lady Genista Broome in pearls, feathers and armpit-length gloves: her presentation photograph. Someone had inked a little moustache over the smile.

There was a copy of *War of the Worlds* on the shelf with many useful underlinings – 'What have we done – what has Weybridge done? Everything gone, everything destroyed' – and an angry nib had filled the margins with notes in block capitals. 'Start here' had been written next to the opening of the first Martian cylinder on Horsell Common. Not a bad idea.

Felix, who had finished his lobster, entered the room, lay down full-length on the green plush daybed under the window, lit a cigarette and began blowing smoke rings.

'PZ had all the writers' couches taken out a few years back – "you sleep on your own damned time" were his exact words – but your guy wasn't gonna take that lying down. A few well-chosen words on the phone to Kiss's office and this beauty was bussed over within the hour. I think it had a starring role in *Those Brontë Girls*: Emily and Anne both wheezed their last on it.'

Miss McAllister, a trifle unsteady on her heels after her working lunch, was watching them from the doorway.

'I see you've made yourself at home.'

'It seems Mr Peyton is likely be tied up on another project for the foreseeable so I thought I'd install myself here for the time being.'

Evelyn took the cover off the typewriter which stood on a small wheeled table to the side of the main desk and tried to feed a piece of Miracle letterhead between its rollers. The little bell thingy kept going ping in a very irritating way.

Miss McAllister raised her eyebrows.

'You don't type? Even Peyton managed that much.'

'Never felt the need,' said Evelyn, stabbing experimentally at one of the keys. 'I've always used a bureau for that kind of thing but I expect it's different for writers. I could have a go, I suppose … It can't be that hard, can it? If a man can do it? Show me where the paper goes.'

'Maybe some other time.' Miss McAllister squinted at her wristwatch. 'You should maybe think about getting back to change fairly soon, Mrs Murdoch dear. The Kramer party starts at seven. Should be a *super* evening.' She smiled and strolled across to the desk and began opening and closing drawers, flicking idly through the papers the Colonel had left. Was she looking for something?

'Will you and Mr Kay be at the party?'

'Sure. We're the parsley round the real guests. Wouldn't miss it for the world: imported wines, very swish.'

'Could you let me have the address?'

'No need. Kiss's minions are sending a magic carpet: six thirty sharp. That should give you plenty of time to get all gussied up. You could shower even ...'

Someone had repaired the guttering above the front step of Evelyn's bungalow. The filthy sitting room was still a wilderness of garden bric-a-brac but the main bathroom now had hot water and had been cleared of paint pots. The rakes and hoes had been removed from the closet where the studio's choice of evening gowns were now hanging from the brass rail like bias-cut butterflies.

Evelyn twisted her hair into Alphonse's tortoiseshell comb and dabbed her mouth with the little carmine stick then stood before the cheval glass in her dressing gown and held each dress up in turn. The beige-coloured one was a near-perfect match for her unsunned skin. The blue was more forgiving but it was impossible to fathom the cat's cradle of straps across the back and in the end the white satin was the only one with fastenings she could understand: a twenty-inch row of tiny silk beads that ran from between the shoulder blades to the small of the back. She had only managed to fumble six of the buttons into their loops when a car horn sounded. She held the dress around her and stuck her head out of the front door.

'Taxi for Mrs Murdoch!'

Not a taxi at all but a blue convertible that had been driven up the back lane to the door of the bungalow by a youngish, blondish, curly-headed man in a sand-coloured blazer. Tanned and very tall, he looked as though he might well do exercises with Indian clubs ('red-blooded' was the phrase they used in *Photoplay*).

The man jumped over the car door without opening it – were there special vaulting horses for practising this peculiar skill? – and strode into the house.

'Monroe, Ted Monroe from the script department.'

He took in the room at a glance: the spillikinned window blinds, the jumble of rusting deckchairs.

'You *live* here? I thought English dames were house-proud. You know: crumpets on the lawn, pants on the piano, that kind of thing.'

'I only arrived yesterday.'

'What happened? D'you throw a party?' He grinned at the forest of turpentine bottles still on the sideboard and scratched at his curls. 'Some party.'

'It was like this when I found it. There's supposed to be a caretaker but he doesn't seem to be taking care. I'm meeting the owner – Mrs Silverman? – tomorrow. I'm hoping she can get her Jap chap to pull his finger out.'

The twitch of Monroe's eyebrows made Evelyn wish she had put it another way.

'You ready to go?'

'I shan't be a moment, it's just that I can't …' When she turned back into the bedroom, the heel of her slipper caught in the hem of her unfastened gown. As Monroe's tennis reflexes broke her fall, the dress slipped from her shoulders and her hair tumbled out of its comb. She regained her balance but hard, warm hands kept hold of her bare upper arms. His deep tan made the smile flash whiter.

'Why, Mrs Murdoch! This is so sudden!'

The script would have written itself but to her surprise Ted Monroe loosened his hold and merely stooped down to retrieve the comb.

101

'The frock they sent has rather a lot of buttons.'

He craned his neck to look behind her. She had them all out of whack, he said. He edged round and his fingertips began tickling down her spine, refastening the satin loops.

'Kiss's people told me to come get you. You're his new signing, that right? What happened to the big fella?'

'Mr Peyton was called away.'

'So soon? He only lasted a few weeks. Own office, private line, nice duplex apartment ... Never figured out what he actually *did* apart from hang out with Kiss a lot but he played a mean game of tennis. And poker. You play much poker, Mrs Murdoch?'

The buttoning fingers had slowed down. 'Elocution, isn't it? Thistle sifters? Peter Piper picking pecks?' Each consonant was a puff of warm air against the skin of her back. 'I have a black-backed bath brush. Do you have a black-backed bath brush, Mrs Murdoch?'

He placed both hands on her shoulders and turned her back round, making the gores of the long skirt flare out like the petals on a petunia.

'There you go. All you need now is the orange blossom. And a nice fit –' he nodded approval '– very nice.' (Far too beastly tight, in other words.)

'I may not be available for button duty later but I shouldn't worry, there's usually a zipper in the side seam somewhere: the buttons are just for show.'

She slapped him quite a bit harder than she intended. Film actors usually kissed women who did that (after they had ruefully rubbed their cheeks). He didn't even rub his cheek.

'I think you've seen too many movies, Mrs Murdoch. And where are you off to in your glad rags? Got a date? I thought I was supposed to be taking you to the Kramer party?'

*

Ted Monroe drove very fast and the sun was only just setting when they pulled up in front of Mr Kramer's Beverly Hills mansion. Monroe put on a gentlemanly show of opening the passenger door and squiring her past the butler but once inside he made his excuses, leaving Evelyn stranded in the marble hallway.

Evelyn had only a limited experience of parties. She had once been taken to a *Dorffest* during her stay in Bavaria where a man in lederhosen had played 'Der Wacht am Rhein' on a tray of cowbells. Her daily bulletin to her father (in her best German) was full of the joys of *schuplattler* and *glühwein* and the sausage-eating game that led to a saucy exchange of forfeits and kisses with Max, the young son of the house. Her father's reply (sent express) imposed an immediate curfew for the rest of her visit.

There had been times, during her nine months in Postal Censorship, when a colleague would persuade 'poor Mrs Murdoch' to join them at a party to which she hadn't strictly been invited. 'No one will mind,' they would insist, 'it's open house', 'they love surprises', 'come as you are', but one always felt an interloper, always imagined the hosts having last-minute loaves-and-fishes panics in the pantry at the prospect of an extra guest, and it was never a success. Her colleagues would make an introduction or two but they never really took and she would be left marooned by the door, empty sherry glass in hand, counting the minutes until she could decently slip away and catch her train.

Hollywood parties were much more familiar. Gowns came fresh from the dressmaker, orchids from the icebox. Hair was curled and plaited like a German loaf glistening with sugar glaze. The husband, often in tails, sometimes in uniform, would fasten anniversary diamonds in the boudoir mirror, there would be a long walk down a curved staircase to a room lit by chandeliers, a Jeevesy gent in a wing collar would announce that dinner was served, then wink kindly at the interloper who reached for the wrong spoon.

Mr Kramer's guests were gathered in what *House Beautiful* had called his 'blue salon'. Most of the men were in open-necked shirts and the women wore slacks and sundresses. Queen Guinevere had swapped her green velvet kirtle for a pair of candy-striped halter-necked beach pyjamas. Miss McAllister, who had been working late, had only had time to replace the pilgrim collar of her office dress with a bib of white glass beads. She was standing, drink in hand, by the French windows gossiping with Felix Kay who was wearing a crumpled yachting blazer and deck shoes. Both writers had instinctively positioned themselves on the edges of the room, recognising that they were essentially *figurants* in the scene, while the more famous guests, voices loud, necklines low, performed their solos and duets centre stage.

'I wonder what Mrs Murdoch will be wearing this evening? Should be amusing. Kiss's secretary told me that Kiss had her pick out a whole bunch of ritzy gowns left over from that Seventh Avenue picture.'

'*Satin in Manhattan?*'

'That's the one,' Miss McAllister chuckled. 'I told her "black tie" and you know how stuffy the English are.'

Felix Kay laughed a trifle uncomfortably.

'Not very sisterly …'

'Sisterly?' hissed Miss McAllister. 'She's no sister of mine, brother. I'm damned if I'm going to let myself be high-hatted by that dame.' She deepened her voice to match Evelyn's. '*Do you think I might have a cup of tea?* Nuts

104

to that. Whose side are you on, anyhow? Don't tell me you're carrying a little torch at long last? Have we finally found your type?'

Ted Monroe was fighting his way through the crush to join them, a highball in each hand.

'What happened to her ladyship?' demanded Miss McAllister. 'Don't tell me she's powdering her nose because I won't believe you.'

Monroe took a long swig from his glass.

'Left her in the hall. I'm not Kiss's errand boy.'

Miss McAllister craned her neck to get a better view of the door. Her face fell: Evelyn Murdoch standing on the threshold in blue silk slacks and matching blouse.

'Who spilled?'

'Don't blame me, Connie dear. She figured it out all by herself.'

Evelyn took a swimmer's breath and walked down the two steps into the room. She strolled over to the window to join them, treading an uneasy Charleston across the white carpet in brand-new, shiny-soled shoes.

'No black tie?' giggled Miss McAllister, smiling down at Evelyn's slacks. 'You should have let me call Wardrobe.'

Evelyn tried to picture herself in this sea of polo shirts and playsuits 'all gussied up' in her floor-length duchesse satin. It was practically sabotage … She thought back to Miss McAllister nonchalantly opening and closing HP's desk drawers. Perhaps it *was* sabotage?

'I'm from Woking, Miss McAllister, not Western Samoa. We have movie theatres and everything.'

Evelyn turned on her heel (very smooth on Mr Kramer's shag pile) and retraced her steps to the door followed by Ted Monroe. She lit a cigarette and chose one of the smaller glasses from a passing tray.

'It seems almost a pity to spoil Miss McAllister's fun. I suppose I ought to thank you for "putting me wise".'

Ted Monroe frowned.

'You look surprised, Mrs Murdoch. You actually have the gall to look surprised. What kind of a heel did you think I was?'

Evelyn puffed on her cigarette. 'I'm sure I don't know, Mr Monroe. What kind of a heel are you?'

He pushed his forefinger against the very tip of her nose and leaned in close.

'Don't, Mrs Murdoch. *Please* don't start with the dialogue. I already *dream* in dialogue.'

Mr Kramer's famous blue salon followed the fall of the hillside in a series of shallow steps. A very small man in very large checks was promising the earth to a tall brunette who had made a study of the terrain and taken care to position herself on one of the lower slopes. Evelyn began mentally measuring the furniture: were there outsize chairs for dainty débutantes? Small doorways for heroes?

Conversations hung in the steam-heated air; well-bred, slightly artificial voices talking fast and wise like the shuffled pages of a screwball comedy.

'So, six weeks with the shrink and the daughter's telling everyone she's a lesbian.'

'A *lesbian*? Practising?'

'I doubt it, knowing her. Remember when she took up the piano?'

Two men smoking cigars became an impromptu double act.

'We haven't cast the dame yet but the Danish blonde is out in front.'

'Sure she is. She's built that way.'

106

An extravagantly ugly woman wearing purple satin harem trousers and a whole jungle trading post of black and white beads looked pointedly at Evelyn and turned to a friend. 'You see what I mean?' It was several seconds before Evelyn registered that she had actually been speaking Spanish.

She felt perilously close to tears but instead headed back to the cool of the front hall. Party sound effects drifted out after her: the jazzy rattle of a cocktail shaker; the chink of champagne saucers; the easy chitchat of men and women who knew what enjoying oneself should look and sound like. What would Jesus do? Jesus would have another little drink.

Walter Kramer's decorator had built what he called a Den, a womb-like, leather-armchaired nook leading off the main room. It was lined with Royal Stewart tartan and hung with certificates, trophies and countless signed photographs of Mr Kramer shaking hands: Roosevelt; Mussolini; Churchill; Rin Tin Tin. There was a knotty pine bar arrangement in the corner where a waiter was being kept busy mixing drinks to order for the guests who were propping up the counter.

'Can any of you American blighters make a decent martini?'

An English character player called Cedric Sedgwick had dressed for the party in a gaily striped blazer, cricket jersey and paisley cravat. His own choice? wondered Evelyn. Or did he leave such decisions to Wardrobe? The actor was scowling at his glass through his monocle.

'Chap at my club used to make the best martinis. Had cups for it. It needs to be *veddy veddy* dry and you need to make the ice from purest imported spring water.'

At the other end of the bar, Sir Mordred from *Knights of Love*, now nattily dressed in plus twos, Argyll socks and a slightly crooked toupee, was leaning back to admire the top of an empty beer bottle where he had constructed a rickety little sculpture using the contents of a dozen monogrammed matchboxes.

Evelyn clambered on to the stool beside him and drained the glass in her hand.

'Attagirl! Fancy another? Silly not to, only way to make sense of the whole grisly affair. Jimmy! Another nicely iced martini for our friend here, Miss er ...'

He seemed pleased by her English name and accent and toasted her in gin as he introduced himself: Frobisher, Baines Frobisher, but she must call him Binky. Brits ought to stick together, wasn't that right, Cedric? The striped man inspected Evelyn through his eyeglass for the merest moment before turning back to Baines Frobisher who wasn't to forget: kippers next Sunday; usual crowd; no riff-raff.

'Very informal: "come as you are" – whatever that is.'

Cedric did not smile or bow or acknowledge Evelyn in any way and nor did he invite her to whatever it was.

Binky Frobisher led her away from the four-ale fug of the bar and back into the main room.

'*Eppsolutely ghaastly*, isn't it? D'you know I think there's a critical size at play when it comes to this whole parlour-cum-rumpus room arrangement. Anything bigger than a tennis court and you risk turning the whole thing into a jumbo-sized hotel lounge with lots and lots of photographs of yourself in it. Look at it!' He waved his glass in the air. 'None of it's on a normal, common-or-garden domestic scale ... I mean that divan thingy over there by the window must be fifteen feet long – longer. And all those whatnots and whatnot, and all these *tables – gemütlich*, they call them – but you expect a box of headed paper and a pen on a stand.

I keep thinking I'm going to be paged – or caught mashing by the house detective.

'And that saloon-bar affair's no help.' He jerked his head back towards the cocktail corner where Cedric Sedgwick was now telling anyone who would listen that the secret was merely to let the shadow of the vermouth bottle fall on the pitcher of ice – normal conversation seemed beyond him.

'And far too much Art,' continued Binky. 'You could get all this modern stuff for peanuts after '29 – always supposing you had any peanuts left, obviously. Kramer cleaned up but it's a mite excessive, don't you find? Crying out for turnstiles. Do you think they do a postcard of that one?' He leered wolfishly at an unnecessarily anatomical rendering of a large purple zantedeschia. 'Reminds me of my first wife.'

Evelyn heard herself making a giggling sound. Silly noise. She straightened her face and tried to concentrate on the rest of the furnishings. None of the walls in the house had been painted or papered in the normal way. The salon was a quarrelsome blend of flints and copper sheeting. An aquarium had been set into the cobblestoned chimney breast and framed by an antique mirror trimmed with wormy chunks of flame-red coral, the shapes echoing the fire beneath.

'Don't the poor fish get hot?' wondered Evelyn, blinking anxiously at the tank.

'There's a refrigeration unit built in round the back of the fire,' said Binky.

Their host had finally materialised and was giving a stray starlet the full private tour. There was a large oil painting of pink and white peonies hanging above a demi-lune table, the nut-coloured background the same shade as the suede wall behind it, making the flowers look like part of the decor.

'Not my favourite artist but he keeps the florist's bills down,' said Mr Kramer (a well-worn gag).

Mr Kramer's paintings were chiefly of flowers and Paris streets. Binky Frobisher was unimpressed.

'Fantin-Latour and Utrillo? Oh dear. It's like a Montmartre florist died and went to heaven ... *Ghaastly*.' He emptied his glass and gave Evelyn a wink. 'I hear the merry clang of dish covers. I think they're about to serve up the first sitting in the dining room. I must grab some Beluga before the vultures descend. Cheerio!'

The guests drained away to watch the birthday boy blow out his candles, leaving Evelyn by herself in the darkening salon. Mr Kramer's paintings were lit individually by tiny bulbs on brass brackets but the rest of the room's kindly lighting was invisibly delivered by a complicated rheostat system hidden behind the cornice which the butler could dim with the twist of a switch. The only other light source was a single spotlight over the main chimney piece. Evelyn moved across to it and positioned herself in its path then turned towards the gilded overmantel. She hardly recognised the woman on the far side of the glass. The high, strong light – a good six feet above her head – cast dramatic shadows across her face, throwing her cheekbones into relief, honing her jawline. She adjusted the set of her head, checking the unfamiliar profile now lengthened and glamorised by Alphonse's magic comb.

'*Cleffer* girl.'

A tallish man in white buckskin jodhpurs and a surprising amount of eye-black had joined her.

'Now: count to seven and watch that lamp like you couldn't live without it.'

He looked up at the ceiling, then across at Evelyn's reflection.

'Some it takes them years to learn. Some I haff to chalk the floor every time but this lady –' he gestured to an invisible audience '– this lady she gets it in one. See the face now?' His reflection joined hers in the mirror. 'A million dollars –' he saw the disapproving frown cross her face '– OK maybe *half* a million. You should get one for your apartment. The man pointed to the spotlight. 'One of the studio guys will fix it for you. You got a high ceiling? Get a high ceiling. Move to a church.'

His name was Otto Von Blick and Miracle had brought him over from Kiss's studio in London to direct Magda Malo in a new movie called *The Borgia Pearl*. What was it about? asked Evelyn (her first words so far). A continental shrug. It was about $300,000 dollars-worth of movie made to look like a million with a few feathers, some lights, a little smoke.

'Miracle had her playing Guinevere with some *schmuck* you-should-excuse-me who thinks he can direct. Direct? *Funerals* he should direct. They see a girl in one of my moofies, they put her under contract and then can't understand why she's no damned good.'

Guests unable to bag a seat in the dining room were drifting back to the drinks table and he lowered his voice to confide that he would now be reshooting Miss Malo's Arthurian love scenes.

'With *Lancy-lot?*' purred Evelyn.

'Ha!' A delighted laugh, a passionate kiss on her hand, heads turning. 'You see those rushes! You're with Miracle?'

He pocketed her business card and gave her cheek a pinch.

'I like you, Mrs Murdoch! Very *cleffer* lady. Cute I don't need. Cute I got.'

She was to come and watch him at work on Stage Six next week. He produced his own card from a slim gold case. 'Come and see what I make with Magda. Poor little Magda …'

The problem with Miss Malo, he explained, was that she didn't speak any language properly.

'Poor kid, what a life: half Danish, half Hungarian, raised in Tirana. Her file says she's trilingual –' he pulled a face '– four times lingual if you count Yiddish, but you know I speak a little Albanian myself and trust me: her Albanian is not so good. And English? I've had parrots with more English. They say to me is all OK. She can learn it *pho-net-ic-all-y* or we can do the whole thing with blackboards and bitsy bits of paper stuck on the furniture, but this is because they kind of figured the lady – twenty-two years old according to her publicity – could actually *read* and you know what?' He chuckled and shook his head. 'But on screen? A goddess. And a puppet.' He moved his hand as though there were a toy glove on it. 'She's like a beautiful blonde acting machine.' He sighed. 'The camera tells such *luffly* lies. Lucky for us she's a good mimic. And so beautiful.' He bunched his finger ends together and kissed them ecstatically. 'And I taught her the basics.'

'The basics?'

He too was a good mimic. It was as if Magda Malo herself were whispering the phrases into Evelyn's ear: *For you? Anything*; *You are my favourite man*; *I want to hear all about it*; *Nussing nicer darling*; *You read my mind*.

'She learns quick.' He nodded towards the piano where a man so old and unattractive he could only have been a producer was lighting Miss Malo's gold-tipped cigarette. 'You are my favourite man,' the actress murmured. A tray of champagne was paused in its tracks. 'You read my mind.

'You see?' laughed Von Blick. 'Just the basics. And she does *ex-actly* what I tell her. No *motivation* nonsense. Her motivation is seventeen hundred a week. Not like Mr

Brains Frobisher over there. "Character immersion", he calls it. Never again. As I live and breathe, never, ever, *effer* again. This guy needs a midwife, not a director. And forceps.' He mimed an ugly pulling motion with his clawed right fist.

The volume of her own laughter surprised her and the other guests turned to watch.

'Contralto,' he demanded, tweaking at the stray lock of hair on her forehead, and she immediately cut the sound and resumed laughing an octave lower.

'Cleffer.'

Miss Malo left the party on the arm of her producer friend and his limousine had hardly rolled out of the drive before Von Blick was kissing the hand of a latecomer, a tall, honey-blonde of about eighteen dressed in a knee-length gown of bronze velour. Had she been waiting outside in the car?

Von Blick took a crumb of white chalk from his pocket and marked a tiny cross on the glossy black curve of the grand piano.

He ushered Evelyn to a nearby sofa – 'You stay right here, *Liebling*' – then led his new protegée to the spot where they had been standing.

'Action!'

The girl found the director's chalk mark at once and began drinking it in with her limpid hazel eyes, beaded lashes casting mysterious shadows on the slopes of her high cheekbones.

Their host had returned (minus his art-loving starlet) and he greeted Von Blick with a two-handed handshake. The director drew him towards the piano and began conversing in an undertone. Kramer looked – and stayed looking – at the pretty new face.

'Malo, *schmalo*: this girl is the goods. She sings too.'

'They all sing. Believe me, Otto: they *all* sing. But call me,' nodded Mr Kramer though nothing more had been said, 'call me Monday.'

A man sat down at the keyboard and began doing a Marlene Dietrich impersonation. Mr Kramer began to laugh, everyone began to laugh.

'You aren't laughing, Mrs Murdoch?' said Von Blick.

'It doesn't mean I'm not amused.'

'Maybe. But you should look in the columns: *everyone laughing.* Maybe you can afford not to laugh? But don't be too sure. These other ladies here, they cannot afford it. Magda and my new little friend over there, they under-stand this. They are not amused maybe but when the bigshot laughs they have their cue. See?' He cocked his head towards the girl in brown velour who gave the slight-est possible nod then let her golden head fall back in a silent ecstasy of mirth.

Von Blick smiled his approval and relieved Evelyn of her empty glass

'*Noch einmal?*'

'*Sie haben meine Gedanken lesen.*'

'Ha!'

He snapped his fingers at a man with a tray.

'Very cleffer. Lousy accent but *sehr schlau*. Pleasure talking with you, *Liebling*. Don't forget: Stage Six next Friday. I'll call you.'

Felix Kay darted over from the dining room the instant Von Blick left Evelyn's side.

He took one of his brown cigarettes from the packet in his pocket – thrifty habit – and struck a match on his fingernail.

'You seemed pretty palsy-walsy with Von Blick. Have you guys met before somewhere? I guess speaking German must be a help?'

Evelyn struggled to keep her breathing even. So much for cloak and dagger.

'Just schoolgirl stuff.'

He took her elbow, parked her beside a Georgian silver salver studded with tiny squares of fish roe on toast and began posting them into his mouth.

'Kramer needs a larger dining table. It's murder in there.'

'I don't think caviar is kosher, Mr Kay.'

'Felix, please, *Felix*. No I don't think it is either. Don't anybody tell my mother or I'll starve to death. My wife is crazy for caviar. Bernice, have you met Mrs Murdoch?'

And he launched into a peculiar comic routine in which he had a one-sided conversation with the non-existent Mrs Kay. Evelyn would later learn that Mrs Kay was a regular partygoer, giving Felix a licence to speak his mind. Like a ventriloquist, he cast himself as the straight man to her insulting remarks.

'Yes, she could stand to gain a few pounds but she's a hell of a lot prettier than Connie.' He cocked an ear towards the invisible woman on his arm. 'Yes, it is a pretty blouse, isn't it?'

He stepped out of character and reached across to straighten Evelyn's collar, rubbing the silk between his fingertips.

'Nice. Blue suits you. Connie told me about the stunt she tried to pull. I tried ringing your house to let you know it was a gag but the line was dead. I'm glad you found out in time.'

She shook her head at the sheer pointless malice of her new colleague's little scheme.

'*Peculiar* thing to do.'

'You mustn't mind Connie, she's been having a really bad time. They've got her working on some last-minute rewrites. The studio bought this book about an amnesiac heiress in the dust bowl: *Wrong Road South*. It made the bestseller lists and the *New York Times* called it "a modern Odyssey".' His accent grew starchy. '"No contemporary novel hits harder or delves deeper into the modern American psyche." Miracle beat off a number of rival bidders, renamed it *Driving Her Crazy* and now they want to rework it as a musical. Connie's been tearing her hair out. She's too good for this place – or thinks she is. Did you know she wrote a play? It opened – and closed – a couple of weeks ago: *Dry Goods*, not the catchiest title. The *Herald* said it was *jejune* … never seen Connie *cry* before …'

Evelyn found it hard to care.

'That hardly explains her behaviour. I simply don't see what she'd gain by it.'

'Oh you'd be surprised. Everyone entering that office is a threat – let alone anyone in a skirt and a yellow convertible. If she can get you to make yourself conspicuous – let alone ridiculous – your stock would fall pretty fast. Kiss would have been mortified if his *protégée* made a *faux pas* at a *soirée*.'

'I'm not his *protégée*, Mr Kay.'

He popped the last caviar toast.

'Whatever you say, *Liebling*.'

Chapter 7

T HE DEAD TELEPHONE sprang to life. The voice at the other end began *in medias res*.

'I should get there by nine thirty. I daren't risk the steps down so meet me by the love seat.'

At twenty past nine Evelyn strolled up through the wilderness and out through the arch in the yew hedge. Mamie Silverman was already waiting for her, seated at the wheel of an open-topped car. She was wearing a black Italian straw hat over a gaily coloured silk headscarf and her face was almost entirely obscured by a gigantic pair of tortoiseshell sunglasses perched on a nose so thickly powdered that it looked more like papier mâché than flesh – as if it were attached to the glasses. The Invisible Woman.

Evelyn would forgive her for not coming down to the pool house. Her hip was acting up but she had taken one of the pink pills so it should ease off in a while. Evelyn was so *tall*. Zandor hadn't said she was tall. Poor Zandor's plane got stuck in Memphis and he had to go back East before he even got here. Had Evelyn met Zandor yet? Mamie had known him since the first time he came to the States when he made that kidnapping movie – the one he got Best Adapted Screenplay for? Like a brother to her.

'When Wolfie died he came over and cooked me pancakes with sour cream and cherry jam. Poor Wolfie *loved* pancakes.'

Evelyn arranged her face to register sadness at the old woman's loss.

'Helped me bury his little collar in the yard. Always so kind. So when I saw him at some party last week and he tells me he's got an English lady coming and asks me which hotel do I think, I said hotel *nothing* I have a cosy little house in Bel Air going begging.

'My husband lived in the main house here with his first wife and the girls, but he never liked it much. I say let's get it painted white, buy some nice couches. Manny says let's move to Malibu. Manny says only bums live in Bel Air, *millionaire* bums, but bums. We move about a lot. We've got a house out on the ocean but Paula says we should try Pasadena. A lot of old money in Pasadena ... You ought to meet Paula, my stepdaughter. Her big sister Celeste, Sissy, got married but Paula still lives with us. Paula spent a lot of time in Europe, they finished her in France.'

Mamie Silverman struggled out of the car and looked around her at the garden.

'Yuki does a good job. I hope he isn't keeping the pool house too warm for you. I know you English aren't used to the heat.'

The hatted head rotated bird-style. 'Where is that lazy Jap son-of-a-bitch?' Her gloved hand pressed on the car's hooter until the gardener came scuttling along the cinder path.

'Yuki, meet your new boss: Mrs Murdoch; Mr Hashimoto.'

He bowed deeply.

'I pay Yuki good money to look after the place. That right, Yuki? I see you're keeping the gravel nice.' Her toes scratched a soft shoe shuffle along what remained of his nasty little pattern.

Mr Hashimoto took a pair of secateurs from the pocket of his apron and made snipping motions in the air. 'Trees very big. Too big.'

'Never mind trees too big. Trees just fine. Miss Paula gave you your instructions four days ago, Yuki-san: clear the guesthouse; make nice, make shipshape. You make shipshape?'

He bowed some more, casting sly looks at Evelyn to see how much had been said.

'You make shipshape for my dear flend Mrs Murdoch? Mrs Murdoch ruvry Engrish rady. Savvy? You lazy Jap.'

Another low bow.

'An honour to welcome honourable lady,' then (in Japanese) he added, '*you ugly old she-goat!*'

Mrs Silverman smiled blandly and continued issuing instructions.

'You give Mrs Murdoch basket, yes? Fetch basket? Wishy-washy?' The kid fingers mimed washday while the gardener looked on with the raw fish eye of a man keeping a straight face. He did some more bowing as he replied.

'*Shitty old goat. Go and wash your face with shit.*'

Mamie nodded at him dementedly, earrings rattling.

'What say we leave Mr Hashimoto to get some work done and I'll give you a tour of the main house?'

'I'll catch you up,' said Evelyn as her landlady hobbled towards the porch. 'I dropped my handkerchief.'

Mr Hashimoto was retreating at speed through the yew hedge.

'You very busy, Mr Hashimoto?'

He nodded repeatedly, muttering further obscenities under his breath, stopping only when Evelyn began to speak very softly, telling him that unless he put her house in order and cleaned up that mess in the driveway she

119

would talk to honourable lady and Mr Hashimoto would have to find a new job – with no references.

'I fix phone yesterday.'

'You need to fix a lot more than that.'

The bowing grew deeper and more rapid. '*Stinking foreigner. Your mother's belly button sticks out.*'

The chap running the Japanese course arranged by the Holborn office had made a point of teaching them all the insults he knew and it was tempting to give as good as she got but Evelyn remembered the carpet of swastikas and thought better of it. Perhaps she ought to start a dossier?

Mrs Silverman had only got as far as the front door and was squinting through the glass at a sunless hallway thronged with dustsheeted furniture and shrouded light fittings.

'You sure you can be bothered with the tour?' She plunged her hand into her bag and began rummaging for the keys she had forgotten to bring.

'It's a dump, anyway. Manny's first wife chose it – chose the architect anyway. They didn't have much of a say after that. The guy insisted on designing every last thing: cupboards, couches, door handles, light switches – even the piano, *lousy* piano. He told all the journals at the time that it was his masterpiece but then he didn't have to live in it. Manny says he came over after they moved in to check them out and told them they weren't to hang any of their pictures – and Manny had a lot of pictures. A dealer picked them out for him, smart guy. I miss those pictures. We had them all with us when we had that place up at Laughlin Park but practically all of the walls at the Malibu house are glass so most of the paintings are still either at the bank or up in the attic here in Bel Air. We put a few in the pool house. You like the pool house? It's really a very snug little place. Manny says they were going to get the same architect but he didn't want the job so they got a local outfit. My stepdaughter says it looks like they got it from a catalogue. Maybe they did. That was why they had to let the bushes grow. The bigshot architect heard about it and said that if it was visible from the drive, he'd come over and torch the place.'

Mrs Silverman said that she had never understood why her husband hadn't just sold the house like a regular person but he had some sort of fetish about real estate. His most recent plan was to build a house on the Pacific but Mrs Silverman wasn't a fan of the ocean. In fact, for two pins Mamie would move to New York but she couldn't because that was where the first Mrs Silverman had her apartment – as though New York were an hotel or a country house where the two wives would be sure to run into one another ('It's a big town but it's a small world').

'I miss Manhattan. I miss the theatre. People here say New York's always either too hot or too cold but I never minded the cold. I got my sables for that.'

Mrs Silverman limped back down the house steps to her car.

'Zandor was keen we should look after you. You married? Divorced?'

'He was killed,' said Evelyn. Again.

The gloved hand pinched at hers.

'You ought to come to dinner, see the ocean, meet Manny.'

Evelyn, rather dreading her solitary Saturday, was mentally selecting something to wear but the old lady started the car without naming a date.

'I'll call you.'

It was what they said instead of goodbye.

*

121

'Mrs Murdoch got some messages.' Connie McAllister looked down at her notepad when Evelyn arrived at the office on Monday. 'Kiss's office called, Von Blick called – oh yes and *God* called. And *these* came.' She made a parade of lifting a pile of Manila document wallets from the wire tray on her desk. 'And *that*.' A nod towards a basket of red and white carnations: the card read 'Sorry for the delay in meeting. Kisses Kiss. *Maradj elfoglalt* (Keep busy)'.

Evelyn walked past the flowers and unlocked HP's office, leaving the door open (no need to escalate hostilities). She uncradled the white telephone and asked for the sign-writing department. She held a hand over the receiver and smiled through the door at Miss McAllister on the far side of the main room.

'I'll have a word with one of the telephonists. Ghastly for you to have to take messages all the time.'

'Ghaaastly.'

It was the last word she uttered to Evelyn for several days.

The first Manila wallet contained a ring-bound script of something called *The Lady and the Lumberjack* and a small, cream-coloured envelope with a British postage stamp and no censor's mark.

I'm so glad I've got you to write to [wrote Deborah]. Not that much happens. Some mad old bat from the Women's Voluntary was doing the rounds yesterday evening. Said we ought to keep rabbits but the key word is 'keep' because next door's bunnies all tunnelled to freedom within the week and Mr Meakin in the big old house on the end had his eaten by a fox off the heath. I found him bending Mother's ear on the subject which was thoughtless of him, to put it mildly, as Mother immediately put her feet up on the fender and asked where they had been seen and how big were they and now makes me beat about under her bed with the yard broom which is tiresome but less tiresome than starting a private rabbit farm. The WVS woman says 'one can always beg scraps of bolted lettuce and what-have-you from one's green-grocer'. Do you think she's even so much as *seen* a greengrocer? You can bet your life her cook does it all. Stupid bloody woman (excuse my French). There was a picture in the paper of the allotments in Kensington Gardens which are full of magic cabbage all grown up and gorgeous. 'Potemkin cabbage', Mr Meakin says. Is that an actual variety? Mrs Meakin has moved in with her aunt on the Isle of Man but Mr M seems to be managing all right on his own. Keeps giving me beetroot. *Overtures*, Mother says.

The second Manila wallet contained a letter written on pistachio-coloured writing paper engraved 'From the desk of Walter Grendon' inviting Evelyn to 'one of my four o'clocks' on Sunday week.

The third wallet contained a long and extraordinarily detailed memo from PZ Homberg to Zandor Kiss which had been copied to practically everyone in the studio. He was still very worried about *Knights of Love*. Yes, the rewritten dialogue read well enough but the back-and-forth chat between Lancelot and Guinevere was going to look 'cutty'. Von Blick should make the scene 70 per cent on Miss Malo with Hooper off-camera. The second of twelve long paragraphs focused on Miss Malo's make-up which may have been 'just dandy' for the villainess/vamp in *Cairo Boulevard* but Guinevere should look more whole-some: 'Tone down the lipstick or the audience is going to side with Arthur.'

A Miss Della Cavendish, Mr Kiss's personal secretary (and personal shopper), had sent another copy of the H. G. Wells novel with a note inside explaining that Mr Kiss would be in Washington until the weekend but hoped to catch Mrs Murdoch at Cedric Sedgwick's Sunday kipper party. Meanwhile, she was to liaise with Felix Kay on possible *War of the Worlds* treatments in readiness for the story conference with PZ on the 14th.

Felix had had the same memo. He brought his coffee into Evelyn's office.

'The studio has had the rights to this Wells book since '26 – they bought a whole bunch of novels when the talkies came in – but it never happened and then your friend Peyton suggests it and Kiss reckons the time is ripe. He's given PZ a one-page outline but he wants us to work up the cute-kid angle.'

'*Cute-kid angle?* It's about a middle-aged man.'

'Not now it isn't. They needed to find something for little Rindy McGee, help her break out of B-pictures before she gets too old to lisp. You've seen her stuff?'

'Er, not really my cup of tea.'

'Me neither but she gets more fan mail than the rest of the studio put together.'

Rindy was the only child of a bit-player calling herself Bitsy Devine, Felix explained. Mrs Devine had planned her daughter's screen career from the womb and had picked out a name to match. But the agent she found reckoned that nobody ever had an adult career with a name like Baby Devine – except maybe in stag pictures – and had rechristened the child Dorinda McGee. Curls, dimples and a flair for acrobatics had made 'America's Pussycat' an immediate hit.

'They say she'll be twelve next birthday but she's seven for professional purposes,' said Felix. 'PZ says it'll all be over once she gets a brassiere.'

The studio was making the most of the time remaining and any number of pre-existing narratives had apparently had golden-haired children insinuated into their storylines (Florence Nightingale had acquired a niece). H. G. Wells's eyewitness account of the razing of the Home Counties was to be recast with a small child who was heading across country with a performing dog to find a big sister who had been trapped by the Martians.

'A performing dog?'

'They have a dog on contract: yappy thing, about yay big, crooked ears, made quite a hit in a two-reeler called *Brandy Goes West*. "Brandy" doesn't play too well in the Bible belt so they're trying to think of something else. The smart money's on Biscuit.'

'Will the dog still do as it's told with a new name?'

'Who knows? His trainer does it all with hand signals so I guess the name's no big deal.'

Felix closed the connecting door to the main office and led Evelyn over to the window.

'The dog isn't the only thing getting a new name. Anything with "World" and "War" in the title is gonna be a red rag to the Senate Committee and they're already on Kiss's case. The old silver fox probably reckons the kid and the dog and a new title will throw them off the scent so no one will notice the whole plucky-little-nation-with-standing-menace-from-the-skies schtick he's got in mind, but he'll have to get up pretty damned early to get it past Kramer and PZ. They're dumb but they're not stupid and they aren't interested in being held up for "Incitement to war", cute kid or no cute kid. They already had a pretty close shave. Did you see Kiss's Spanish Armada movie?

That little black moustache on the King of Spain? No wonder the Nazis have got him on that list of theirs. I think the moustache was your guy Peyton's idea. Very forceful personality. He some kind of army type?'

Evelyn met this with a resolutely dead bat.

'Surely not. He'd be in uniform somewhere.'

There was a sharp knock at the door. Miss McAllister had brewed Felix a fresh cup of coffee (Evelyn had ceased to exist). She peered over Felix's shoulder.

'You working on that Martian thing? I saw Ted Monroe reading that.'

Felix waited until she had closed the door before letting out a heavy sigh. 'It would have been kind of nice not to have Monroe breathing down my neck for a change. He and I started at Miracle on the same day but he was the one who "connected". He's a good writer but most of his best work is done after hours. He and PZ play back-gammon and blackjack together. You ever play with a real card brain?'

Evelyn shook her head (now was perhaps not the moment to explain that games of chance were Frowned Upon).

'Before he and PZ are halfway through a deck Ted will know the odds on every ace. Cleans him out every time. Doesn't make him a better screenwriter but you know ...' he hesitated '... it kind of *does*. Suddenly he's PZ's golden boy. They go to the fights, play golf at the Hillcrest. PZ even talks about optioning that book he wrote. Can you imagine anyone making a movie of that prime piece of dreck?'

There was a faint raccoon-like rustling outside the office door at floor level. Evelyn opened it to find a workman in Miracle overalls with a hodful of paints and brushes and little sheets of gold leaf in tissue paper. The man squatted back on his milking stool and resumed work on the glass. 'H. P. Peyton' was rubbed clean with the merest lick of white spirit.

'What do you want on here, ma'am?'

Evelyn handed him one of the cards reading 'Special Consultant'.

'You and everyone else in the place.'

Felix retrieved his cup and headed for the door.

'I'll rough out the H. G. Wells with kid and dog. You keep on with the book and think beautiful English thoughts that we can throw at the art department and we'll try and run it by Kiss at the Sedgwick party.'

Evelyn pointed out that she hadn't been invited.

'Don't be so *Briddish*. It's open house. Drive over and pick me up and that way we can arrive together. Sedgwick won't mind. Besides, he'll have seen you schmoozing with Von Blick and he's probably dying to be the scheming count in *The Borgia Pearl*. Cedric can play that kind of thing in his sleep.'

Felix Kay's house – 'Skywater' according to the mailbox – was not shipshape. The plans for the building, displayed in a frame in the hallway, showed a Modernist green-house set in a tidy forest of weeping figs. The architect had staggered the two-storey structure so that its flat roofs would form shallow rectangular puddles to reflect the surrounding trees and sky. His line-and-wash idyll showed the owners seated at an open window, downing cocktails, reading Cocteau as they enjoyed the scents rising from the sunken herb garden.

On sunny days – and most Los Angeles days were sunny, after all – the house retained something of the fantasy but on Sunday morning the overflows of the roof-ponds had filled with autumn leaves and water was coursing down the walls and seeping through the bitumen into the rooms below. The sunken herb garden had become a slimy sea of dead leaves and liverwort and the front door was reached by a wobbly workman's plank.

Evelyn found Felix Kay re-siting one of the zinc pails dotted around the sitting room. The bucket gave a painful clang against the poured-concrete floor.

'Interesting house.'

'I'm minding it for a friend. It's very German School: early Günther Fink – a little something from his suprema-cist period. There was a piece in the *Atlantic* about him. He likes everything to have a flat roof whatever the climate; he built a pair of houses up in the Rockies a few years back – they aren't there now: you'd think a guy from the Alps would know better. He hates the whole inside/outside thing so you get a lot of glass and a lot of water: "Ze house is not a shield but a membrane" –' Felix Kay did a very good German accent '– a permeable membrane, in this particular case. Suits me, though: my pal was planning on selling the place but the tin pails put the buyers off and I get to stay a while longer. It's a good location – no pool, sadly. He really wanted a swimming pool but Fink told him swimming pools were *bourgeois*. That guy really knows how to hurt.'

The sitting-room walls were a greyish-beige, as if the owner had fired the decorator at the undercoat stage. There was very little furniture, all of it ugly – but Evelyn was used to ugly furniture.

All of the chairs at her mother-in-law's house were of an uncompromising, almost skeletal form. Shortly after her sons were married Mrs Murdoch had had a sudden urge to update the family parlour and a group visit to one of the big London stores was arranged. The furni-ture showroom was a sea of moquette and cretonne and chintz piped with endless caterpillars of fluffy braid.

These unfamiliar comforts were all arranged in companionable roomscapes on the sales floor. Sometimes one of the armchairs in a group would be noticeably larger than its round-shouldered overstuffed wife. Sometimes there was a stool to match, as if they had been breeding.

Encouraged by the commission-hungry salesman, Mrs Murdoch had agreed to try out his 'Excelsior Suite'. The chair had a softly angled velvet back (a slippery slope) and she had lowered herself suspiciously into its red plush embrace but rose to her feet almost immediately. 'Oh no! No no. No thank you' – a look of reproach at a man who could countenance earning a living selling something that would keep a good Christian woman's spine so perilously far from the straight and narrow.

Mrs Murdoch would probably have approved of Günther Fink's plushless interior – as would Silas. Silas had preferred hard chairs. Evelyn could imagine him, straight-backed in the corner of that putty-coloured room (not reading Cocteau) on a chair that appeared to have been fashioned from matchwood and an old tweed skirt. There were big brown geographical watermarks on the room's low ceiling. Evelyn reached up to the sodden plasterboard panels with her fingertips, tracing a large stain shaped exactly like the Isle of Wight.

'Not much of a day for a party.'

'The guy on the radio promised sunshine by lunch.'

Cedric Sedgwick's cosy Beverly Hills retreat had been concocted in the Tudorbethan style with half-timbered walls and barley-sugar chimneys.

The sun had come out as promised and the guests were poised by the open French windows in their white flannels and buckskin shoes waiting for the croquet lawn to dry off. A tall young man smiled at them from the doorway.

'Come and meet Fox,' said Felix. 'Foxton Meredith? Plays Galahad in the King Arthur movie? We saw him at the train station. Fox and I were at college together.'

Sir Galahad was being stroked and petted by Myra Manning, his new best friend from the *Hollywood Examiner.* Early reports on his performance in *Knights of Love* had been good (so good that some of his scenes had been cut to avoid upstaging the leads) and Miss Manning was keen to get a story. More roles were talked of and signet-ringed hands slapped his slubbed-silk back as guests passed to and from the buffet at the far end of the Olde English drawing room.

Felix was wearing the same old weekday blazer and a shirt that looked as though it had been ironed in the dark by a drunk but even Evelyn could see that his friend's wardrobe was in another league. His jacket was palest fawn and his necktie, a cubist study in chartreuse and gold, seemed to have been picked to match his pale-green eyes. The tie was loosely knotted, giving him a raffish, almost schoolboyish appearance. Although no taller or slimmer than his friend, his easy stride gave an illusion of height and he fell into poses with greyhound grace.

How did she do? He took Evelyn's hand in a firm, frank grip, his face registering warmth and interest for an invisible camera. He smelled deliciously of a lemony cologne. His sex appeal was clearly something that required constant exercise – like a throwing arm, or a springer spaniel – and he set about winning her over with professional skill. *Such* a becoming dress – *perfect* for that English complexion. He was *so* glad Felix had finally gotten someone sympathetic to work with. The green eyes were unnaturally bright, thought Evelyn: a two-martini glitter – maybe more than two martinis …

'I was talking to Myra – you know Myra, don't you?' He turned the beam of his smile towards Miss Manning who was looking beadily around the room and scribbling into her notebook with a silver pencil.

'She's a few stories short of a column this week, Mrs Murdoch. Maybe you and me should elope.'

The actor had turned back to Evelyn to deliver his line (first the eyes, followed by the slow turn of the head) then looked above and behind her, scanning the room for a gracious means of dispensing with her company.

'Oh dear. Poor Felix,' said Fox Meredith suddenly.

Felix was over by the piano talking to an older man. He had produced a paperback from his pocket but the man was moving away from him rather hastily without taking the book. Meredith took him by the arm but although his tone was sympathetic he was obviously exasperated by his friend's lack of *savoir faire*.

'Now wasn't the time, old man. You can't expect the guy to buy the book at a kipper brunch. I told you I'd talk to him. He'll be at the club later. Smile! It's a party, remember. Let me get you another drink. Better still, you go and get Mrs Murdoch another drink. I ought to mingle.'

Meredith's smile brightened again as a tall man in a candy-striped blazer and cricket clothes entered the room.

'My liege!' A mock bow.

Had Raymond met Evelyn? Raymond Games; Evelyn Murdoch. Mrs Murdoch was over from England working at Miracle. Raymond was King Arthur in *Knights of Love*.

'How do you do, Mrs Murdoch?'

The actor was famed for his diction and he spoke very slowly, like a wound-down gramophone, clearly relishing his own enunciation.

131

'Do you want to be in movies, Mrs Murdoch?'

'Don't be silly, Mr Games.'

A lightning change of tack.

'As a writer, I mean. Or continuity perhaps? I'll wager you have very sharp eyes. Pretty eyes.'

His hand came to rest on an area roughly two inches below the small of her back.

'Telephone me.'

The actor reversed smoothly out of shot and twirled into the arms of Myra Manning but Raymond Games was old news and the columnist used her kiss on his cheek to check on some new arrivals over his shoulder: two men in yachting blazers had come in, both tall, both dressed with too much care – like a music-hall double act that might break into a soft-shoe routine at any moment. One of them was Joseph Weiss.

He had not seen Evelyn. She moved over to the buffet table where two women were gossiping in an audible whisper.

'But he was *married*!' protested one. 'They had twin boys, for heaven's sakes.'

'Sure they did,' laughed the other. 'She set the alarm clock. First thing in the morning he wouldn't care if she was wearing a side-saddle. Didn't you see *House Beautiful?* There was a piece about their bachelor beach house. "A very economical arrangement", apparently.'

'*Economical?* That's a new word for it.'

An Englishman in club colours was fastidiously dissecting a sandwich to remove all trace of tomato – 'They're bad for my ulcer' – while his companion began lifting dish covers with either hand as though he were about to play 'Die Wacht am Rhein' with giant cowbells.

'I thought we were supposed to be having kippers.'

'Don't be absurd. Have you ever cooked a kipper? Ghastly pong and every cat for miles around. Poor Cedric tried it once and Myra Manning nearly choked on a bone. People were queuing up to thump her between the shoulder blades. Not a mistake you make twice.'

On the far side of the room a tall, silver-haired man in a pink Norfolk jacket had arrived and was holding court with a group of blazered studio executives who were all nodding their heads in agreement. The man waited while one of them relit his large cigar then smiled across to Evelyn and beckoned her to join them. She was about to go over and investigate but found her path blocked by Joseph Weiss.

'Mrs Murdoch! I told you it was a small world.'

He turned to his companion.

'Conrad, you must meet my new friend from the Super Chief. Mrs Murdoch is over here working with Miracle Studios: Evelyn Murdoch; Conrad Dengler.'

One sensed, rather than heard, the click of the heels.

'*Guten tag.*'

'Very well, thank you.' (Not caught out that easily.)

Their host was putting a record on the Victrola and his guests eagerly cleared space for dancing. In the confusion, Evelyn escaped to the library nook, which was cosy with club fenders and fire irons and a pair of antique globes with bottles inside. The walls were lined with Harris tweed and tiled with framed snapshots. A handsome bronze of a horse's head had been trepanned between its ears to support a brass light fitting and placed in the centre of a pietra dura table depicting a bouquet of parrot tulips in a mosaic of lapis, jasper and malachite. Evelyn took careful hold of the lamp in order to move it aside and admire the stone flowers but the horse was held in its place by the electric cord which fed through the statue into a dime-sized opening drilled through the stone. She looked down at the floor but there was no flex there either. Another hole drilled through the carpet? Through the floorboards? Through the centre of the earth? As a child on a beach at Worthing she had once tried to dig through to Australia. What was Hollywood's antipodes? She prodded her forefinger at one of the globes, mentally skewering a knitting needle through California and wondering where the point would emerge.

'Madagascar?' she mused aloud.

'Madagascar?' Conrad Dengler's deck shoes had made no sound on the room's thick carpet. 'Madagascar? That's most interesting. Why do you say that?' His voice was low and urgent and his eyes darted to each side of the room like a silent screen villain about to whisk a Gish sister into white slavery.

'It looked like a perfect solution at one time, didn't it?' he smiled. 'It would have solved a difficult situation, don't you agree?'

Before he could say any more, they were joined by a worried-looking Joseph Weiss. He was sure Mrs Murdoch was not interested in African geography. Cedric Sedgwick's record was still playing and Weiss raised hands and eyebrows to invite her to dance with him but his move was intercepted by the tall, pink-jacketed man who grabbed hold of Evelyn and kissed her wetly on both cheeks.

'Evie, darling!' His loud voice was a strange mix of Balliol and Budapest. 'You look marvellous!'

Zandor Kiss put a pink cashmere arm around her waist and magicked her away from Weiss and his friend in a sort of syncopated wiggle.

'You follow well, Mrs Murdoch. You rumba? Everyone should rumba. My Miss Cavendish back at the office will see to it. They have a man right there at the studio. Little dago – Gonzales? Morales? That guy could teach a cripple to rumba,' promised Mr Kiss. 'Very easy: a little like a *paso doble*' (as if that explained everything).

He stopped dancing as soon as they reached the terrace, giving a final half turn so that he had his back to Joseph Weiss. 'So, how come you know the Kraut?'

'On the train,' breathed Evelyn, matching his hugger-mugger tones. 'Told him I was in voice culture.'

'Very good, that we can fix. Maybe we can have you coach the McGee girl. I want her talking like Anna Neagle. Is your house OK? Mamie Silverman is a very nice lady. Very – what is the word?'

'*Szimpatikus?*'

'Exactly! Crazy like an Albanian donkey but *szimpatikus*.'

Keeping her voice low she asked if he had any idea when Colonel Peyton would be returning. Kiss gave a slow shake of the head and put a finger to his lips. The Colonel was a very busy man.

'But if I'm supposed to be his assistant …'

'This town is full of weasels. You can be useful, you can listen; you can come to things like this and listen.'

'Yes, but what am I to do the rest of the time?'

Kiss took her hand and began absently polishing the back of it.

'What does anyone do in this place? You've seen the studio: all those offices, all those pretty telephones. What do any of them do? Read some scripts. Make a few notes. You know shorthand? Make it up. *Look busy*. Have you read the Mars book?'

Evelyn said that she had and reminded him that she lived in Woking.

'What?'

'Woking? It's one of the towns attacked in the novel.'

He shook his head. 'Not any more. We cut Woking. We'd have the Legion of Decency on our backs. Minds like sewers, these Decency people. Anyhow, we'll find you plenty to do. They're having a meeting in PZ's office at eleven o'clock tomorrow. The Kay kid can bring you. You can be consultant – like on your business cards.'

'But surely that would mean treading on the toes of all the other writers and consultants?'

Mr Kiss made a dismissive gesture with his hand. She wasn't to take any notice of those *farkuk*. He obviously hadn't expected her to understand him and he looked at her blush in surprise.

'It said "conversational Hungarian" on your papers. What kind of conversations were you having, Mrs Murdoch?'

'My school's singing teacher was originally from Györ. He didn't like the English very much.'

When she arrived back at the bungalow the terrace was clear of mud and weeds, a pair of steamer chairs had been angled to face the sunset and a splendid Bonnard landscape had been hung on the newly painted wall opposite her bed.

Friday's *LA Times* was on the kitchen table. There was a three-column photograph of the smashed interior of St Paul's Cathedral on its front page. 'Offering from Mars,' read the caption. 'The beautiful high altar in London yesterday desecrated by raiding planes as silent Nazi missiles fall far and wide.'

Chapter 8

FELIX KAY WAS wearing a less Mad Professor jacket than usual when Evelyn arrived at work the next day and was straightening his tie and combing his hair in the mirror behind the office door.

'We're seeing Kiss and the big cheese at eleven,' he explained.

At exactly five minutes to they walked across to the executive building where Kiss's personal secretary, Della Cavendish, was at her desk about to wrap a slim jeweller's box in a sheet of Japanese paper. The gift tag read 'To Darling Rindy from Uncle Zandor'. Miss Cavendish wasn't at all happy about it. The child was way too young for that kind of thing. She snapped open the leather case and held a rivière of pale-green stones up to the light.

'They'd match your eyes,' oozed Felix.

'Didn't think I was your type, Mr Kay.'

Her face resumed its all-purpose smile as she turned to Evelyn.

'Mrs Murdoch, isn't it? I remember buying the dress. Zandor said I was to give you Miss McGee's address and phone number.' She took an index card from her blotter. 'And he had me call Mr Morales about some dancing lessons. He's got a two-hour slot after lunch.'

One of Miss Cavendish's telephones began ringing. She put a hand over the receiver.

'PZ's still tied up in another meeting so nobody's here yet.' Miss Cavendish suppressed a yawn. 'Maybe you could wait outside, Mr Kay? Work on the tan? Rest your sex appeal?'

They took a seat facing the office window. Axminster lawns were ringed by formal flowerbeds planted with toy-like standard roses, each bush cunningly grafted so that the blooms were half red, half white like a ready-made set for *Alice in Wonderland*. On the rust-coloured soil beneath the plants a team of Japanese gardeners were grubbing up perfectly healthy pansies ready for the autumn switch to begonias.

A half-familiar face was practising golf shots on the lawn. He squinted across at them to check their status then resumed his manoeuvres, taking care to remain in clear view of the office windows. He then began doing surprising things with a set of dumb-bells.

'Funny place to exercise. Is there not a gymnasium for that?'

'Who'd see him? Poor guy gets typecast as college professor, lab-coat types. It happens when they wear glasses.' Felix gave the man a long stare. 'I guess he's gunning for an action picture.'

There was an urgent rap on the glass from Miss Cavendish.

The corridor leading to PZ's suite was lined with photographs. Everyone at eye level was a star but there were lesser mortals down by the skirting boards and up near the ceiling. Felix raised a scuffed suede foot and pointed to a picture in the bottom corner: a military-looking chap sporting dog's-tooth checks and an Errol Flynn moustache.

'HP takes a good picture, doesn't he?'

'Cutting it very fine, Mr Kay.'

138

A woman in a trim brown tailor-made and horn-rimmed spectacles was standing by the door to the inner office carrying a pile of yellow folders. The door read 'PZ Homberg, Chief Executive'. Evelyn rubbed experimentally at the letter C as she passed and the wafer of gold leaf wrinkled readily across the polished maple veneer.

PZ's private desk was high up on a dais at the far end of the room with the usual bank of snapshots (was there anyone anywhere who hadn't met Charles Lindbergh?). There was an American flag on a short pole, a brass outline of the United States tooled into the wall behind the desk and a row of wall clocks: Los Angeles; New York; London; Berlin; Bombay; Sydney. London was ten minutes slow.

A conference table ran the length of the room and had been laid for a three-course meeting, each place supplied with blotter, notepad, pencils, water jug and a crystal ashtray the size of a hubcap. Half a dozen men drifted in but lurked by the picture window, seemingly reluctant to commit to a seating plan.

The woman in brown, Trudi Hansen, PZ's 'executive secretary', knew their little game only too well.

'Do sit down, gentlemen.'

She herself remained standing at the top of the table and there was an awkward musical-chairs moment while they all jockeyed for seats – near but not too near.

'The important thing is to stay out of spitting distance,' warned Felix.

No sooner had the last man taken his place than the far door opened to reveal Zandor Kiss, Ted Monroe, Walter Kramer and a tall, dark man in rimless spectacles smoking a long cigar: PZ Homberg.

'You kidding? He's on my Drop Dead list. Actually he's top of my Drop Dead list – and there's some stiff competition.'

The head of Miracle Studios wore a well-cut flannel suit and a necktie of dull grey silk, a lawyerly subfusc entirely at odds with his manner. He took in the *placement* at a glance and immediately strode to the wrong end of the table, signalling Miss Hansen to join him. Zandor Kiss bagged the chair to his right and pulled up another for Miss Cavendish who sat at his elbow, pen poised. Ted Monroe, oblivious to any pecking order, took the empty chair next to Evelyn and immediately poured himself a glass of water and loosened his tie. Mr Kramer sat at the other end of the table and lit the first of ten cigarettes. He remained silent for the entire meeting but made the occasional note with a gold fountain pen ('look busy').

'OK people! What we got? Trudi?'

Miss Hansen consulted the first of her yellow folders.

'They've had some early snow up in Vermont so now *The Lady and the Lumberjack* is five days behind schedule. Eighty per cent of the work has been done in the studio but Dolores Del Ray was flown up for two days of exterior shots by the old swimming hole – the swim itself is being done right here in the tank – but then they got the two inches of snow.'

PZ was unimpressed by the delay. What were they paying the writers for? Write some snow.

'Way ahead of you, PZ.'

Ted Monroe skimmed a few paper-clipped sheets across the table's high-gloss surface.

'We change the swimming hole to a ski lodge – that way we can still use the log cabin. The second unit got some footage of the snowfall and Wardrobe have sent up some winter sports outfits and a sable coat.'

A small man in a bow tie and a diamond-patterned sweater pulled some sketches from a portfolio.

PZ appeared unconvinced.

'Can she ski, even?'

'For eighteen hundred a week she can ski.'

Miss Hansen thought not.

'Miss Del Ray has a "No Dangerous Sports or Activities" clause in her contract. She broke her ankle trying to ride a camel in that Von Blick thing she did and her agent isn't taking any chances.'

'The McGee moppet's playing the kid sister. She can definitely ski,' said Felix. 'She skied in that Santa Claus picture.'

'OK, but what about the bathing suit? Publicity was dead set on the bathing suit. The magazines have the photos already.'

'She can wear tight pants and a fancy sweater,' said Monroe. 'A *tight* fancy sweater. We'll see her getting off a sledge or a snowplough then along the path, enter the old log cabin mid-shot, shrug off the sables —' Ted Monroe rolled his shoulders and puffed out his chest suggestively '— then we unleash the pedigree Pomeranians.'

'Greyhounds'd be better,' said Felix. 'More class.'

'Listen, they could be *raccoons* for all the camera will see of them. We'll be zooming in for the close-up: a snow-flake on her frozen cheek … maybe we'd better make it a low-necked sweater …' Monroe paused mid-flow. 'Always assuming that the snow holds. If not, run with the swimming-hole idea. She OK with swimming, or is that too dangerous for her?'

Miss Hansen signalled to an underling who scuttled back to the main office in her high-heeled shoes. There was the shriek of steel filing-cabinet drawers as the relevant contract was whisked from the archive and brought back for inspection.

'Swimming is OK,' read Miss Hansen, 'but no high diving, no water ballets and her hairdresser to be on permanent standby.'

'I wish I had her agent,' laughed PZ. 'OK, run with the snow thing but make it snappy and get them to send a daily weather report. What's next? Ted? Any more of those treatments we talked about?'

PZ and the great American public were very taken with the whole fish-out-of-water comedy format in which an aristocratic female was brought to heel by a man in a checked shirt (her comeuppance usually featured mud and a lot of torn lace) and the studio was keen to feed the appetite it had created. *Duchess in the Dirt* was due to start shooting the following week and *Countess in Calico* was also in the pipeline. Ted Monroe wondered aloud if the same gag would work with a male lead? Maybe an older guy plus a pair of juveniles – *The Duke Goes West*? Some English bozo pitches up in New Mexico, the Rolls-Royce breaks down, he high-hats the local talent and ends up in a horse trough – plus the cowboy gets the girl. It could be a vehicle for Games, he thought, or possibly Frobisher? Ted Monroe could see Baines Frobisher in a horse trough.

'You and me both,' agreed PZ. 'Did we find a part for him in the toga picture?'

Miss Hansen consulted her notebook.

'Games to play Caligula, Frobisher as Uncle Claudius, two hundred pairs of sandals and about a mile of bedsheets – Von Blick's got a Harvard Latin professor on the payroll.'

'Prestige pictures are a pain in the ass,' sighed PZ. 'Let me see something on that Duke idea by Friday, Ted. How'd *The Cowboy and the Countess* go down?'

'They had a preview out in Barstow last week,' said Miss Hansen, pinging the elastic from two piles of index cards and passing them to her boss.

PZ flicked through the pasteboard comments in the first batch.

'"Funniest movie I ever saw",' he read. '"Laughed so hard I peed in my girlfriend's hand".'

An awkward, snuffly moment while sniggers were swallowed.

'How about the current version of *Knights of Love*?'

'Not so good.'

Miss Hansen lowered her glasses and read from the top few comments.

'Eighty per cent not in favour: "About as sexy as a stained-glass window. The no-good, cheating dame should learn to speak English. My girlfriend and I lost interest after twenty minutes. Any more movies like this and I'll have to marry the bitch." The general feeling was Not Enough Sex.'

'Sounds to me like they supply their own,' said PZ, waving the cards away. 'It's easy to overreact to a bunch of cards – everyone thinks they know better – but nobody ever had a hit with twenty per cent approval. What are we doing to fix it? Zandor?'

'Sex, we've got –' Zandor Kiss nodded to a publicity man who handed round photographs that featured a pouting, wimpled Miss Malo displaying un-Arthurian amounts of décolletage '– and Von Blick is going to be reshooting the love scenes with some new dialogue from Mr Kay here.'

He signalled to Miss Cavendish who dealt everyone a few foolscap pages and PZ's rimless spectacles flashed as he compared the old scene with the latest rewrite.

'We need to do something about that "cheating dame" thing,' mused Felix, 'make Guinevere more sympathetic.' He paused for the briefest moment. 'Maybe she should have a casket on the table with some baby shoes she's been knitting: one made, one never finished? She could take them out and fuss with them a little then lock them back in the box? The music will do the rest. Every mother in America will get the message: Arthur doesn't cut the mustard.'

'That ought to get it,' nodded PZ. 'Nice job, Felix.'

Felix seemed taller suddenly.

'OK, OK, OK. Now, Zandor, what's happened with that British Air Force doco idea you pitched us? *Lions in the Sky*? They win the war yet?'

Zandor Kiss said that he was flying back to London later in the week and had meetings lined up with the British War Office about making a film showing the day-to-day running of an RAF squadron.

'Easy on the war stuff but everyone loves airplane pictures.' PZ turned to Ted Monroe. 'Work up a treatment – plenty of aerial stunts. One page, not too much dialect and –' he jabbed his cigar towards Kiss '– *no Krauts*.'

'OK. New business? Trudi?' An impatient nod to Miss Hansen.

'The new scenario for the Martian picture. Mr Kiss to present.'

Zandor Kiss placed his fingertips on the table's edge and closed his eyes (Ted Monroe rolled his).

'We hear the orchestra. An unearthly sound: strings – maybe a theremin?'

'A *what*?'

'New electric thing,' said Felix. 'Very high-pitched, sounds like Deanna Durbin in a tight girdle.'

PZ shrugged and signalled to Kiss to continue.

'The camera zooms in through the cockpit of a space-ship – pilot's point of view. There's a panel of buttons and speedos and above them, through the window, we see the Earth getting closer and closer. Then we pull back and see a wrinkled claw come into shot and move one of the levers.' Kiss opened his eyes and his voice grew louder and more dramatic. 'The claw lets go the lever and points out of the window in the direction of the Earth, then it balls into a fist and we hear someone say, "You are an inferior race."'

'Wait a minute, wait a minute. You got the Martians talking English? You sure about that?'

'We could use Esperanto,' suggested Felix. 'Worked fine in *Codename Ramona*. That way the only people we offend are the Esperanto people.'

'And boy do they get offended,' sighed Miss Hansen. 'We're still getting the letters.'

'How would it sound?' asked PZ. 'We got someone?'

'*Vi estas malsupera raso.*'

PZ frowned in Evelyn's direction. The whole table frowned.

'Who *is* that?'

'Mrs Murdoch,' said Kiss. 'She's cultural consultant on the project. She's from England' (more an apology than an introduction).

'I thought they spoke English there. What's she doing talking Esperanto?' demanded PZ suspiciously.

'It's an international language,' murmured Evelyn.

'So?' said Ted Monroe. 'English is pretty goddammed international. *Yiddish* is international.'

He took up one of his colour pencils and did a rapid doodle on his blotter: a little green Martian with a speech bubble reading '*Oy gewalt!*'

Kiss carried on with his potted scenario. It was not one that Mr Wells would recognise.

'Dissolve. We zoom in on an English village – signpost, roses, cobblestones, the whole shebang – and next thing you know there's a thatched cottage on fire and the old church spire's been knocked down and a little girl in a sailor dress is running after her dog. Our hero – clean-cut, Leslie Howard type – gets off his bicycle and takes the child by the shoulders. "What's the matter, young lady?"'

PZ produced a roll of adding-machine paper from his pocket and began making notes on it.

'He puts the child on the crossbar of the bicycle and they ride off through what the Martians have left of old London town – cue hordes of Cockney refugees and comic types – and then they make their way back out into the countryside dodging the Martian death ray until they get to the school where her big sister teaches.'

'So far, so good. Rindy McGee's a cinch for the kid if she can do the accent.'

'Mrs Murdoch here is taking care of that.' He turned to Miss Cavendish and told her to make a date for some voice coaching.

'OK, who you got for the male lead?'

'We're testing Fox Meredith,' said one of the nameless men. 'Plays Galahad in *Knights of Love.*'

'His limey accent is pretty good,' interjected Felix. 'He was in legit for two years back east ... He played Bert in *Violets Below Stairs.*'

The room looked blank, waiting to see how it played with the boss.

'That thing at the Broadhurst? I saw that. I think the butler did it.'

It seemed safe to laugh and they all did so.

Mr Kiss pressed on, speaking faster now, sensing that he was losing them.

'Meanwhile – and ziss is the luff interest – they find the schoolteacher sister trapped inside the old chapel.'

'Anyone in mind?'

'Von Blick's trying to sell us this little blonde he's been building up,' said another of the men. 'Cute.'

Kiss ignored the interruption. 'And the schoolteacher is hiding from the Martians in the chapel with all the girls in her class and she's reading them a story so they won't panic.'

'Reading what?' PZ got up from his chair and began orbiting the table.

Suddenly everyone was an expert. Kiss himself was all for a Bible story – 'Somevone smoting somevone' – but PZ said nuts to that, bring in the Bible and you'd kill any picture stone dead. Someone else thought a classic would be better – like when Olivia de Havilland does it in *Gone With the Wind*? *Henry V*, maybe? Or *Tom Brown's Schooldays*? – and PZ said that *Tom Brown's Schooldays* was an RKO picture and was he out of his goddamned mind and then Evelyn heard herself suggesting that the schoolteacher might find a forbidden book under a hassock.

'Under a *what*?'

No sense getting flustered.

'A hassock, a knee cushion. One of the girls could have hidden a romance or something to read during prayers and she could read to them from that.'

PZ scratched his chin.

'A ro-mance ... that's not bad. And one of the schoolkids can say how she always wanted orchids or orange blossoms or persimmons or some such and another one says how she always dreamed of white lace and six bridesmaids and all the time we're hearing the death rays going off and then we get a close-up of the sister and a look that says maybe they none of them live to get married. Maybe there could be light falling on her face from a stained-glass window. You know like in that *Hunchback* movie?'

Ted Monroe was unconvinced and wasn't afraid to say so.

'You're slowing the whole thing down to a crawl,' he continued, scratching more doodles on his blotter (the

147

water jug blocked Evelyn's view). 'What happens to the Martians while we're having all this boy-meets-girl baloney? They gonna be bridesmaids?'

'Screw the Martians.'

But Ted Monroe wasn't letting go.

'Mr Wells happy about all this?'

One of the nameless executives said that Mr Wells would be very happy with his percentage and that the great man would be AOK with any treatment they saw fit to use.

'Wait a minute: you're turning a modern masterpiece into *A Million Martians and a Girl* and you're trying to tell me that Wells is AOK about that?' barked Monroe. 'And the dog? Is he AOK about the fucking dog?'

A collective shimmy of excitement. Only the PZs of this world used that kind of language. Even the big man himself looked impressed.

'No little dog in the book?'

'No little dog in the book. The kid I can just about stand, but *a dog*? I bet you just love the dog –' he turned on Evelyn '– veddy English. Martians wiping out a whole civilisation and we got to worry about a stupid little thing like a dog. If the Martians really were coming the guy would wring its neck.'

'Only a Nazi would wring its neck.' Evelyn spoke more loudly than she had intended. 'We have to care about little things. We have to. That's what makes us civilised.'

There was a heavy silence while the rest of the room waited to know if they liked the dog.

PZ liked the dog. He continued circling the table.

'You bet your life it is. It's exactly what makes us civilised. Which reminds me: where are we dogwise? We got a name yet?'

'They've pretty much settled on Randy,' said Miss Hansen.

'We already talked about that: the Brits won't wear it,' said Kiss (more sniggers from mid-table).

'Dandy?' wondered Evelyn.

'Dandy? Dan-dy … I like that.' PZ paused mid-prowl then nodded towards Miss Hansen. 'Get a memo to the dog people. See if he'll sit up and beg for "Dandy".' He gave Evelyn's back an approving smack. 'Good work. Nobody ever lost money on a dog picture. Martians?' He rocked his head from side to side. 'Maybe not so good.'

Evelyn felt a little taller.

PZ reached across for a printed scenario and the whole room rustled as everyone joined him on page fifteen.

'We got any art on all this?' he said, resuming his seat.

The art director produced a folder of rough sketches which PZ examined one by one before throwing them into the centre of the table. There were several of the Martians (little green chimpanzees) and their three-legged death-ray machines (the resemblance to the Miracle water tower was unmistakable: 'Boilers on stilts, I tell you, striding along like men').

England itself was a selection of tuppence-coloured views – St Paul's, Tower Bridge, Big Ben, Anne Hathaway's cottage – all in various states of destruction, all strafed with the beams of searchlights. Oh dear. PZ was back on his feet to have another look at the sketches. He rescanned the artwork and looked along the table. Kramer was shaking his head.

'You all thinking what I'm thinking?' PZ leaned across to Zandor Kiss and poked his club tie with an angry forefinger. 'You're going to need to be very, very careful here. We gotta keep a close eye on you, Zandy, baby. You think we don't read the papers? Saint Paul's Cathedral? Not in my studio you don't.'

149

Kiss, an expert back-pedaller, lost no time in blaming the art department and their lousy clichés. One of the executives, marginally braver than the rest, said that Chaplin's Hitler film had got some great press in New York. PZ, only partially reassured, closed down the discussion.

'We'll talk some more in my office tomorrow. Miss Hansen will tell you when.' He nodded to Felix. 'Carry on with the treatment but I don't want any jackboots, you follow me?'

He gathered the sketches into their portfolio and handed them back to the man in the diamond-patterned sweater.

'You do good work.'

'Thank you, sir.'

Without further ceremony PZ walked to the far end of the room, sat down at his desk and began dictating a stream of memos into his recording apparatus. The others rose from the table and filed out into the corridor. As they trooped past the wall of pictures Mr Kiss turned to Miss Cavendish.

'We should get Mrs Murdoch's picture taken. One of the studio chaps will do it for you. Miss Cavendish will arrange it. It'll make her a nice souvenir.'

A souvenir. Not especially encouraging.

She walked with Felix to the commissary.

'I don't think there's any point you and me knocking ourselves out over this Martian treatment,' said Felix. 'Looks to me like PZ and Kramer have had the Senate Committee on their backs again. Last thing they need is Kiss and his little green Nazis. Kiss thinks Miracle is his personal propaganda unit but he picked the wrong guys.'

'You'd think they'd be glad to do their bit,' mused Evelyn as they took their seats in the cafeteria, 'rather than tiptoe round the war like that, being *Jews* and everything.'

She could have bitten her tongue but Felix didn't seem to be offended.

'Sure, they tiptoe. They're keeping their heads down. Nobody likes a whining Jew and FDR isn't going to let a few bleeding hearts make a mess of foreign trade. Sure, they go to *schul* and eat herring, but they don't want to rock the boat. This isn't Warner Brothers. PZ and Kramer are playing a long game: business is business.'

'Yes, but you'd think they would want to show some sort of solidarity. I mean, would Negroes do that?'

'Would Negroes do what?'

'I mean if the movie business were run by rags-to-riches coloured people, would they avoid making films about Negro things?'

'Ne-groes? Are you crazy?' It seemed that she had, finally, offended him.

'It's just a hypothesis. *Martians* then. If the Martians ran Hollywood. Would Martians do that?'

He relaxed, ready to make concessions now they were back in the realm of the possible. '*Martians*, maybe.'

Chapter 9

S HE MUSTN'T FORGET to look English, said Miss Cavendish, when she telephoned Evelyn in Bel Air on Thursday morning to remind her about Dorinda McGee's elocution lessons. Mr Kiss had rung from the airport and was very specific: 'sumsing in tweed'. Publicity would be sending a photographer to capture the new voice coach at work.

Evelyn's reflection looked very English indeed in the glass front door of the McGee mansion, and she did a tiny double take at the sight of herself back in her dismal grey suit.

A swarthy man in a butler costume answered the door. Behind him a woman's voice drifted down the wide oak stairs.

'Craven? Is that the masseuse?'

The butler raised an eyebrow and Evelyn shook her head and gave him one of the cards with 'Voice Culture' on it.

'I have an appointment with Miss McGee.'

'Miss McGee is in the rose garden, madam.'

The house, mildly medieval in style with mullioned windows and a heavy beard of ivy, was set in a large formal garden ringed by a moat-like rill. Twelve identical child-sized canoes were secured to the landing stage with twelve identical mooring hitches.

To the rear of the house beyond the swimming pool (heart-shaped) were a series of flower beds, neatly arrayed like the hospital kind and all planted with a pale-pink hybrid tea called 'Pussycat' which had been named in honour of the star by the American Rose Society. It was all as tidy as a park but the pattern had been wrecked by a newly-dug bed drilled with fully grown, shop-bought vegetables. A ten-foot section of white picket fencing had been leaned against the stately yew hedge. Behind it, neat rolls of turf waited to be relaid once Miss McGee had finished playing at self-sufficiency in her own little Potemkin pumpkin patch.

America's Pussycat wore blue denim dungarees, a red gingham blouse and two dozen large freckles which had been drawn across her nose with a brown pencil. There was a crudely sewn patch on one knee of the overalls and a three-cornered tear on the other. The child was poking implausibly at the wet red soil between the rows of pump-kins with a very shiny new trowel while a photographer adjusted his lights and a youngish man in a sherbet-co-loured jacket made suggestions from the touchline. There was a wide-brimmed Panama on the grass next to him and a moat-like ring around his brilliantined hair where the natty hat had sat.

'Give her the worm,' he ordered as the photographer screwed in a fresh bulb. One of the McGees' Japanese gardeners reached down for a teacup and tipped an earth-worm into Rindy's waiting palm.

'Try to look scared, disgusted.'

But the veteran of *Dolly Daydream* needed more specific direction. Did he want scared or did he want disgusted? Or did he actually want both at the same time? Could she do both? Sure she could do both.

'Now give me grumpy-but-cute. And you look too clean. Rough it up a little.'

The child slipped a small mirror from her bib pocket, reached down for a clod of mud which she smeared across her cheek like a grown-up powdering her nose then turned to the lens as her face slotted back into the agreed expression: biting her lower lip, curling her upper lip and scowling at the task before her. The bulb flashed and Evelyn stepped into shot. The man in the sherbet jacket held out his hand.

'Mrs Murdoch? Clinton Parker, I'm Miss McGee's press agent. Sorry to hold you up but we're snatching shots between showers – we want to get the exterior stuff in the can.'

Once the cameraman was satisfied, Mr Parker shepherded his client across to the front gate where she played a short scene with a movie extra in a mailman's uniform who was pretending to take delivery of a parcel labelled 'Bundles for Britain' while the press agent told the photographer which interiors he wanted.

'Make sure you get all the baby pictures on the piano but be sure and keep the cocktail cabinet out of shot.'

Evelyn was not particularly fond of children. She just couldn't speak their language. It didn't seem especially hard, but, try as she might, she could never quite catch the right tone of voice – you *are* a clever girl! What *smart* shoes!

Silas had wanted children very much – and very soon. Other people – people in songs and films, anyway – made love (or, just possibly, 'whoopee') but Silas made *babies* which did rather make one want to stay downstairs by the fire and read another chapter of *The Grapes of Wrath*. War had put an end to the nightly fumbles but his attentions were almost constant when he came home on leave during training and his letters always ended by asking if she had any good news to tell him.

As soon as they had returned from their Torquay honeymoon, people she hardly knew began listening for pattering feet, watching the colours she chose in the wool shop and assuming that she would be keen to practise her maternal skills on surplus infants. Even Silas's death hadn't put an end to it. A near neighbour in Woking had a little girl of five and fondly supposed that poor childless Mrs Murdoch would like nothing better than to have it left for collection like so much luggage while its mother went shopping on Saturday mornings. She was no *trouble*, said her mother, who must, Evelyn decided, have understood something quite different by the word.

The child, Wendy, a short tubby blonde that burst into tears on the slightest pretext, had been told to call the nice lady at No. 9 'Auntie' Evelyn. Did *Auntie* Evelyn have a jewellery box? Mrs Buckingham (Auntie Betty) next door had a jewellery box, a musical one with a ballet dancer inside. Mrs Buckingham had given Wendy a brooch. Mummy was looking after it until Wendy was grown up enough to wear it. If she was *Mrs Murdoch*, was there a *Mr* Murdoch? Did *he* buy brooches? Mrs Buckingham always saved up her rations so that they could make biscuits. Could Auntie Evelyn make biscuits? wondered Wendy. 'Why is that child crying?', demanded old Mrs Murdoch. No jam in *her* rice pudding after that nonsense.

Happily, Dorinda McGee, born 1928 but aged seven for professional purposes, was not and never had been a child.

The pressman introduced Evelyn and explained that this was the nice lady who was going to make sure she sounded like the real deal when she played the English kid in the Martian movie. Manners were not the child's strong suit.

'What do I want a dumb old dialogue coach for? I can do accents,' protested Dorinda. 'I did French in *Mamzelle Mischief.*'

'Mrs Murdoch here is from London, England.'

'How eppsolutely ghaaaastly,' said Rindy, perfectly mimicking Baines 'Binky' Frobisher (who had played the crap-shooting butler in *The Littlest Lady's Maid*).

'Ah well,' shrugged Rindy, 'I suppose it's this or the clarinet. As long as she don't make me *practise*. The clarinet guy made me practise.'

'She picked it up real fast when we made *Little Girl Blues*,' conceded the press agent, *sotto voce*, 'but Artie Shaw she's not.'

Back at the house, the masseuse had finally arrived and was being led to my lady's chamber while a second young woman, tricked out in a pink nurse's uniform and white lace-up shoes, was shown to a chair in the hall. The white leatherette suitcase by her side said 'Myrtle's Beauty Boudoir: Bringing Beauty to You'. And she was using the unforgiving minutes to rub at her fingernails with a chamois-covered wand.

'Manicurist,' explained Rindy. 'Mother always has the full service on Thursdays, ready for the weekend. The foot woman was just here, the face man's coming at three, then the girls from the hairdresser's. My contract says I have to have twenty hours of school classes a week but I can do pretty much what I want on Thursdays.'

Did she have many hobbies, Evelyn asked – a bore's question if ever there was one – but Rindy McGee was more than happy to boast of her accomplishments. She had mastered five musical instruments, could tap dance, play tennis, ride and ice skate. She hurled a mean lasso and was alarmingly well-versed in circus knife-throwing (this last skill had been taught her by Otto Von Blick).

'I sing, too, and ski.'

'You don't say.'

'And I can cry real tears any time I want. I just think of the time the puppy got hit by the ice truck.'

Acquiring so many accomplishments came at a price, however, and her ignorance of regular schoolgirl topics was encyclopaedic.

'I can learn my lines OK, but anything else forget it,' explained Rindy placidly as they headed up the main staircase.

'You guys go on up and start with the Moses-supposes stuff,' said Parker. 'We'll be right with you. We just need to get a shot of the canoe run.'

The young star's apartment ran the length of the house's attic and was accessed via a concealed door on the top landing which the child opened with a deft dab at the linenfold panelling.

'We had kidnappers when we lived over in Los Feliz,' Rindy explained. 'Craven – he's our butler – scared them off but now Mom isn't taking any chances. Did you read about the French kid they grabbed? *My* ransom was going to be twice that.'

The walls of the hidden staircase were lined with magazine covers: Rindy in an Easter bonnet; Rindy in a cowgirl outfit; Rindy with Santa Claus; Rindy with Charlie Chaplin; Rindy with the President. No Mussolini – not yet at least.

The long room was half nursery, half boudoir, with a hundred teddy bears, a double bed canopied in pink net and a baby grand piano (did they even make upright pianos in America?).

Rindy McGee wiped the mud from her face and began changing into a white blouse and flannel pinafore dress.

'The photographer will be up in a minute. You want to freshen up?'

Evelyn peered at the triptych of Evelyns in the mirror of the pink-flounced dressing table and tucked three stray strands of hair into place. The child gave a hoot of laughter.

'That's *it*? Is lipstick against your religion, or something? You look about ninety. That's what they do for grandmas in the make-up department: just a quick smear of pan-cake then a bit of toothpaste combed through their hair and plenty of No Lipstick. Ages them fifty years. That's what you look like.' The baby-blue eyes looked Evelyn up and down. 'How old are you anyway? Thirty-five? And all that *grey* … Is that an English suit?'

But Clinton Parker, who was helping the photographer manhandle his equipment up the stairs, wouldn't hear a word against Evelyn's ensemble.

'The suit's perfect: a little bit of Olde England. The copy will write itself.'

The photographer began setting up his lights while Parker arranged a pair of giltwood chairs face to face beside the piano.

'Just make your mouth into an O and, Mrs Murdoch, you put your hand under her chin. Here, put these on –' He produced a pair of lens-less horn-rimmed spectacles from his pocket. 'Try to look old and grouchy.' Evelyn caught him winking at Dorinda via the three-way mirror. 'OK, do your stuff: *round tones.*'

Ladylike accomplishments had not been a particular priority at the boarding school that Evelyn's father had chosen for her but there had been a class called 'Elocution, Deportment and the Modern Home' in which the sixth form was taught how to recite poetry, choose soft furnishings and give notice to domestic staff. She had a dim memory of deep-breathing exercises, brown cows and rugged rocks but had prepared for her new role by buying a pamphlet on stage diction in a second-hand bookstore whose shelves were filled with dog-eared publications on voice culture left over from the days when everyone in town was either teaching elocution or learning how to speak. The well-thumbed paperback she had chosen began with the cardinal vowels and worked its way through to lesson twenty (Shakespeare) via pickled peppers and black-backed bath brushes.

Photographs taken, Rindy McGee sat down at her dressing table and set about removing the fake freckles. A dozen photographs showing all the possible hairstyles for *War of the Worlds* was tucked around the frame of the mirror: ringlets; a topknot; pigtails. All had been defaced with glasses and inky Franz Ferdinand beards except for one showing the star with hair pulled up into two bunches like the ears on a very surprised spaniel.

'It stinks but it takes years off me, Mother says. Besides, I'll match my co-star. He's pretty cute for a dog,' admitted Rindy, 'but *equal billing?* Mother's mad as hell.'

'I don't think your mother would like you to say that word.'

'She wouldn't care. I can do pretty much what I want so long as it isn't in public. I have to *lisp* in public.'

The child was entirely unsurprised when Evelyn told her that there were no dogs or children in the book. Five would get you ten that the original story was bunk, she said. It wasn't a book once it got sold to the studio: it was a movie and movies were for people who couldn't read – or so her friend Teddy Monroe always said.

'You see me in *Alice in Hollywoodland?* That was my first starring role. I was six years old but they put "four" on all the publicity. Teddy did the script on that. Teddy's a swell guy. He wrote me this.'

Rindy went over to the piano stool and produced a red folder bound like a script and labelled '*The Magic Mink* by Theodore Valentine Monroe'.

The magic mink was a fur coat belonging to a wicked stepmother and every night the animals whose skins had made it would come back to life and climb into the heroine's bed to keep her warm and tell her all about their previous lives in a Russian palace and what the stepmother got up to when she wore the coat. Monroe had illustrated it with his own scribbly line-and-wash: stepmother getting drunk at a society party; stepmother robbing a bank; stepmother in jail. The mink themselves were sketched in scratchy black ink, with fluffy backbleeds of sepia watercolour capturing the softness of their fur. The stepmother's hair was a crude dab of gamboges, her Cupid's bow three dots of vermilion.

'Neat, isn't it?' Dorinda replaced the book in its hiding place. 'I told him he should get it published, make it a series. Maybe do one about an alligator purse or something? But he kind of lost interest. Mother hit the roof when she saw it – Mom wears a lot of mink.'

A black maid entered carrying a large, striped dress box.

'Just put it on the bed, Beulah,' said the child with a total lack of curiosity.

Rindy explained that she was being confirmed on Friday week and that there was to be a big party afterwards as it was the day before her birthday and that Evelyn could come if she wanted but if Rindy were Evelyn she'd try to think up a prior engagement.

'It would be neat if you came but it's sure to be a yawn …'

Evelyn, slightly at a loss, said surely Rindy would enjoy seeing all her little friends but the child gave a contemptuous snort and said they were just a bunch of studio people's kids her pressman had invited. None of them was coming to the church beforehand. Half of them were Jewish in any case. Or *half* Jewish.

'They never say which half. You Catholic?'

'Methodist.'

'Figures. We're Catholic.' Rindy pulled a tiny gold and diamond crucifix from inside her blouse and kissed it. 'Father Mulvey says my talent is an Act of God.'

Evelyn smothered a smile. Did the Almighty really act in that way? She had always imagined him busy with earthquakes and tidal waves – things one couldn't insure against. Not *tap dancing*.

Evelyn hadn't intended to take Otto Von Blick up on his invitation, assuming that, like 'call me', it was just something people said, but he had personally telephoned to remind her: 'It'll be part of your education. You can watch me spin straw into gold.'

She spent the first hour of Friday morning being photographed for the studio wall – the 'souvenir' Kiss had promised her – before strolling the four blocks to Sound Stage Six together with Felix Kay who had offered to keep her company ('I sweated blood over that dialogue').

The original director of *Knights of Love* had been so enamoured of the Technicolor Camelot the art department had created that all of his love scenes were in mid-shot and (as the amateur critic in Barstow had so rightly said) 'about as sexy as a stained-glass window'.

The film had been wrapped over a fortnight ago and the technicians had already struck the set but Von Blick's close-ups had no need of battlements or staircases ('a few feathers, some lights, a little smoke'). Camelot was reduced to a Gothic looking glass and a few yards of tapestry and the remains of the more elaborate Arthurian world lay in pieces around the hangar-like room. Just inside the main door the top of the Round Table was angled against the wall, its surface ringed with knightly names gilded into place by the sign-writing team. The names on Arthur's side of the circle – the side that would face the camera – were all from Thomas Malory: Galahad, Percival, Gawain; but the other half were pure Tinseltown: Sir Grumpy, Sir Sleepy, Sir Dopey …

The interior of the building was in almost total darkness but over in the far corner, through a jungle of ladders and rigging, Von Blick and his team could be glimpsed like a witches' sabbath in a focused beam of working light. Queen Guinevere was seated on a gilded plywood throne while a dozen specialists prepared her for close inspection by the cameraman's two-inch lens. The queen's loyal page, its sex hard to determine in the red-velvet get-up and yellow wig, was propped against a leaning board blowing bubble gum and waiting for the cue to rush forward with its all-important line ('My Queen! The King is come!'). Behind the throne, a man with a pocketful of steel combs and a jar of pomade was reglazing the Medusa coils of hair emerging from Magda Malo's headdress. Meanwhile, the make-up man waited his turn, fiddling with his pots and brushes and harrying his young assistant to find him a smaller sea sponge.

Running repairs completed, Guinevere resumed drinking iced Coca-Cola through a straw. Thick, soundproofed walls and no windows kept the temperature subtropical. The air was heavy with a sickly, punchbowl smell of lemons from the insecticide used to keep the flies off the actress's painted skin. Sweat ran down her neck from beneath the heavy golden wig.

Felix and Evelyn trod water at the edge of the pool of light but Von Blick turned to smile a greeting before picking his way across a floor wormy with black cables like giant liquorice bootlaces.

'Aha! My cleffer English friend!'

He took Evelyn's hand and pulled her into the light. The make-up girl in the photographic studio had redrawn her face in a bizarre palette of colours designed to look well in monochrome, but once the shoot was over Evelyn's black lips and greenish cheeks were wiped away with an oily rag and replaced with a rosy simulacrum of youth and health: lips strawberried over, skin matte and creamy. The girl seemed very pleased indeed by the improvement and gave Evelyn a stick of the stuff to keep. Felix hadn't noticed the change but Von Blick spotted the Miracle brushwork at once.

'Madame Murdoch here is ready for her close-up,' he teased away a stray eyelash with his thumb, 'but Mademoiselle Malo she is not ready.'

A four-page memo from PZ had been copied to Evelyn (and twenty-seven other people) explaining that they had had a directive from the Hays Office ruling that the neckline of the actress's slinky green gown was 'indecently low'. A seamstress with a pincushion attached to her left wrist was making last-minute adjustments with a yard of what might well have been *mousseline de soie*.

The director turned to Felix.

'Does that look indecently low to you? You'd see more on the beach but it wouldn't be fifty feet wide and we have to follow the code here, don't we, Mr Screenwriter? "Do not make vice attractive, do not make gambling and drunkenness attractive, no prolonged passionate love scenes." Which leaves us with what exactly? *Little Women*? Little women –' the lipsmacking leer of a cartoon wolf in the henhouse '– sounds like a stag picture for midgets.'

'Otto? Otto!' Magda Malo wasn't getting enough attention. 'I can't see you! Who you talk to?'

The lovely face peered forward and, as her eyes adjusted to the gloom, she spotted Evelyn and Felix lurking behind the cameraman. Her larynx powered up like a siren. Who was that *schmuck*? They promised her a closed set! It was in her contract! Get her agent on the phone! (Her English was strictly need-to-know.)

'Relax, *Liebling*. Without this *schmuck* we'd all be making a silent movie. And you need to be nice to Mrs Murdoch here. We got a memo today. She might be doing your dialogue coaching for *The Borgia Pearl* and she's a friend of the big wet Kiss you like so much, so be nice, yes?'

Miss Malo's twenty-five words of replacement dialogue had been chalked on a blackboard beside the camera where her lover was supposedly standing. Von Blick had taped a small hand mirror just to the right of the lens so that she could gaze lovingly into her own eyes as she spoke. The director stepped back and made right angles with his thumbs and forefingers to frame the scene then climbed on to his chair and began firing off endearments and instructions to the actress and technical crew in preparation for the take, playing one against the other, flattering and insulting them in their various native languages with the fluency and diplomacy of a Swiss maître d' in a station hotel.

'How does the ugly bitch look from up there, Federico?'

'Turn your upper body away from me, *Liebling*, raise your chin three centimetres, drop your voice good and low *like this*.' Von Blick sank to baritone. 'Count to seven and watch that lamp like you couldn't live without it.'

After ten more takes the director called 'cut', took *Liebling*'s hand, kissed it and gently pulled her from her seat and stationed her behind the camera. She must humour him. The instant the lights came back up, Von Blick took his star's place on the Gothic throne and turned to look longingly at his own reflection in the little glass as his rumpled pockmarked face troped irresistibly towards the 300 watts of starlight six feet above his head before delivering the line. Without beauty, without make-up, that slow tilt of the head and the puppet-like drop of the eyelids enabled this middle-aged German Jew to conjure the magical effect he was striving for. Literally a trick of the light.

Take twenty. Nearly an hour had passed when another stranger entered the charmed circle, shattering the mood. It was Miss Della Cavendish, notebook in hand, who came with an urgent status update on Mr Von Blick's forthcoming life of the Emperor Caligula.

'Wardrobe are doing a draft budget for Miss Hansen. They need to know how many vestal virgins. The Harvard guy says we only need six but Mr Kiss wired me to check with you.'

'Six!'

'The professor says the Plu-tarch guy is quite specific.'

'Six! Six actual virgins, I could see your problem. Six *actual* virgins would be a very tall order in this town but this is a *movie*, Della baby. Six-*teen*. Minimum. Sixty maybe. And tell them to go easy on the Wardrobe budget if you get my drift.' He shook his head. '*Six* virgins, he offers me! I'm making an epic here, not a petting party.'

'We finish? We not finish?' Magda Malo, her face a lovely alabaster icon, impatience on a monument.

'OK, *Liebling*, back to work. Let's try a dry take, just an itsy-bitsy rehearsal.' He reached out to pat her pan-caked cheek but the hand behind his back had its fingers crossed. 'Tilt head, breathe, smile, look down, look up, say line.'

Von Blick winked at the cameraman and put a finger to his lips.

'Perfect! Cut and print! *Danke schön*, gentlemen. *Bravi!*' A soft, solitary round of applause.

Magda Malo rose from her throne and went back to her trailer, tailed by Wardrobe, holding the damp green fabric clear of the floor.

'Finally, *finally*, when it doesn't matter, she does what matters,' smiled Von Blick, 'but we got it in the can. Nobody likes retakes on a finished picture but what they don't realise is that it isn't finished till it's finished.' He turned to Evelyn. 'Good to see you again, princess. Are you free on the ninth? I'm having a house-warming. You come, yes? I show you my paintings.'

The director waved a hand at Felix, registering his frayed collar and flyblown jacket. 'You be *chaperon*, Mr Screenwriter.' The title made Felix sound vaguely important but Evelyn wondered if Von Blick simply couldn't remember his name.

Chapter 10

THERE WAS A SLOW-SPREADING bloodstain on the lilac silk sofa cushions where a busty young blonde lay, holding an ice pack to her face. Over by the door, her press agent was shouting into the telephone.

'Hello Mrs Ginsburg? Is the good Doctor home? I hate to bother him on a Sunday but it's kind of an emergency …'

The press agent put his hand over the mouthpiece as he whispered to a friend at his side. 'Best thing that could happen. Now she'll *have* to have it fixed up. Crazy Danish broad kept insisting it had *character*. I told her: when they want character they get Barrymore. This Ginsburg guy's got a whole pattern book: Hedy Lamarr, Colbert, anyone she wants. It'll be the making of her, mark my words.'

The glass doors leading on to the patio would normally have been misted with desert dust but a squad of men with chamois leathers from the maintenance company had just finished polishing them to a crystal shine to be ready for Wally Grendon's famous weekly lunch when poor Miss Larsen arrived and decided to take a turn around the garden. Her host had little sympathy beyond agreeing that it was all *ghastly* and kept looking at his watch until the men in white coats pulled up in a private ambulance and led the weeping girl away.

'Thank God she arrived early,' said Wally as he flipped the cushions.

Evelyn had been in two minds about Mr Grendon's invitation – she hadn't even been introduced to the man – but Felix told her not to be a sap.

'I'll be there, everyone will be there.'

'But what does he even do? Will I have seen him in anything?'

'Not since the talkies.'

Wally Grendon's acting career had ended under something of a cloud (Felix didn't elaborate) but he had made a lot of good friends and the studio had kept him on as a set designer and he had a nice sideline in interior decor. His own Beverly Hills house had begun life as run-of-the-mill Spanish Colonial, said Felix, but Wally had transformed it into something altogether grander, adding a Greek Revival porch and a lot of Georgian sash windows. The only nod to the German School was a wall of plate glass leading out to the kidney-shaped swimming pool.

'They say Manny Silverman's having a new pool built over at his Malibu place,' said Felix. 'It's gonna be shaped like his liver.'

The interior (which was changed at least once a year) currently favoured the Rococo. Lampshades were beaded, pelmets tasselled and the ceiling of the thirty-foot 'salon' was lavishly iced with fancy plaster mouldings.

'Grendon's potty about that stuff.' Binky Frobisher had arrived and greeted Evelyn with a kiss on both cheeks. 'Gets it made up by a chap who used to be a dentist. Wally rips a few feet of crenellated ogee or whatever it is out of some Irish castle and the chap makes moulds of it that he can run off by the yard. One day Wally will smile and his teeth will just be a row of egg-and-dart.'

Dentistry again.

'Our host usually favours bright colours – as you can see from his taste in cravats – but he keeps the walls very plain so he can show off the Art. All for sale, of course,' explained Binky. 'He gets it all shipped in by his New York dealer friends. Very nice commission. I don't think he owns a single canvas.'

The most prominent exhibit was a large naked woman executed in green and yellow oil paint hung opposite a gigantic white settee, custom-built to run the length of the room (and, not entirely coincidentally, the length of the beach-house set for *Lady in Fear*).

Binky handed Evelyn a glass of champagne with a lump of sugar in the bottom. She took a sip and turned reluctantly to the gigantic green buttocks. Even in galleries, nudes made Evelyn feel uneasy. People who would balk at a tight skirt or an indecently low neckline made a special case for nudes. Postcards were smut but nudes were Art. Mr Grendon's naked lady had been painted from behind as though the artist were sneaking up on her. There was a dimpled cleft snaking down her plump back as if she could be thumbed in half like a breakfast roll.

On the other side of the fireplace hung a canvas showing a team of men digging the foundations of a skyscraper in the shadow of a tenement building festooned with drying laundry. Binky began doing that art-lover gavotte that people did: standing back to admire the composition, leaning in to puzzle at the signature through his eyeglass.

'Wally won't have any trouble selling that one. His faggot friends all love the Ashcan School – all those horny-handed sons of toil. They think it gives a room the he-man touch,' Binky simpered conspiratorially. 'Same thing with the nudes: fooling nobody.'

The Highland terrier draped over Wally Grendon's arm had been dyed lilac to match his upholstery. His two white Persian cats, bookended on a radiator and keeping a weather eye on the salmon in aspic, had not.

'Wally made the Pet Parlour people try the same stunt on those two one time.' Ted Monroe had arrived, drink already magically in hand. 'Not a mistake you make twice. They settled out of court, mercifully.'

'Who, the pet people or the cats?'

Both Persians had pounced down from their perch and were engaged in testing a small Louis Quinze divan to destruction with their flexing claws, their muttered dialogue more growl than purr. Kowtow had liked to claw furniture (but only ever Silas's chair).

Evelyn tweezed a shrimp tail from one of the lunch dishes and held it furtively at her side. A ball of white fur materialised instantly: pleased, but unsurprised. It claimed the treat then began polishing Evelyn's shins optimistically.

'How very *civilised*,' said Ted Monroe. 'You like animals, I take it?'

'Only cats.' She dropped another shrimp.

'You got cats back home?'

'I did have – one. He was called Kowtow.'

'Was?'

And she found herself telling Ted Monroe about the little black cat that she had taken with her to the house in Woking. Her husband had never really warmed to him, and the day after war was declared he had smuggled Evelyn's little friend down to the vet's surgery, returning with the empty basket and a quarter of peppermint creams (Silas's favourite). 'I didn't want to upset you, dearest, but it was for the best.'

'Chin up,' he had said when he found her in tears beside the basket. 'You can stroke me instead.' Quite racy for him.

'My husband said it was more *humane* but that wasn't how it felt to me, I'm afraid.'

A breeze blew in from across the terrace and she shivered at the memory.

'Cold?' Ted Monroe's warm hand cupped her elbow and he edged her in the direction of the fireplace. She looked up into his face, feeling the transforming beams of a high key light above her head.

'I have to get back to work,' he began, still holding her arm. 'PZ wants treatments for all that cowboy and countess stuff – but I'm glad I found you here; I wanted to apologise about the meeting the other day? I was just so mad at Kiss. If you're going to make *War of the Worlds* then make War of the goddamn Worlds not *Rin Tin Tin and the Men from Mars*. I hope you'll forgive me. You must let me make it up to you. Are you doing anything for lunch Saturday?'

She shook her head then felt herself raising her chin and looking at his earlobe like she couldn't live without it. There were a lot of laughter lines around his eyes. She held her breath waiting for a more specific invitation but instead he merely looked at his watch. 'Jesus, I really gotta go. Want me to introduce you to anyone?'

She followed his gaze as he looked hopefully around him and, to her surprise, saw that there were a number of familiar faces among the latecomers: Raymond Games admiring his reflection in a speckly old looking glass; Myra Manning giggling in a corner with Foxton Meredith; Connie McAllister (sticking to a strict no-solids regime) and Ida and Wanda Van Clark who were admiring one of the couches with a very thin, very suntanned woman in buttercup yellow. Mrs Van Clark was vastly relieved to spot someone she knew and made a beeline for Evelyn the instant Ted Monroe left her side.

171

'It's Evelyn, isn't it?' she gushed. 'I hardly recognised you in your California wardrobe. We met on the Chief? This is my sister, Carmen. Evelyn Murdoch: Carmen Stone – Mrs Ronald Stone III,' Mrs Van Clark explained, clearly proud that there should have been so many. 'Wally's fixing up their house in Palm Beach.'

Mrs Stone was examining the bullion fringing on an onion-dome lampshade.

'Ronald wanted French provincial but Wally says that's so *vieux jeux* so we're going to have something more *moderne*. And some of *those*.' She pointed at the obstacle course of small chairs dotted about the room.

Wally Grendon had pioneered the 'hostess chair', an armless, wingless, button-backed arrangement whose seat was barely a foot from the floor. It was designed for women to sink into, their skirts billowing about them, their *embonpoint* on display, their faces angled adoringly in the direction of whoever they were speaking to. He had plenty in stock and had arranged them in chatty groups like deserted deckchairs when the park was closing. Low chairs meant low tables and there were many of these, each supplied with an ashtray and a silver-mounted conch shell filled with Turkish cigarettes – cork-tipped and regular – all elaborately monogrammed.

'Cunning, aren't they?' said Mrs Van Clark's sister, lighting one. 'Wally has them made to order in London. I went there once. Crazy little arcade place. Two old dames up in a garret rolling tobacco. Ronnie and I were staying at the –'

Mrs Ronald broke off mid-swank as Otto Von Blick exploded on to the scene.

'Wally baby!' He threw his arms wide and zigzagged his way through the furniture, smile on full power. 'They showed me the work you did on that Sun King *schlock*! You're a genius! He looks a foot taller!'

Von Blick folded his host in a bear hug, peeling one arm away to gesture theatrically to the room.

'Louis the Fourteenth would have *luffed* this guy – and he could have saved him a fortune.'

Von Blick's arm snared a drink from a passing tray and he downed it in one Cossack gulp before making a rapid circuit of the room, pausing to kiss cheeks and punch biceps, his clutch of stock phrases as limited as his protégée's: *call me Monday, never seen you look better*. It was only a flying visit, he explained, as he was off to another party – 'Dietrich's cooking lunch for twenty – stuffed cabbage and Dobos Torte: how can I resist?' He spotted Evelyn on his way to the door.

'So, how did my English lady enjoy my love scene?'

'Nothing nicer, darling.'

He laughed. A magic, musical sound which brought Wally Grendon across the room to refill Evelyn's glass. Raymond Games, who had his hat on ready to leave, took it off again.

As Evelyn walked Von Blick to the terrace doors they passed the piano where Foxton Meredith was picking out 'The Wedding of the Painted Doll'. His wardrobe was as natty as ever but he was looking very much the worse for wear.

'I see Mr Meredith is on the daiquiri diet,' chuckled the director to Evelyn. 'He should have stayed home and slept it off. Beauty is a commodity; a young actor needs to keep his stock high.'

A farewell kiss on both cheeks.

As he drove away, Raymond Games took his place by her side.

'It's Evelyn Murdoch, isn't it? We met at Sedgwick's? You're looking *maaaahvellous*.' He spoke at dictation speed and his vowels were round and resonant, like the little diagrams in Rindy's elocution book come to life. 'California obviously agrees with you.'

He took her hand and kissed it. He thought that he might be falling in love with her, he said. It was one of his best and most effective lines, particularly potent when bestowed on typists and telephonists and make-up girls and on mousy Englishwomen of a certain age. *Oh Mr Games, you shouldn't say such things* said their frightened, grateful little eyes. He lunged into Evelyn's neck and inhaled noisily.

'Ravishing scent.' (She wasn't wearing any.) 'Like being back in Sussex.'

There were traces of make-up around the roots of his eyelashes and a stringy little bogey of glue at his temple where the edge of his wafer-thin bespoke hairpiece met the skin of his forehead. He gave up the flirtation and got down to business.

'Cynthia and I are having a few friends over next Sunday. I'll see that your name's put on the list – not everyone here has been asked so keep it *sous le chapeau* … Under your hat,' he translated patiently (one never knew who was and who wasn't *comme il faut* in this madhouse).

'*Naturellement*,' said Evelyn.

'I do hope you can join us. Lots of chums. Any friend of Otto's …'

He drifted off, clearly perplexed by his failure to fascinate, and Evelyn took a corner seat on the low divan under the window. The darkening day was still mild and all of the terrace doors and windows had been thrown open, the better to view the western sky where a trio of baby bluebirds were bouncing on a palm frond against the ultramarine and orange sunset like a scene from a butterfly-wing brooch.

A few of the remaining guests had taken their cocktails to the twilit tables around the swimming pool and there was an earthy whiff of pine and sagebrush wafting in through the window. And vanilla. And lavender. Joseph 'call me Joe' Weiss was at the table immediately outside. Krauts at six o'clock.

It was several minutes before Evelyn even realised that Weiss and his friend were speaking German. German-German with unmistakable traces of a lilting Bavarian accent. She could see a face and the back of a blond head reflected in the glass of the open window which meant that she too was potentially visible. She sank deeper into the cushions.

Weiss had begun telling a dirty story.

'And the gypsy scum to her brother says, "You do it better than Daddy," and he replies, "That's just what Mother says always."'

His companion laughed at the joke – a hearty, attractive laugh – then reminded him to speak English. German would attract attention and, besides, in this land of migrants and half-breeds, there was always the danger of being understood.

'About the other business: it will be better if we leave the senator to his own devices. He works for us. He just doesn't know that he does.'

'The senator is a businessman and all businessmen are isolationists,' murmured Weiss, in his accentless English. 'Look at Hollywood: run by a pack of Jews but they also are businessmen. They have their foreign markets to consider. German distribution may be lost to them but we weren't the only players: there was a movie about a Spanish whore; Spain complained; Paramount *burned the negative. Businessmen*, Klaus. We can speak their language.

Isolationism is a better friend to us than the Bund playing soldiers with their little storm troopers. That only makes trouble, creates ill-feeling. You will see that I am right.'

Night had fallen and the butler put a dance record on the gramophone and threw the switches that floodlit the garden and pool. The two murmuring men got up from their table and sauntered back inside. Joseph Weiss surveyed the room as he entered and immediately spotted Evelyn.

'Mrs Murdoch! We meet again.' He bowed and held out that soft, hot hand. 'Allow me to introduce another of my colleagues: Evelyn Murdoch; Klaus Huber. Mrs Murdoch is over here on an assignment with Miracle Studios.'

'Assignment.' An odd word to use.

It was the same man who had been lunching with Weiss in Chicago (minus the Bavarian bow tie). The older German shook hands as Evelyn rose from the divan and she saw him give a sharp look through the open window to his previous seat by the pool. How long had she been in Hollywood? Where was she staying? What movies was she working on? How long had she known Grendon? It was more like a grilling from a border guard than normal party prattle.

'Do you rumba, Mrs Murdoch?'

Well, yes, she did (after a fashion), thanks to two fractious hours with the snake-hipped Mr Morales, an effete Latin American who had amused himself by smiling abuse at her in gutter Spanish. '*Brava!*' he had smarmed after her first attempt. '*It's like trying to fuck a dead sow.*' She wondered what he would say about Klaus Huber's dancing.

'So, a place in Bel Air? Very nice too.' Like his friend, Huber prided himself on his idiomatic English although he scorned to mask his accent. 'A very decent *billet*, so important to have a *funk hole*. I heard you're very *thick* with Zandor Kiss.' Heard? Heard from whom? 'Tell me, what *ekk-saktly* is Herr Kiss's nationality these days?'

An innocent question – until a German asked it.

'I have no idea.'

'Perhaps Mr Kiss enjoys dual nationality? The German Reich is actually very keen on dual nationality ...'

Joseph Weiss made a move to cut in on their dance with a hand on his colleague's arm but the older man ignored the warning touch. After a whole day of cocktails, discretion was beyond him.

'Herr Kiss could *propaply* pick and choose, no? House in La Joya, hotel suite in New York, a flat in Eaton Square and, once upon a time anyway, a *bel étage* apartment on the Quai Voltaire ...'

'Yes, but you were talking of nationality, Herr Huber, not a property portfolio?'

'A Jew is a citizen of anywhere and nowhere. He has no nationality and therefore no loyalty.'

Evelyn could feel her party smile slipping from her grasp and he immediately spotted the loss of facial control.

'Aha.' The watchful German flared a nostril, curled a lip. Conrad Veidt could not have done it more witheringly. 'Another bleeding heart. Another liberal conscience. And yet here you are, Mrs Murdoch, safe from *blitzkrieg* in sunny California. "Land of the Free", the song says, but this is not a liberal country, Mrs Murdoch. They have a delightful country club here in Los Angeles – I have the honour to be a guest member – but half the people in this room would not be welcome there. And the only black and yellow faces in this shining city are parking cars or mowing lawns or wearing tap shoes. I say again: this is not a liberal country to throw stones from, Mrs Murdoch.

177

And England? You have a lot of *Jewish* friends in Woking, Mrs Murdoch?'

Joseph Weiss finally succeeded in pulling his colleague away. Some guys he had to meet.

It was only as the two men retreated to the bar that it occurred to Evelyn that she had not told either man where her family lived.

Chapter 11

THE MARTIANS HAD all disembarked from the *Mouzinho* at Pier 94 and were filling in their Alien Registration forms ('I came in by: *space ship*'; 'I expect to remain in the United States: *permanently*') and promptly set about getting jobs as Los Angeles gardeners, combing the gravel driveways with the legs of their diabolical machines.

Evelyn woke in a cold sweat and her brain immediately began playing back the rushes of the previous night's conversation. How did the two Germans know about her 'assignment'? And now that they had found out about it how much longer before New York pulled the plug and air-freighted her back across the Atlantic like a box of lemons to cold, grey, Jewless Woking and her rickety old desk in High Holborn? Might she have jeopardised the entire New York operation? Would everyone – Lady Genista, the whole bally lot of them – be deemed *persona non grata* and sent home to Blighty thanks to her bungling amateurism?

Three thirty. It must be nearly dawn on the East coast by now. What time would someone like Lady toffee-nosed Genista roll into work on a Monday morning? Did she even work Mondays? Probably spent her weekends at Long Island house parties playing tennis and drinking cocktails and taking Pomeranians for walks in tight sweaters.

Evelyn finally fell back to sleep and dreamed that Silas had been employed as a dental consultant on *War of the Worlds* and was given his own laboratory where he was fitting all the Martians with little pointy green dentures.

Writers' Block was deserted when she arrived except for a woman called Mercedes. Mercedes was attached to the studio's vast army of cleaners and polishers but her sole task was to water and groom the potted plants, polishing their leaves and snipping off any dead foliage with scissors worn chained to the belt of her uniform. It all seemed extraordinarily labour-intensive but the whole of America was like that: one monumental job-creation scheme. There were men to press the buttons in the automatic elevators, men to open and close doors, men to park your car. There were coin-operated cigarette machines everywhere and yet every bar or restaurant retained a young woman in a heavily-boned playsuit wielding a tray of filter-tips.

As soon as Mercedes had left, Evelyn shut herself in her office and asked the operator to please connect her to the mysterious New York number she had spotted in the XYZ section of HP's Rotadex. It was more than twenty minutes before the exchange rang back – it seemed that the whole of Los Angeles called the East Coast at that time on a Monday morning. Lady Genista was not available so she explained her difficulty as guardedly as she could (walls, ears) to a man called Gregory Fenn who sounded exactly like David Niven and was remarkably hard to rattle.

'The man's name was Klaus Huber.'

He cut her short.

'No names, no pack drill. Not on the blower.'

'Oh yes, of course, sorry.'

When he next spoke his accent had undergone a curious change, like an actor stepping into character: less public school, more public transport.

'I expect you are telephoning about your role with our West Coast branch? I realise that the, er, lady who conducted your preliminary interview may have indicated that there was a permanent position available but there has been a shake-up of personnel and I'm afraid that, in the unforeseen absence of your immediate superior, the post as such no longer exists and you are therefore surplus to requirements our end. Obviously we never like to sever all ties with any ex-employee, casual or otherwise. We'd still be happy to keep you on our books – in a purely unofficial capacity, you understand – so that if a freelance project of any significance were to come your way you could avail yourself of our expertise. You with me?'

'But –' Evelyn struggled to find the necessary job-seeking jargon '– the gentleman I mentioned seemed very much aware of my background. I was quite surprised.'

'Standard procedure on our competitors' part,' said the unflappable Gregory. 'We would expect them to keep abreast and his close interest in such matters has long been anticipated. The firm has taken considerable pains to advertise your reputation in your particular field. No one could be better qualified. We are all, naturally, disappointed that our man will not, after all, be working with you but, on a more positive note, it's very comforting to hear from our sources that you have landed on your feet over there. Your, er, prunes and prisms initiative sounds sound, as it were. We wish you every success.'

'And you're quite, *quite* sure that this won't threaten the smooth running of the business? The gentleman seemed …'

Fenn again cut her short. 'Yes, yes, yes, I dare say. They all blow hard but he's very small fry, I can assure you. Ring again if there's anything *major* to report, obviously. Nice to have had this little chat. They tell me that you are being kept pretty busy so I must let you get on.' People always said that when they were desperate to get you off the line.

Evelyn replaced the receiver. 'They tell me'? Who told him? Which of her new acquaintances and colleagues was doubling as the eyes and ears of NYHQ? Any of the professional Englishmen fitted the bill but they might just as easily be working for the other side.

Gregory Fenn put down the phone then took the day book from the shelf but decided against logging the call and put it back. Genista Broome, who had spent the last week at the British Library of Information, was decanting the remains of her desk drawers into a suitcase. She looked at her watch in surprise.

'Was that the Murdoch woman? Goodness, she's keen. It must be about seven in the morning over there. I thought she was being recalled? Can't say I'm surprised. She was always a bit of a fly in the ointment.'

'She's pretty much been cut loose now that HP's got himself installed in Bermuda but we can't exactly deport her and any change in the status quo is more likely to arouse suspicion than not. I don't think the Krauts know quite what to make of her actually, so she's proving quite a handy little red herring from our point of view. I get the impression that she isn't entirely comfortable being there under false pretences but they're hardly going to drag Saucy away from steaming open diplomatic bags in Nassau just to give her someone to translate for. Anyway it's hardly our problem. She's Kiss's pigeon really and our man says he's got her doing a bit of dialogue coaching – eminently qualified by the sound of her. You led me to expect something high-pitched and Home Counties but she has rather a pleasant voice – I've always been partial to a nice *contralto profundo*. Voice coaching should be right up her alley and she might as well stay there out of harm's way. I know I would. Have you seen this morning's paper? "London a shambles with death toll soaring". Far better to stay put.'

'Does she often telephone? She was given strict instructions not to – I didn't even give her a number.'

'Really? Well she found it somewhere: most enterprising. It appears that she's run across a couple of our old friends from the Los Angeles German legation – presumably thanks to your antics at Grand Central station – and one of them has put the wind up her by mentioning Woking. You know how excitable amateurs get. I told her to take two aspirin and ring me in the morning – or, rather, *not* ring me in the morning.'

Fenn stumped over to the tea urn while Lady Genista did up the straps on her case.

'How goes the library?'

'Absolutely frightful. And freezing. My new colleagues have dragged a desk and six chairs into the stationery cupboard which has the only functioning radiator. It's pure Marx Brothers. We take it in turns to man the information line back in the office proper, which is something of a lonely furrow, as you can imagine. I had exactly one call last week and that was from Sybil Harper wanting to know how many cigars Churchill smokes a day. Any news on your transfer to Press Liaison?'

'Gone very quiet,' admitted Fenn, 'and the extra-galling thing is that while I was soft-soaping the press-liaison people I took my eye off the ball and missed a very cushy number: Historical Adviser at Miracle Studios. Desmond Colley nabbed it, jammy little tick. Didn't even read History but he managed to dazzle them with the Great Modern Novel.'

Lady Genista looked blank.

'*Pacifist*, wouldn't you know it,' spat Gregory, 'but says he rolled bandages in Spain. He'd been lying low in Lisbon, though I think his eyesight would probably spare him the bother of a tribunal. Arrived on the clipper last week. Used to fag for my brother Miles. Miles says the novel's frightful muck: *Burnt Umber*? Name like that. I don't suppose for a moment anyone at the studio read any of it but there was a suit of armour on the dust jacket and that appears to have done the trick.'

'Wait a minute … *Colley*? Isn't he a communist?'

'Not practising.'

'Yes, but he's written tons of articles: "Crisis of Capitalism", all that. The Yanks would hate that.'

'So they would …' Gregory Fenn drained his teacup. 'Pass me that telephone.'

Evelyn replaced the receiver and walked dazedly through the main office and across to the kitchenette where she found Miss McAllister pouring a sachet of white powder into a glass. Evelyn's fingers trembled as she reached for the coffee percolator.

'I seem to be feeling a trifle off-colour this morning.'

'Wally's parties get me that way too,' said Miss McAllister, who seemed to have suspended hostilities. She held out the now foaming glass.

'Want some?'

Evelyn took a cup of black coffee back to her desk where the morning messenger boy was depositing her post. He had stopped calling her 'Toots' since the sign on the door changed to 'Special Consultant' but his salute was decidedly satirical.

There was a seven-page memorandum from PZ commending Evelyn's notes on the *War of the Worlds* dialogue. On the second sheet he said that Mrs Murdoch should work on Rindy McGee's accent as originally planned: 'this will be a skill worth having whatever transpires vis-à-vis *War of the Worlds*'. Mr Kiss was copied on the memo and Evelyn wondered how he would feel about 'whatever transpires' (hardly a vote of confidence). Pages three and four contained a detailed analysis of the costume designs that had been submitted by the art department ('The big sister teaches school. You have made her look like a Gibson girl. Lose the S-bend corset').

The only other post was a typewritten card 'from the desk of Della Cavendish', which had fallen out of the same envelope, informing her that Miss McGee would be expecting her at eleven sharp. It was already half past ten.

Rindy McGee was waiting for her on a bench by the canoe run.

Evelyn had not been looking forward to voice coaching (accents were never her forte) and she decided to follow the scheme outlined in her second-hand textbook. Rindy had heard it all before.

'*Which witch is which*? That thing where you blow the candle? I did that already.'

'It's your vowels I'm concerned about. You tend to over-egg things. Nobody really talks like Mr Frobisher, you know. Little girls especially.'

Evelyn opened the revised *War of the Worlds* script at one of the passages she had marked.

'Keep the sound short and crisp. "Dog" not "*dahg*". Keep your mouth as small as possible: "the rotten dog has got to stop".'

The child had a quick ear but she bored easily and was soon trying to change the subject.

'Von Blick is a pal of yours, isn't he? Must be if he let you on the set for those retakes. That was me in the yellow wig, by the way: Guinevere's page. I don't get a credit but PZ told me it would be good for my education to see Von Blick in action. Malo was furious when they let you in – she always insists on a closed set – and then Von Blick made that crack about you being ready for your close-up. She *hates* it when anyone else gets any attention. Especially if they're easy on the eye.'

Rindy looked Evelyn up and down. 'That grey suit made you look like something out of a social-problem picture. You look almost human today.'

Evelyn still didn't feel it. She managed to struggle through an hour of vocal exercises before driving back to the studio where she met Miss McAllister just coming out of Writers' Block. There was a cameraman on a crane by the entrance to the 'slum' side of the building.

'The second unit are filming a gunfight,' said Miss McAllister, who had a bale of scripts under one arm. 'My head won't stand it – even my apartment is quieter than this. I should get out while you can. They're on a break but you won't be allowed out once they start up again.'

Evelyn darted upstairs to retrieve the afternoon post then drove back to Bel Air where she took a lunch tray out on to the terrace. Mr Hashimoto was dead-heading the hibiscus bushes. He looked sideways at her as she bit into an apple.

'Mrs like flute?'

She said that yes she did and he offered to get her some wholesale from his brother who had a smallholding out in Gardena.

'My Jane like flute,' he confided. 'Every day make juice.'

He reached inside his overalls and produced a photograph protected by a little celluloid wallet. A large, smiling woman with tightly curled yellow hair.

'Very pretty,' he insisted – odd the way his Rs and Ls came and went.

'Very,' lied Evelyn. 'Is Mrs Hashimoto a gardener too?'

Mr Hashimoto gave a short bark of laughter and shook his head as he explained that no, Mrs Hashimoto was not a gardener and nor was she Mrs Hashimoto. They had been living together down in Gardena for eighteen years and she was the mother of his two grown-up children, but Jane remained his *con-cu-bine*. He pronounced the word very deliberately, like Rindy doing dialect. He wanted to marry her but the law didn't allow it, he said, not in California. Michigan, yes, but no Mrs Silverman to work for in Michigan.

He slid the photograph back into his wallet and pulled his secateurs from the pocket of his overalls.

'Garden he much better now, yes? Tell boss all shipshape?'

Evelyn's afternoon post contained the usual pile of scripts from Miss Cavendish, a Saturday-night dinner invitation from Mamie Silverman, a pasteboard folder full of photographs and a letter from home.

Deborah began by apologising for writing again so soon but she felt that Evelyn ought to know that mysterious pink cards had been pinned up in the window of the paper shop and on the noticeboard of the public library offering lessons in Elocution and Stage Diction by a Mrs Silas Murdoch who was apparently a fully accredited examiner for the Guildhall School of Music and Drama. None of Deborah's business, obviously, but couldn't that be classed as *fraud*?

Gregory Fenn had been quite right; the 'firm' had taken considerable pains, the masterstroke being the supply and fitting of a brass plaque by the front door of the Murdoch

187

home with Evelyn's name and bogus credentials engraved upon it. This elaborate forgery (complete with verdigris) had been installed in the teeth of vigorous and vocal protests from Evelyn's mother-in-law.

Lord knows what would have happened if I hadn't been there [wrote Deborah]. It wouldn't have been quite so bad if she could have remembered who you are – 'Evelyn? Evelyn who? Sending men to drill holes in my porch!' – all that. She got quite shirty with the man but I don't think her teeth actually broke the skin. You've got to be so careful with tradesmen. She shut the man from the gas board in the cellar on Friday. Made a pass at her, apparently (as they all do).
Fortunately the telephone number on the pink cards they've pinned up doesn't exist – you know what she's like when the phone goes. She can get quite abusive with callers even when she *does* know who it is – especially if they call on the Sabbath. I started off putting the phone out in the front passage as far as the cord will stretch because it takes her a minute to rouse herself out of her chair, but she has been known to get there in time if they let it ring so I now keep it under a cushion inside the seat of the hall stand when I go out and so far she seems to have slept through. That's if anyone ever rings up in the daytime – it wouldn't be good news if they did.
One of the church visitors left her a newspaper and all of a sudden she's riddled with remorse about Woking not being bombed yet but my suggestion that we salve her conscience by moving to Liverpool fell on deaf ears – do you think she has flaps on them like hippopotamuses? Or is that nostrils? Then we had a

prayer of thanks for being spared and God bless and keep poor dear Gilbert and not a peep from her about not getting any letters from poor dear Silas so we may be over the worst.

There was a freshening wind blowing across the canyon and Evelyn piled her post on to the tea tray and took the lot back inside. A dead robin was lying on the doorstep, flatter in death like a pressed flower. There was no sign of its killer. The Bengal was proving a very hard cat to love. The fur clung tightly to its lean, wiry body with only the skimpiest dewlap, and while it would just about tolerate stroking, its proud head and silky striped flank always pulled away from the caress. Poor Kowtow had been a very affectionate animal. Evelyn thought again of him dying alone and uncuddled on the vet's enamel table.

She changed into her flannelette nightdress and curled up in an armchair to finish her letter.

Thank you for your lovely funny card. Looks a bit like Torquay, what with all the palm trees. Is it winter there yet? It jolly well is here and she's already insisting on a fire in the parlour all day long which I bank up when I come home to give her her lunch.

The side of that concrete coal bunker fell off last week. Mrs F and I shovelled up most of it but we couldn't budge the fallen slab so every tin pail in the house is now a coal bucket. Spiders everywhere and an awful wet smell about the place. It's a lot like living in the coal hole but it may turn out to have been a blessing in a way. The WVS got wind of our spare bedrooms and came round again to evaluate us for evacuees and we haven't heard back so with any luck we've failed the inspection. I'm hoping they'll realise

189

that I've got quite enough on my plate minding the Outlaw without delousing some little Tottenham tearaway in my tea half hour. And they all wet the bed – we hear all about it in the surgery.

You'd have thought they'd send the children further afield than Surrey in any case … One of Dr Ashmole's new patients, a Mrs Dewsbury, had her three evacuated to Anglesey for the duration. She seems pleased as punch about it being so far off, partly because it's safer but chiefly because no one expects you to visit them when they're 300 miles away. Dr Ashmole always puts her down the bottom of the list ('sick headaches', oh really) so I get the full story in the waiting room. Two boys and a girl: Dennis, David and Diane (saves on name tapes I suppose). She says she's not got the nine shillings they've told her she's to pay towards their keep every week but she still manages a wash and set once a fortnight and the Plaza every Friday so a big pinch of salt on all that, don't you think?

I went up to town on my day off last week to finally try and sort out poor Silas's life insurance but I hadn't taken his birth certificate with me – you'd think the death notification would suffice – so it was a wasted journey. I had quite a time finding the office. There was more bombing all round Lombard Street the night before and the men were still clearing paths through the rubble: bricks, furniture, lampshades, biscuit tins. I saw a bedroom slipper with a foot still in it. I thought it was all offices round there.

I was just on my way back to Waterloo when the siren went so I had to run along to the public shelter. We were all squashed up on to the benches when the lights went out. A man came a bit of a cropper

down the steps and we all shoved up some more and
he sat down next to me. Very pleasant chap. Gave
me his newspaper to sit on. I thought it was all going
to be another false alarm but it wasn't. I'd always
flattered myself that I'd be all right if I was ever in a
real raid but I wasn't all right at all and I screamed
and grabbed the man's hand and he was terribly nice
about it. By this time the other people had all started
rolling out barrels – I swear I would pay money never
to hear that rotten song again – and he brings them
all up short reciting *The Charge of the Light Brigade* of all
things and so someone else piped up with 'The Lion
Ate Our Albert' and I gave them my *Lady of Shalott*
and the hour fairly flew by. Funny, because when
we got outside again I saw that he wasn't someone
I would have talked to in the ordinary way. Well-
spoken, no spring chicken, but very well turned out
and a nice smell of soap about him. He walked me
to the station after the All Clear. Different trains. He
lives over at Horsham but sometimes goes to one of
the cinemas in Woking if there's something good on
and had I seen *Major Barbara*?

Your box of fruit arrived this morning. The Outlaw
says they'll be just the thing for Harvest Festival so
I have hidden them in the mending basket with the
oloroso.

The ink was a different colour for the final page and
Deborah's handwriting less copperplate as she squeezed
in a rather alarming postscript.

I was planning to trek back up to the insurance office
some time this week but something has come up. I
won't worry you with it till I have more particulars.

191

The report we got was very vague. Will write with more gen ASAP.

Then a scribbled PPS:

I'd be grateful if you destroyed this letter when you've finished with it. If you died (not that it's likely, but you never know …) they might send it back here and if I died in the meantime – every danger after last week – then it would be there for poor Gilbert to find and he might get the wrong idea about *The Lady of Shalott* and all that nonsense. Unless he died too, of course …

Evelyn frowned as she refolded the letter. *Report?* What report?

The last bit of post contained a gilt-edged portfolio with one of Zandor Kiss's business cards clipped to it: 'They don't do you justice'. Inside were half a dozen prints of a long-necked, dark-haired woman, shoulders shrouded in a wisp of white lace, a collar of gold at her throat. Heavy black crayon gave the almond eyes a startling, Nefertiti-like outline and a thick layer of paint had rendered the skin supernaturally smooth, not like skin at all, more like royal icing or velvet painted by Ingres. An unearthly light haloed the hair and flickered mysteriously on the roll of studio paper behind the head. There were two cabinet portraits and a mixed pack of *cartes visites* for her to send to friends and admirers. She could all but hear Mrs Murdoch quoting from her library of soft-bound, hard-lined Wesleyan tracts: 'No gold, no curling of hair, nothing apt to attract the eyes of bystanders to create and inflame lust.'

She placed the photographs on the dressing table and after she had brushed her hair and dabbed vanishing cream on her face she tried to replicate the pose the photographer had coaxed from her: parted lips, surprised eyes.

The framed picture of Evelyn was one of the few things that Silas's captain had returned. The glass of the frame had broken in transit and when Evelyn removed the familiar wedding-day snapshot she found another picture behind it: a signed photograph of a smiling Nova Pilbeam. Behind that was wedged a hand-coloured French post-card. Miss Pilbeam, 'Wimbledon-born star of *Nine Days a Queen*', was fully dressed but the young French lady was sitting up in bed stark naked holding a bone-china cup and saucer. Her bosoms were the exact size and shape of iced buns. She too was smiling.

Silas always brought Evelyn a cup of Horniman's Black Label in the mornings. Was the tea-drinking mademoiselle his ideal? Had his wife's flannelette nightgown been a daily disappointment?

Chapter 12

'**Y**OU ONE OF the sweet people?'
No, Evelyn was not one of the sweet people. The uniformed woman seemed disappointed and bustled back into the house.

The driveway of Rindy McGee's mansion was swarming with lorries and motors belonging to the flower people and cake people and fairy-light people who had been busy transforming the inside of the house for the young star's (official) eighth birthday party. Chinese lanterns were strung across the front of the porch, the strawberry trees were blooming with giant tissue-paper blossoms and a gross of yellow rubber ducks were being emptied into the canoe run under the watchful eye of Clinton Parker. Rindy's press agent was having a very busy day. Ducks launched, he began marshalling a small pack of press photographers to the various points of interest, beginning with a large kennel in the shape of the Petit Trianon. It was uninhabited.

'The dog's due at two thirty when the main guests arrive. Make sure the handler takes it straight to the doghouse so the guys can get some shots. Everybody loves a dog.'

In the main hall a pair of Japanese boys in brown Holland overalls were coiling garlands through the banisters. Mrs Zaklinsky, the McGees' cook–housekeeper, had nothing to cook and no house to keep and had only to drift from room to room in a Battenburg lace apron telling the hired hands to wipe their feet.

The main living room now contained a twelve-foot banqueting table covered with pink damask and every conceivable variety of cake and sweetmeat ('a land of milk and honey'). There were cornucopias of oranges and peaches and grapes at each end of the spread but the display was dominated by two super-sized birthday cakes: an igloo made from marshmallows and a model of the Golden Gate Bridge fashioned from peanut brittle and spun sugar which had just been unboxed by Monsieur Verard, Rindy's *pâtissier*, whose violet delivery sedan was parked in the drive. A smallish, red-headed boy in velvet knickerbockers and a lace shirt front appraised both structures with a connoisseur's eye. A dimpled pink finger was picking hungrily at the candy cabling of the bridge.

'*My* last cake was shaped like the Hoover Dam. It cost *for-ty-nine million dollars* – the dam, not the cake. You seen the Hoover Dam? I made them take me when we were shooting out in Nevada. Nine-ty-six men died making it. Did you know that?'

'The cake?'

'No, dope,' said the child witheringly. 'The dam.'

'How horrid.'

Hollywood children had quick ears. English, wasn't she? Where the war was? Was her husband fighting the war? What did he die of? Did he kill a whole bunch of people? Evelyn shook her head. In his penultimate note Silas had revealed that one of his patients had contracted septicaemia following the extraction of a third molar. It happened a lot in the heat, apparently, particularly when they didn't use the special peroxide mouthwash. 'As if I supplied it for my own amusement,' he had written, tetchily.

195

More guests were starting to arrive and the photographers – dog and ducks safely in the can – were gathered in readiness by the time Bobby Canfield made his entrance. He wore grey flannels and a white silk shirt and club tie under a sleeveless cashmere sweater. His brogues twinkled like nutshells beneath the perfect break of his bespoke grey flannels. He was nine years old (said so in *Photoplay*).

Having posed for the cameras holding his chocolate meerschaum pipe, the star of *Puppy of the Baskervilles* joined Evelyn and Little Lord Fauntleroy at the buffet table. Master Canfield was not a party hound.

'This *sucks*. The picture-snatchers need to make the evening editions so my agent told Dad to drive me here early. Any sign of the birthday girl?'

He prised a cube of marshmallow from the back half of the igloo and slyly coughed it into his mouth. There was the faintest flush of razor burn on his upper lip. He turned from them and stared, unimpressed, at the full-sized portrait of his hostess which hung above the fireplace surrounded by birthday cards showing puppies in perambulators and kittens in wellington boots. Rindy had been painted holding a frilly white (rented) dog and wore ballet shoes and a very short pink lace tutu.

'They got her legs insured for *half a million dollars* – if you believe what the publicity people put out when she signed her contract,' said Master Canfield. 'They always pull that insurance stunt but nobody thinks about what it really means. There's a guy sells matches who sits on a little cart outside the train station downtown. Only half there. I guess he forgot to get insurance. I'd sooner have legs,' said the boy, who had clearly given the matter a great deal of thought, '*way* sooner.'

He looked sideways at Evelyn.

'You a nanny, or what?'

'Voice culture.'

'Figures. Too pretty for a nanny. My nanny had a moustache. You any good? They want me more la-di-dah for my next picture: *The Boy in the Iron Mask*. I'll ask Rindy.'

Guests began arriving in greater numbers and, at the stroke of three, Dorinda McGee cascaded down the main stairs in a blur of bubble-gum ruffles and an electrical storm of flashbulbs. She was accompanied by a clutch of smaller and younger eight-year-olds. Each one had its hair locked in sugar-watered ringlets and each wore a pastel-coloured frock that barely covered the pastel-coloured panties beneath. Their faces had been dusted with powder and their lips glazed with Vaseline for the waiting cameras. Rindy's mother signalled for her to sit on the bottom step and the girls collapsed around her, bridesmaids at the wedding of the painted doll.

Rindy blew out the eight pink candles that had been inserted into the igloo, leaving the guests to tear it apart while she repaired to the piano to crack a few more smiles.

'Just the keyboard, no need for the whole thing – she's the little girl next door, don't forget – but make sure you get Steinway's name in,' warned Clinton. 'We owe them.'

His work complete, the press agent strolled over to the cakes and began jabbing at the now lopsided igloo. He smiled ruefully at Evelyn.

'It's a very fine line. Every kid wants a piano and a swell birthday party but we gotta think of the hick towns, you know? Places the train don't stop.'

Evelyn thought again of the mesmerised figures lining the platform as the Super Chief passed through Colorado and New Mexico and wondered aloud how many of their children had their own *pâtissier*. Clinton was unapologetic. Nobody minded the *pâtissier* (he pronounced it *pad ECA*). All kids liked sweet stuff but grand pianos didn't play so

197

well; grand pianos looked *greedy*. And besides, the cake guy was only hired for parties. They'd even managed to work the whole sweet-tooth thing into a sponsorship deal with Smilebrite children's toothpaste (cherry, banana, aniseed and wildstrawberry flavours and more sugar per ounce than a marshmallow igloo).

The birthday girl remained at the piano, picking out the chords of 'If I Only Had a Brain' and gazing around the room at the children Mr Parker had invited. Her personality had shut down like a Klieg light the instant the photographers left but at the sight of Evelyn she ran across the room and made a deep, sarcastic curtsey.

'Why, Mrs Murdoch, *how veddy, veddy naice* to see you! Which witch is which, wondered Wilbur – see? I've been practising. I never practised with the other coach we had. I like you a whole lot better. I told PZ. The other dame was *eppsolutely ghaastly.*' She dropped the accent and began peeling herself a grape. 'I don't know any of these bozos – not *personally*. I told you I wouldn't. They're only here for the columns. Nice dress, by the way, whole lot nicer than mine. Kingfisher is a good colour for you. This dress is lousy – Clinton picked it out. I suppose it could have been worse: they were going to make me wear gingham and come as Dorothy. I auditioned for that, you know –' Rindy stared into space and clasped her hands together '– "There's no place like home!" My agent was spitting tacks.'

The child pinched disdainfully at her candyfloss frills. 'Oh well, at least I don't have to wear corduroy knickers like poor Buster over there. The dress I'm wearing to the Von Blick party next month is a whole lot better. Mother says everyone will be getting their penguin suits out of mothballs. It's going to be real *fawncy*, very East Coast. Mother's going to be having fittings with the dressmaker

198

all day Tuesday: ivory panne velvet. Mine's midnight blue. I look very *swan-yay* in midnight blue. Shame you won't get to see it.'

Rindy's trained face registered sadness as if she were mentally picturing the dead puppy or a failed audition but the welling tear dried fast when Evelyn pointed out that she too was on the Von Blick guest list.

'Since when did Voice Culture start getting invited to parties? I guess you Europeans got to stick together.'

She turned to look out of the window and her face fell.

'Oh no!' Rindy pointed out to the garden. 'There's no escape. I thought we'd done with all the press for today but here comes the Manning Menace. I swear to God she's pitched a tent behind the boathouse.'

Myra Manning, wearing a leopard-skin turban and a collar of wrestling furs, was making her way across the stumble stones through a sea of celluloid wildfowl. Rindy ducked down behind the piano.

'"Myra Manning: Pal to the Stars" – I don't think I've ever uttered a line of dialogue without her or one of the other ghouls on set. "Good publicity", Clinton says.' A world-weary sigh fluttered the ruffles on her collar. 'I guess I'd better attend to my guests. *Do* help yourself to drinks.'

After an hour, the party had reached the lemon-ade-and-marshmallow equivalent of the three-martini stage. A musical prodigy in a sailor suit was vamping through 'Whistle While You Work' while an undersized adolescent with a wide, chocolate-sundae smile was standing beside her on the stool, belting out the lyric. He was wearing a scaled-down copy of Ty Hooper's costume in *The Cowboy and the Countess*. A missing front tooth (a silver dollar from the tooth fairy) added to his air of saloon-bar menace.

The soles of Evelyn's sandals stuck to the carpet as she turned to leave. A small girl in peppermint tulle lay full-length on the white sofa and was lobbing doughnuts into one of the crystal lampshades. Mrs Zaklinsky, watching from the wings, was unperturbed. She had men arriving with ladders who could deal with that and the steam-cleaning people were booked for later that afternoon. The housekeeper made a mental note to call the piano tuner as she noticed a solitary guest diligently wedging marshmallows between the strings of the Steinway. Nothing money couldn't fix (and it wasn't her money).

'Ain't they *cute*? Not often they have any real fun. You got kids?'

Evelyn shook her head and Mrs Zaklinksy looked suitably saddened (or perhaps merely thought about dead dogs).

Cute? Really? Why were their hands always sticky? Was it something they secreted? And why did they smell so strongly of soiled nappies and talcum powder or the sickly sweets they had eaten or the syrupy medicines they had just been dosed with or the paraffin stuff rubbed into their hair to keep the insects off? And that was just the reasonably well-behaved ones, never mind the kind that ran amok in railway carriages or shattered the silence in libraries or charged up and down the decks of the *Mouzinho* while their mothers smiled indulgently.

Like dogs – and very much *unlike* cats – they always assumed that one was thrilled to have them clambering on to one's lap and pulling at one's hair or scarf or buttons and launching into recitations of boys on burning decks or travellers knocking on moonlit doors. Worse still, once out of range of their various minders, they reverted to almost simian behaviour: biting their fingernails or scratching their private parts or picking their freckled noses and eating what they found there. Old Mrs Murdoch would have called Rindy 'precocious' but at least the child could hold a normal conversation.

Mrs Zaklinsky was retrieving the wreckage of the Golden Gate Bridge from the upholstery as Evelyn made her way to the door. Could she be kind enough to let Miss McGee know that Mrs Murdoch would return next Wednesday afternoon?

Evelyn had eaten her Saturday breakfast in her pyjamas then dozed off in a sunlit easy chair in front of the French windows.

The Martians' birthday cake was a scale model of Anne Hathaway's cottage sliced in two by a spun-sugar death ray. They were holding the party at Rindy's house and the spacemen were taking it in turns to fire their disintegrator pistols at the chandeliers, each discharge producing a loud, rapping sound.

'Room service!'

Ted Monroe was standing on the terrace behind the glass doors. He was dressed for a morning's golf and carrying a large wicker picnic hamper.

'Sorry to disturb your beauty sleep but I got you something. Close the door behind me.'

He set the squeaking basket on the Persian rug and loosened the loop holding the twin lids together. Half a dozen kittens jumbled out.

'I told the pet store they were for Betty Grable – the guy was a big fan – now all you have to do is pick the one you want. I said I'd get the rest back to him by noon.'

One by one he pinched the tiny animals up from the carpet until Evelyn had the entire litter in her lap: one black; two tabbies; one ginger; one black and white; and one jumbled mixture of the other colourways: a shade card for the breed.

'And the ones I don't want go back to the shop?'

'Sure. And then some nice old lady buys them. Or they get an agent. Or the guy gets hold of Betty Grable's address. *Relax.*'

The warm kittens slithered about on the satin of her kimono, mashing each other's backs and faces with miniature velvet paws as they struggled to the top of the heap, each one strenuously auditioning for a birthday card. Ted Monroe was taking furtive peeks at his watch but she found it almost impossible to choose, to offer a home to one and not the rest. And yet people chose orphans ... and evacuees ... As soon as the thought occurred she began to feel that she really ought to pick the ugly calico runt with the big black smudge above its nose. The kitten with cold sores and impetigo and rats' tails and broken glasses mended with sticking plaster, a permanent scab on its knocked knee. The kitten wetting the bed or picking its nose. The Tottenham tearaway.

'How can I possibly decide?'

'How did you choose your old cat?'

She smiled sadly at the memory of the Pets' Parlour man opening the cage behind the shop window and inviting her to take her pick. 'Let the kitten choose you,' the man had said – the voice of long experience – then smiled as the smallest of the litter climbed into the wide cuff of her winter coat and began sleeping there like a mandarin's secret Pekingese. She'd named him Kowtow, not because he was remotely exotic or oriental but because he had once gone to sleep in a sleeve. She had taken him with her in her trousseau to the house on Hook Heath. Old Mrs Murdoch had a horror of mice but it was not equal to her horror of pet animals. Kowtow, a natural evangelist, had tried to win her over – without success: 'Silas says they're unhygienic, and he ought to know.'

Evelyn slid down on to the floor and plunged a hand into the wrestling kittens. The stripier of the two tabbies dug its tiny crampon claws into the silk of her dressing gown and began the wobbly climb to her shoulder and pushed its face against hers. She nudged back with the end of her nose and the little furry body slid back down to the warm pool of fur in her lap.

'That one?'

Ted Monroe got up from his chair and reached for the chosen kitten. She could feel his fingers through the fabric of her kimono as he gently separated the tiger tabby from its brothers and let it stand on his outstretched hand for a moment before it began climbing his jacket.

'Definitely this guy. Knows what he wants. I told the pet-store man I'd give them some milk – I wouldn't mind a saucer of something myself.'

'Oh, how rude of me. May I get you some coffee?'

'You stay right there. I'll get it.'

He returned with a tray bearing a large soup plate of milk, the bottle of vodka, a carton of orange juice and the remains of a box of crackers.

'Breakfast of champions,' he insisted.

He fed the kittens their milk before bundling the rejects back into their basket and closing the lid. He scrunched a scrap of paper from his pocket and lobbed it at Evelyn's new friend.

'You like animals, don't you?' she said. 'Rindy McGee showed me the book you wrote for her – the one about the mink coat. Wouldn't you rather be writing books?'

'Everyone in that office would rather be writing books. Kay wrote a book, McAllister wrote a play, I've written a novel or two myself. Trouble is, we all quite like eating.'

The chosen kitten had tired of its paper ball and was heading for the wide-open spaces of the kitchen. Monroe scooped him up and set him back on the shoulder of his sports coat. The kitten peered down at Evelyn, inviting another furry nudge.

'You got any mink, Mrs Murdoch?'

There was no escaping the kiss – the movies had taught her that much: 'He takes her in his arms, bends her head back and kisses her hard on the mouth again and again, till she struggles for breath.' But Evelyn was unprepared for her own response. Whenever she had watched screen kisses back in Woking she would feel her sister-in-law start to squirm in sympathy as the camera zoomed in on the stars' parting lips, but Evelyn had never gained any vicarious pleasure from the clinches, never lost sight of the actress doing the kissing: her lovely Beverly Hills home; her pedigree Pomeranians; the director just out of shot calling for another take as he fed his leading lady the lover's line while she looked adoringly into the mirror taped just to the right of the lens.

During their rapid courtship, Silas's kisses had been rare – a peck on the cheek on meeting, a brisk hug and lip-kiss of farewell once they were engaged – but Evelyn had been more relieved than disappointed. Very occasionally a film (or the sight of another couple stealing an embrace in the darkness) would trigger a longer, bolder display of affection but never anything to trouble the censor.

He had taken her to see *Wuthering Heights* as soon as it came to Woking.

'I hope he was a perfect gentleman, up there in the dress circle?' Deborah had said (Deborah could be a little coarse at times). 'His brother can get quite carried away ...'

Evelyn had protested, as primly as she could, that Silas wasn't the type to make a pest of himself but Deborah had only laughed. *Still waters*, said Deborah, those Murdoch boys. But even this sisterly hint hadn't prepared her. Evelyn had told herself that that sort of thing didn't interest him but of course it interested him, of course it did – as she realised when Silas turned the key in the lock of their honeymoon hotel room and, one by one, switched off the lights. Those new, married kisses had had the antiseptic tang of hydrogen peroxide and a faint smell of pink disinfectant that made her think of drilling and rinsing and tied her stomach in a stubborn knot. Ted Monroe smelled very faintly of cologne and his kiss tasted of vodka and oranges.

His face swam back into focus. She could feel him raising his wristwatch to eye level as he pulled out of the kiss. Was she free that evening?

'I can't. Mamie Silverman invited me to dinner.'

'Too bad.'

But he didn't suggest another date and with a parting chuck under the chin (for the kitten) he was back off down the hill to his golf game. Evelyn watched him drive away then made herself some fresh tea and sat on the front porch where the urns now overflowed with flowers. Mr Hashimoto was putting a second coat of white paint on the fence beside the empty swimming pool. The warm autumn air was so still that she could hear the crackling lick of the brush against the wood. She closed her eyes but her reverie was interrupted by the kitten pouncing on to her lap.

Mr Hashimoto had taken an immediate shine to the animal and knelt down to pet it with a gentle, paint-spattered hand.

'He got a name?'

As she leaned in to kiss the kitten's head the sweet scent of the newly potted tobacco plants rose up like a gas and transported her back to her mother's handkerchiefs.

'Happy. His name is Happy.'

The door was opened by a young blonde woman in her mid-twenties wearing riding clothes who introduced herself as Paula Silverman. The mystery clock on the hall table behind her was just striking seven.

'I won't tell my stepmother you're here. She *hates* it when guests arrive early.'

The chilly manner was enough to make an Englishwoman homesick. Evelyn followed the trim tweed back across the chessboard floor of the hall and down a couple of steps into a large, glass-sided sitting room.

'So, you're the one Zandor feels so guilty about. Cocktail?' Paula Silverman pressed an electric bell then collapsed into the corner of a sofa, arms folded, finger tickling absently at a patch of suede on the elbow of her hacking jacket which hugged her skinny curves like the rind on a fruit – if only fruit had come in pepper-and-salt tweed …

One couldn't beat English tailoring, could one? said Paula. Did Evelyn know that the exact same firm who made her jacket had made the suit Mata Hari wore for the firing squad? Said so in the brochure anyhow. Her stepmother always said it was crazy to spend that kind of money on something and then wear it when you were sitting on some sweaty old horse but that was a tad rich coming from Mamie who had all her underwear hand-made by a bunch of nuns in Pennsylvania.

Mamie wasn't getting ready *per se*, the girl explained, stirring her cocktail, Mamie was trying on the dress she'd ordered for the Von Blick party. It was going to be *white tie*. Evelyn smothered a smile at the candle-snuffing emphasis of her diction.

'*Black* tie used to be good enough until the big Selznick wedding about ten years ago. All the men had tails made and now it's day rig-*err*.' Evelyn sensed that the hick pronunciation was deliberate ('finished in France').

The girl looked at the diminutive gold dial on her right wrist, drained her glass and rose to her feet.

'Want to see the house?'

Evelyn followed her through sliding doors that led down to the dining room.

'Dad's been here a whole three years which is some kind of record. Most of the furniture is from the old Griffith Park place we lived in when we were little. Mother picked it out.'

Paula Silverman sighed sadly as she said this and if Evelyn hadn't known better she'd have assumed her mother was dead (rather than living on Park Avenue).

The tulipwood dining table was ten feet long.

'This is as small as it gets. Mother and Dad used to love giving dinner parties but Mamie hates entertaining at home so we hardly ever use it now.'

There was a butler's pantry between dining room and kitchen where a cupboard had been built to house the eight extra leaves of the dining table and where long rollers stored yard upon yard of heavy Irish linen table-cloths and napkins, all ready-ironed and starched for the Silvermans' non-existent *soirées*.

A Renoir – small girl with small dog – filled the wall behind the host's chair and gave the hostess something pretty to look at while behind her hung an immense canvas depicting a bare-knuckle boxing match.

Mamie Silverman apologised her way into the room, bracelets rattling. She was wearing an embroidered-silk Chinese coat with matching pyjama trousers and a ten-dollar corsage. She pecked the air next to Evelyn's ear, holding her hand up to shut off her view of the boxing picture.

'How's a person supposed to eat with that staring back at them? They look like raw meat. I don't know how

Manny could stand it. No wonder he likes his food on a tray.'

Tour suspended, the three women returned to the sitting room where Paula mixed a fresh batch of high-balls and handed a glass to her stepmother who sat down on one of the couches with her back to the setting sun and stabbed at her drink with a swizzle stick. Thick make-up honeyed over the pale cheeks and the lips had been redrawn on more generous lines in a lipstick the colour of Rindy McGee's party dress. Her face was strangely unwrinkled but the effect was not youthful, more as if the skin had been steam-ironed and stored on a special roller. Her neck knife-pleated as she turned to her stepdaughter.

'You joining us for dinner, Paula?'

'I have a date.'

'But we're going to Nito's … You know you always love dancing there and your father would be so pleased …'

'I have a date.'

Defeated, she turned to Evelyn. Had Paula been looking after her? And how was the cottage? Evelyn's diplomatic murmurs were too soft for her to hear. The room was too big to have a tête-à-tête, complained Mamie, moving to the seat beside her, way too big. A person couldn't get cosy in a room this big.

'So *move*,' snapped her stepdaughter. 'The city's full of houses. Find one you like and move. Or build some-thing.' Paula turned exasperatedly to Evelyn. 'We have this routine every time we have a guest.'

'Manny still hasn't found an architect he can get along with,' explained Mamie. 'We bought a couple of acres up beyond Topanga beach and we were going to get Günther Fink – the guy who designs all the glass houses? – to make us somewhere nice to hang all the pictures and then oh-my-God we finally meet the guy and he wants us to take an *exam*.'

Mamie struggled free of the sofa cushions and retrieved a large folder from a sideboard drawer.

'Do we sleep together? Do we like windows open or closed? How many people for dinner? – can you believe this? – then he wants to know how many paintings we got and then says that's too darn many and they're going to wreck the clean lines of the walls and why don't we sell some? I thought Manny was going to wreck the clean lines of his face when he heard that. There are a lot of bad words in Yiddish you should excuse me and Manny knows every goddamned one of them and now Mr Fink knows them too.

'So anyway, he gives us all these questions and he says, "No consultation please." We're not supposed to tell each other what we like – as if I didn't know already after eight years. I filled in Manny's for him.' She squinted down at the typescript. '"When you have a dinner party do you wash the dishes right away?" Imagine. I haven't washed a dish since I was seventeen years old. One time we hired a new maid and she couldn't start right away so for three days we lived on scrambled eggs and Manny made me trash every plate. Bad enough his wife should have to cook, he said –' Her eyes grew teary and bright as she remembered. 'Then the guy asks how many shoes I got, how many hats, how many sweaters. What is he, some kind of communist? How the hell do I know how many sweaters? Finally he comes up with a plan.'

Mamie was unfolding a large piece of flimsy paper, like a dress pattern with staircases, as Manny Silverman, faultlessly dressed in a dark-blue dinner jacket, ambled over to the sideboard and kissed his wife's cheek.

'I told him if I wanted a submarine, I'd buy a goddamned submarine. Then he asks why I need a porcelain collection: "Nothing impractical can be beautiful," he says. I guess he never met my first wife.'

His daughter winced with annoyance and flounced across to the drinks table.

'So, Paula, you honouring us with your presence this evening?'

'I have a date,' repeated Paula who had her back to the room and so didn't see her father mouthing the four words as she spoke them.

Mamie patted her husband's sleeve. The gesture was presumably intended to be calming but after nearly ten years of marriage she should perhaps have known that it would have the opposite effect.

'Talking of the first Mrs Silverman,' barked her husband, 'she rang the office today saying she's getting married again – nice of you and your sister to tell me, Paula. Crazy bitch. I've been paying her a grand a week plus rent and now the *meshugenah* broad says she's getting married, some *shvontz* in real estate by the name of Stadtler, and the poor *schmuck* – only he's a rich *schmuck* – now writes to me about taking over the lease on the apartment and the wedding's Thursday.'

Despite being nearly $100,000 dollars a year better off, Mr Silverman was oddly depressed by his ex-wife's change of status. While he had her on the payroll she was still notionally under his control. Letting off a blast of steam seemed to calm him but Mamie immediately rekindled his irritation by asking if he had remembered to make their dinner reservation, causing him to bark that the day he needed to book a table in this town he'd shoot himself.

'Right after I shoot you, sweetheart.'

Sometimes not even a table reservation was enough to guarantee dinner at Nito's. The cocktail counter was buzzing with fretful men in black tie demanding that their bookings be honoured but Manny Silverman's ability to march in and pull rank did not seem to provoke them and they watched him jump the queue with an endearing mix of envy and determination: *one day ...*

Blue leather booths ringed the room beyond the tiny dance floor, and the other diners – bald men and beautiful girls – turned to greet the great man and shake his hand as he set a course for his usual corner table. The napkins were crimped into water lilies and there was a centrepiece of fat yellow chrysanthemums alongside a massive black china ashtray that screamed 'Nito's' in bold white capitals (no sense employing a house photographer if the restaurant couldn't be identified). The picture-snatcher was lurking nearby but melted into the background after Mr Silverman beckoned him over and tucked a treasury note behind his display handkerchief.

Manny Silverman held his menu at arm's length. An English actor a few tables away was studying the bill of fare through a monocle and he watched him almost enviously. You looked like a *nebbish* (Mrs Murdoch should excuse him) but it wasn't as dumb as it looked. At least you'd see what you were getting. Maybe he should get eyeglasses?

Mamie shook her head. He mustn't get glasses. Glasses were for old men. In any case what did he want with a menu? He always had the steak. Every time the same steak.

Manny Silverman spat back that he always had a goddamned steak because there would always be a goddamned steak on the menu. Didn't mean that was what he *wanted*. If he had *glasses* he could have something else. He glared at the list of entrées. Tournedos? He could have tournedos, maybe? His wife gave a spiteful shriek of laughter. He was an ignorant know-nothing. Tournedos was steak. He had it all the time. The maître d's always brought him tournedos because it was probably four times the price of the regular sirloin. *Probably?* He liked the *probably*. He gestured towards his wife with his thumb: Never cooked a meal in her life. Never even seen a menu with a price on it. *Probably*, she says.

'You mustn't mind Manny,' murmured Mamie indulgently. 'He bores easy.'

'What's the matter, Mamie? You starving to death?'

Their shouty squabble inevitably drew attention but the other diners were more gratified than irritated: this was why everyone came to Nito's – you got a better class of fight. Evelyn would infinitely rather have been back in Bel Air with a Swiss cheese sandwich. The argument might not even have started if she hadn't been there. They probably dined in peace at home, like trees falling silently in forests.

'So, Mrs Murdoch, how you finding it, living rent-free in Bel Air?'

His wife exclaimed at his rudeness and assured Evelyn that she was very, very welcome but Mr Silverman was spoiling for a fight (maybe the boxing match in his dining room was simply a reminder to calm down?).

'We never had anyone stay in the pool house before but I owe Kiss a couple of favours.'

He looked Evelyn up and down and appeared mildly mollified by the diamond brooch and by Miss Cavendish's choice of gown but was obviously wondering why this no-account broad should be sharing his table and began firing off a string of questions. Was there a Mr Murdoch? What kind of dentist? How did he die? Did he have life insurance? – Evelyn thought with a sudden pang of panic of Deborah's abortive journey to Lombard Street and her mysterious postscript. Mr Silverman's questioning grew more aggressive. What was she doing stateside anyhow? Shouldn't she be rolling bandages or stiffening upper lips back home somewhere? Was she anything to do with the English guy Kiss was showing around? Patton? Peyton, that was it.

Great guy (in Mr Silverman's opinion). Had some stuck-up English dame who used to latch on to him at weekends but a real party hound just the same. Still owed him two hundred bucks but he told some very funny stories. Did Mrs Murdoch know any funny stories? And how come she was such a big pal of Zandor's? It wasn't a question that Evelyn could answer truthfully but she was spared by the arrival of a smiling man with a diamond tie-pin.

'I don't want to break up the party, Mr Silverman, but I've got Helga Hart at my table.'

Otto Von Blick's little protégée, last seen making sheep's eyes at the grand piano at the Kramer party, was sitting with Ted Monroe. Monroe was zooming in close and talking to her very earnestly and the silent girl was moving her head in a slow, graceful roll, as if rehearsing a screen test. She was very young and every inch of skin – face, neck, arms – had the milky lustre of a studio portrait. Monroe took hold of her slim white hand and his cufflinks, nubbly knots of yellow gold, flamed in the light as he raised it to his lips.

Evelyn sat up straighter and put her smile muscles into gear and stole a glance at herself in one of the mirrors lining the room. She looked quite presentable, she thought, the dress suited her: all ready to be looked at (but no one was looking). She had been almost sorry that Manny Silverman had sent the photographer away. It could have

213

been one for the album: 'Self and the Silvermans, Nito's, Los Angeles, October 1940'. Another souvenir.

The tie-pin man leaned in confidentially.

'Monroe says he's going to get PZ to feature her. You ought to meet her. She's very fresh.'

Helga Hart smiled as she rose to leave the table. Her dress was not particularly *décolleté* – Evelyn's was cut lower – but as she walked to the powder room every necktie in the restaurant was suddenly crooked. She had a row of tiny satin buttons down her spine. If there was a zipper Evelyn couldn't see it.

'Very pretty,' agreed Mamie. 'I read about her in one of the columns. It said she only ever has wild flowers in her bungalow at the Marmont.' Mamie plucked uneasily at the orchid pinned to her collar. 'I thought that was kind of nice. We should maybe do that.'

This was more than enough to tip her husband over the brink.

'*Wild flowers*, she wants? Are you crazy? How are the florists in this town supposed to make a living?'

Chapter 13

'SHE'S FILLED THE BLASTED swimming pool with gardenias again.'

An English actor (butlers a speciality) was stumbling through the glass doors to Cynthia Games's drawing room, trumpeting his nose on his silk handkerchief. Behind him was Baines Frobisher.

'She had snow shipped in from Lake Arrowhead to cover the croquet lawn last Christmas. I shan't be staying long,' said Binky, absent-mindedly filling his case from one of the bowls of cigarettes. 'I don't mind hanging on for a few stiffeners but I'm going to buzz off to Sedgwick's fairly soonish and I shall need to time my afternoon extremely carefully. Sedgwick is expecting Dietrich at three and she will almost certainly *sing*. Furthermore, my spies tell me Sybil "Fascination" Harper is planning to put in an appearance here armed with the proofs of her latest column: "Whither Democracy?" perhaps or "Should Roosevelt serve a third term?" Talk about Scylla and Charybdis ...'

Binky caught Evelyn's eye and smiled almost apologetically at this flash of schoolboy erudition.

'The shrivelled fruit of an expensive classical education. There was talk of the diplomatic corps but this pays better, sadly.'

He flicked a speck of ash from his cricket whites. Practically all of the guests were wearing white, their

Sunday-morning uniform of golfing sweaters or tennis clothes. In England white was aprons, collars, gloves, handkerchiefs or a child's socks. Not even brides wore much white any more. But here jackets, suits, coats, even cars were white.

The Games house was white inside and out. Its icing-sugar facade was a meticulous scale model of a French chateau but its interior was a mad mix of ancient and modern with Knole sofas upholstered in futurist prints and gas logs blazing in Adam chimney pieces. The inevitable set of silver picture frames showed Mrs Games shaking hands with Eleanor Roosevelt, Amelia Earhart and Helen Keller. The ceiling of the room nearest the (normally) turquoise swimming pool had been painted the same shade of blue and was lent a watery twinkle by a pair of crystal chandeliers plus two Von Blick-style spotlights: one just above the fireplace, the other above Mrs Games's favourite chair.

Her staff were arranging platters of roast beef and cheesecake around the centrepiece: a giant snow sculpture filled to the brim with caviar. Evelyn stared at the carved ice in disbelief.

'Good heavens ... Is that what I think it is?'

'Yup.' Felix Kay had drifted in from the garden. 'The Brandenburg Gate. Some crazy mix-up with the ice people. They had to take off all the little flags. Cynthia's mad as hell but I kinda like it, particularly as this must mean that the German legation's Sunday lunch guests will be eating their caviar from a pint-sized model of Windsor Castle.'

What Felix didn't know about Cynthia Games wasn't worth knowing. Cynthia Sloan (as was) had met her husband in repertory back in England where she played Gertrude to his Claudius but (as she often complained) experience counted for nothing over here and, rather than submit to character casting, she had settled for the role of helpmeet, spending her time (and Raymond's money) on a series of lavish entertainments – 'My cosy corner of a foreign field' (or so she told the gossip columns) – where writers, artists and visiting dignitaries could hold court while her husband beat them at croquet (snow permitting).

Their hostess cruised past as Felix went to find Foxton Meredith. Mrs Games, like a chatelaine at the village garden party, usually made a point of exchanging words with even the humblest guest at her husband's Sunday free-for-alls (one simply never knew) and one always needed a few *civilians* to dress the set but there were limits. She gave Evelyn a quick once-over, like PZ gauging a costume design, and immediately homed in on her.

'And you are?'

'Evelyn Murdoch? I work with Zandor Kiss. Such a lovely party. Your husband was kind enough to invite me …'

'Was he? I wonder why?'

Cynthia strode away without ceremony, finally tracking down her husband who was selecting a gardenia button-hole from the swimming pool.

'Raymond!' The same low, urgent and ultra-audible stage whisper that had characterised her Lady Macbeth ('A role she was born to play' – *Birmingham Evening Post*). 'Raymond, where is everybody? There's nobody but nobodies, darling. Nobodies and queers.'

Raymond Games looked in through the window and shrugged.

'Kippers with Cedric? But he's got Dietrich coming, don't forget. Hold your nerve, old girl. They'll all make their excuses once she gets out her gramophone records. And Ted Monroe just arrived; he's not nobody. You should humour him. I saw him beat PZ at golf yesterday. Only a brave man ever does that. *Very* sure of himself.'

Mrs Games didn't need telling twice and gave the new arrival the smile she had been saving.

'*darling*! Let me get you a drink. I'm sure you know everybody.'

'I know Mrs Murdoch here.' He kissed Evelyn's cheek. 'How's kitty?'

'The gardener said he'd mind him.' *How's Miss Hart?* she wanted to say but they were joined by Miss McAllister, fresh from a breakfast party which left her several drinks ahead of the game, and Monroe escaped to the bar.

'So how do you know the lovely Cynthia?'

'I don't,' said Evelyn. 'Ghastly woman.'

'Ain't that the truth. You aren't the fool you look.'

Chummy all of a sudden, Miss McAllister helped herself to a highball and linked her arm through Evelyn's with a tinkling laugh. Like an unsuccessful audition for a girl having a good time.

'I see young Meredith over there is going through his repertoire.'

Sir Galahad was standing behind the piano, half-draped in Cynthia Games's green velvet curtains, giving Magda Malo's 'Lancylot' speech in a breathy falsetto, while Felix picked out 'Hearts and Flowers'. Ted Monroe looked across at them both from the bar for a moment then downed his whiskey and announced that he needed to bathe. He strode out on to the terrace, stripping off jacket, shirt and flannels as he went, revealing a cartoon-ishly athletic torso.

'Mr Monroe will be wanting a bathrobe, Griffiths,' murmured Mrs Games as her guest dived into the gardenias. She seemed almost pleased at this test of her nerve, of her hospitality (she had read somewhere that

218

the perfect hostess remains unflappable in the face of all provocations).

'I sometimes wonder why Ted bothers coming to these snorefests,' Miss McAllister was saying. 'But it's all *material*, I suppose. Not that this is his kind of *milieu*. Have you tried either of his novels? *Daisy Don't Dance? Tell the Dog?* The *American Mercury* called him "the recording angel of Nowheresville"' (funny the way they memorised one another's press cuttings) 'and the *Christian Science Monitor* said, "T.V. Monroe's depiction of this urban cesspit left the reviewer needing a hot bath and clean linen." Felix agrees with the Christian Scientists, naturally. Felix says Ted's stories are *ersatz* –' an anxious squint at Evelyn '– that's German for lousy,' she said, helpfully, 'but then he should hear what Ted says about *The 29th Bather* …'

Felix Kay's so far unoptioned novel had been published under the name of Webster Tembo, said Miss McAllister. The bathers of the title were a Walt Whitman allusion. This fact was lost on the wider reading public but hadn't escaped the reviewers who had shown no mercy.

'"As padded as a débutante's brassiere with literary language and soul-searching dialogues,"' recited Connie, not without glee. 'Lucky thing he had an alias. PZ hates a loser. Smart guy just the same. Real smart. I saw Felix knock out a sonnet in three and a half minutes once. Kiss gave him the subject: "A memo from PZ in the style of Hiawatha" – not even Ted could match that. I guess Ted's more a rewrite man. You know he was married, don't you?'

'Felix?'

Smoke shot from Miss McAllister's nose in a short snort of laughter.

'Hell, no: Ted. You wouldn't think it, would you? Only lasted a year. Bet she's sorry now. *And* she got married

219

again first chance she got so no alimony and he got himself a big blue coupé and a cute little gingerbread house in West Hollywood. I only know about the wife because he got tight one night and cried on my shoulder. He does that. All part of the technique. He ever ask you to dance?' Miss McAllister put a hand to her chest and swayed on her heels a little drunkenly. 'He's a wonderful dancer but that's part of the technique too. I kind of prefer dancing with Felix,' she laughed. 'Close, but no cigar.'

'And Mr Kay hasn't been married?'

Miss McAllister gave Evelyn what Deborah would have called an old-fashioned look.

'No chance. But he ought to. And he's a terrific little cook, did you know that?'

Felix Kay and Galahad were now side by side on the piano stool singing 'Over the Rainbow', batting the lyric back and forth between them, taking a syllable each, scarcely missing a beat: 'if hap-py litt-le blue-birds fly be-yond the rain-bow' and instinctively joining each other for the last line. *Why, oh why, can't I?*

Mrs Games's guest of honour, Sybil Harper, had arrived. She immediately set up shop in the den and began chain-smoking Camel cigarettes with a sort of time-and-motion urgency.

'You simply must hear my latest column. I've headlined it "Splendid Isolation". It's tremendous – the best I've ever done. I shall declaim it to you all in a moment but first I need a steak sandwich! It has to be broiled over charcoal and the mustard *must* be French. And you must-must-must *butter* the bread and then and only then cut the slice from the loaf.'

'Makes a change from how to mix cocktails, I suppose,' muttered Binky Frobisher, beating a hasty retreat. 'Do you know she gets $2,500 a speech? Money for old rope.'

'Sybil's remarkable,' murmured Cynthia Games, apologetically, as she moved safely out of earshot and backed into a very damp Ted Monroe.

'Teddy darling!'

She squeezed his biceps and he said something that made her look across to where Evelyn was sitting and Evelyn caught the words 'Very cosy with Kiss and Von Blick'. Monroe went upstairs to dry off and Mrs Games wasted no time, speaking as if their previous conversation had not taken place.

'Ted tells me you're a great friend of Zandor's? It's Evelyn, isn't it? From London?'

Mrs Games pulled a special gosh-it-must-have-been-ghastly face and reverse-curtsied on to the couch beside her. Evelyn must be relieved to be missing the *blitzkrieg* although poor dear Zandor did tend to bore on about it every five minutes. Mrs Games did so worry about Zandor. She and Raymond did their bit for Bundles for Britain and many of their best friends were … *continental* but she did so wish they could let go of the Old Country and stop all that armchair sniping and warmongering. Mrs Games had been rather alarmed by the national draft the previous week but had implicit faith in the President's assurances that 'mobilisation is an act of peace' and didn't doubt him for a moment when he promised that their boys wouldn't be sent into any more 'foreign entanglements'. America was in no mood for it, said Mrs Games.

'And one can quite see why, especially after last time – all that Belgian-babies-on-bayonets nonsense. To hear the other Brits talk you would think that the United States was still one of the colonies, a big pool of eager reservists to be called upon as and when required. As if everyone here came over on the *Mayflower*. Never mind all the Germans and Italians and all the other little hyphenated people. And who cares about a bunch of *Jews* anyway?' Did she even notice herself lowering her voice? Evelyn wondered.

'But I suppose he has next month's election to think of. Raymond and I go to Hyde Park fairly *orphan*' (there was a signed photograph on the piano to prove it – did Roosevelt do nothing but fish?) 'and when we were last there I met the most *fascinating* naval man who insisted that Germany was no threat to *Ameddica* and that we should be looking *East* – the Yellow Peril and so forth. God knows they've sent the advance guard … Los Angeles is swarming with them. They're all very well in the garden but I won't have one in the house. Worse than the Irish.'

Her face froze. Oh Lord, Evelyn wasn't Irish, was she? Or Jewish? Catholic? Ah yes. She gave an approving smile. Methodists had the right idea, them and the Peace Pledge people. She handled the words with care, like Rindy McGee reciting a tongue-twister.

Mrs Games, bored suddenly by the sound of her own RADA-rounded vowels, collared Felix Kay as he passed.

'I mustn't monopolise you, Evelyn dear. Have you met this marvellous man?'

She had obviously forgotten his name. Evelyn smiled at Felix, winking the other eye as he made his bow.

'Why, how do you do? Aren't you the famous Mrs Murdoch everyone's so scared of?'

Evelyn solemnly shook hands.

'And you're Felix Kay, aren't you? *The* Felix Kay? The man who rescued *Gone With the Wind*?'

Cynthia Games's getaway stalled for a microsecond and she gave a slight frown at the possibility that this scruffy young Jew might be more important than she had realised. The sports coat had seen better days but that meant nothing to a writer – *au contraire*. They probably bought them that way, or sat at home on quiet evenings picking at threads with a buttonhook … But, then again, her glass was empty … She made a beeline for a tray of fresh drinks, pink floral tea gown trailing in her wake.

'You got more than the stock two minutes with the lovely Cynthia,' said Felix once she was safely back in the den. 'How was it?'

'*Ameddica First* seemed the general thrust.'

'*Cynthia* first, I suspect, if it came to the crunch. But you're right: she and Raymond are very pro the *status quo*, as you might say.' He cocked an ear to the invisible wife. 'You mustn't say that, Bernice. Cynthia's a very generous woman: give you anything: smallpox; syphilis …'

Foxton Meredith had the sustain pedal down on the baby grand and was singing the refrain of 'After the Ball' to Myra Manning who was now sitting beside him on the stool.

'Oh dear. The fifth martini. Excuse me, won't you? I don't think Myra's going to like Fox's version of this song.'

The Martians wanted a double room with bath with a view of the Surrey Downs. A green, claw-like hand was banging at the bell at the hotel reception then began tapping impatiently on the mahogany veneer of the desk with its talons.

'Mrs Murdoch! Evelyn!'

The kitten was nestling against the nape of her neck and she had a job to switch the light on without disturbing it. The pale face of Felix Kay was pressed against her bedroom window. A taxi had left him by the main gate and his jacket was dark with rain.

Evelyn showed him into the kitchen and automatically lit the gas for tea but he was already at the breakfast bar uncorking the vodka bottle. He took a swig from his glass then placed an elbow on the counter and gave her a rumpled smile.

'Fine time to come calling. I'm really sorry to wake you but I'm in a bit of a jam …'

Or rather Foxton Meredith was. The young actor had done the round of Sunday parties before heading off with Wally Grendon and a few other like-minded souls to a club that Grendon knew down on Sunset.

'The dumb klutz went and got himself arrested. The studio's head of publicity is out of town but his second-in-command is supposed to be arranging something. They were sending Magda Malo on a mercy dash to the bedside of some kid with leukaemia which ought to keep the tabloids out of our hair for a few hours, and the police say they won't press charges, but we still need to cover all the bases just in case they've got a photographer hanging around the station.' Felix lit a cigarette. 'I was wondering if you could drive me over there and fish him out? It would look better if you did it.'

'I suppose so …'

She was about to wriggle out of her nightgown and into some slacks and a pullover when she realised that Felix had followed her into the bedroom and begun rifling through the hangers in the walk-in closet, before settling on one of Miss Cavendish's smarter cocktail frocks.

'We need to play it like you were at the club with him. You're going to be the girlfriend – or maybe the long-suffering sister. Put that comb thing in your hair, wear plenty of lipstick and lose the wedding ring.'

Evelyn disappeared into the bathroom while Felix carried on a shouted exchange, continuing to examine her wardrobe.

'Got your dress for the Von Blick party?'

'I thought the dark-red thing with the belt?'

Over Felix's dead body. Felix pulled the white satin gown from the far end of the rail. Now there was a dress she should wear. Had the height for it. She looked at him, unconvinced, but he crossed his heart and hoped to die. On his mother's grave, he said – not that she was actually in it yet but she had it all picked out.

'Oh I am sorry. Is she not well?'

'Hell, no! Strong as an ox. It just kind of *comforts* her? Suits her, anyway, to talk about it. We feel bad – my brother and me – and she feels good because we feel bad. Go figure.'

He sat on the end of the bed admiring the ancient patchwork quilt of sprigged calico and the pictures that Mr Hashimoto had hung on the freshly painted walls.

'Wish I had a Degas in my boudoir. Even this quilt belongs in a museum.'

He wandered through the other rooms as she dressed.

'A Benois in the spare bedroom? Seriously? When are you ever going to get to see it? We need to hang everything in here, Russian style.' His hand mimed tiling a wall with canvases. 'You could have your own private Frick Collection. You free next weekend? I'll bring the hammer and nails; you mix the drinks.'

As she followed Felix's directions to the police station, he began briefing her like Von Blick extracting a performance. She was Meredith's girlfriend – girlfriend was better than sister. Evelyn asked if such a rigmarole was strictly necessary and he gave a short, unhappy laugh: it was necessary. The desk sergeant had been taken care of. All she had to do was tell the guy she'd come to collect poor darling Frankie (Fox had had the presence of mind to use an alias) and could the sergeant please be an angel and show them out the back way where Felix would be waiting with the car.

'Ritz the guy a little,' said Felix. 'Then just breeze up to Fox and kiss him on the cheek and say "Oh-Frankie-darling-honestly". Fox will take it from there. And don't forget the kiss, the full personality.'

There was a man asleep on the bench beside the front desk of the police station. He had a crush hat pulled down over his eyes and an unlit cigarette between his lips, a black sand of stubble on his chin. On the floor beside him lay an open satchel containing a camera and a copy of that day's *Daily News*. Evelyn looked from the sleeping man to the policeman on duty who winked and put a finger to his lips as she approached. There was a glass-fronted notice-board behind him and she could see her reflection in it. She raised her chin and deepened her voice.

'I believe you're holding a Mr Morris? My car's out the back.'

The policeman came out from behind the desk and led her along a battleship-grey corridor and down the stairs to the cells. There was a strong, unsuccessful smell of disinfectant.

'They've been giving your boyfriend a hard time down there. Wait here.' He was more amused than sorry. He unhooked a bunch of keys from his belt and opened the cell door. There was a short, very nerve-racking delay while Meredith remembered his alias and there were jeers and whistles from the other inmates as the cell door was locked behind him. Evelyn, right on cue, dashed forward and threw her arms around his neck, He didn't smell of cologne any more.

'Oh Frankie, honestly. There is such a thing as too much research, you know. Read a book next time.'

Meredith pulled back from her embrace. An indigo bruise ringed his right eye and his undressed hair fell forward in a foppish forelock.

'I'm sorry, baby.' His blue gaze never left her face and it was some moments before Evelyn realised that he focused on her left eye only, as an actor would in close-up, lending an unnatural intensity to his expression. 'Don and Mary bet us we wouldn't dare go there and you know I could never resist a dare …'

He still had his overcoat, his watch and his signet ring (the desk sergeant had taken care of those together with his Charvet tie and the laces from his correspondent shoes and a pint of whiskey) but every one of the horn buttons had been torn from his sports jacket.

The policeman ushered them out of the rear entrance where Felix was waiting.

'Here he is, Ronnie darling. Safe and sound.'

'Remind me to get you a screen test,' hissed Felix as he shoehorned his friend into the front passenger seat before climbing into the back. Meredith finger-combed his hair into place via the rear-view mirror before awarding a smile to Evelyn and telling her what a darling she was. Even after all those martinis, even with the swollen eye, he had the same easy, manly charm. He was going to be having a few of the guys over next Sunday. Be swell if she could join them. Around five? Lucile Avenue, Felix had the address. He gave her stockinged knee a squeeze, a strange, joyless action like a screen kiss or one of Rindy McGee's cover-girl smiles. Caress delivered, he reached into his jacket pocket. His whiskey bottle was already half empty and he all but drained it. He was asleep before they reached Silver Lake.

'The studio are going to hate all this,' said Felix, 'even if they manage to hush it up. Poor Fox.'

The actor smiled in his sleep. A real smile this time.

*

Make-up had done a fairly good job on the bruising but Fox Meredith was still wearing dark glasses for his party the following Sunday. Galahad's love scenes with Guinevere's lady-in-waiting in *Knights of Love* had been written out together with most of his close-ups (they were working overtime in the cutting room). In the few days since his short stay in a police cell, his planned drinks party had turned into a wake for the untimely death of his screen career. The gossip-mongers, who had only just learned to find him fascinating, had been fed a new scenario, devised in haste by the Miracle publicity team, and as Evelyn arrived Galahad himself was reading aloud from one of the columns.

'"Friends say that Meredith has been suffering from fatigue brought on by overwork and that the young star has vowed to return to the less demanding world of legit-imate theatre." *Less demanding?*' scoffed Galahad. 'Every stage actor I know gets by on bourbon and Benzedrine. Never mind: Dad will be thrilled. The *Theer-tah*. My agent's got me an audition for *The Lead Balloon* next week. They had Leland Trent signed up but his number came up in the draft – not so much a draft as an ill wind …' The actor sighed as he gazed out over his garden, which trickled down the hillside in a series of leafy terraces. The Hollywoodland sign could be glimpsed through the scrub oaks and to the west the sun was preparing for its nightly dip in the ocean.

'It's two degrees in New York,' said Foxton. 'With sleet.'

Baines Frobisher and Cedric Sedgwick, in rival boating blazers, were both admiring the view, glass in hand. They had scant sympathy for Meredith.

'He should count himself lucky a career in legit is still an option. He could easily have ended up as an interior decorator, poaching clients from poor Wally there.'

'You think?' Binky Frobisher pulled a face. 'I don't think Wally would be losing much sleep.'

He waved a hand at the walls of the den which were decked with Polynesian dancing girls painted on black velvet.

'Wally made him a present of them after he persuaded Joan Crawford to chuck them all out – damn near broke her heart,' said Binky. 'That one looks remarkably like my second wife but I think she's my favourite.' He pointed his cigarette at a bare-breasted Polynesian wearing a sort of floral muffler. 'Looks like Sabu with tits.'

Zandor Kiss arrived (to Meredith's evident surprise) and shook the young actor by the hand and wished him luck. He should break a leg, he said, Hollywood's loss was Broadway's gain. Kiss had spotted Evelyn on the other side of the room but made no attempt to speak to her. He was clearly finding her presence on the Miracle lot something of an embarrassment. He did not let it trouble him unduly (he had worse things on the payroll) but she was no longer invited to script meetings. A studio messenger had delivered a copy of an old Kiss project with a note asking her to translate the marked scenes into German. *Bermuda Love Triangle* was about a woman who tries to rekindle her husband's interest by making a play for her sailing instructor until the Atlantic weather takes a nasty turn. 'The Krauts will love the guilt angle,' wrote Kiss but added there was no hurry. Evelyn had done as he asked (her open German dictionary at her side in a desk drawer in case Miss McAllister spotted it) and thoroughly enjoyed the task but she knew full well that the Germans would never actually buy the film – they had long ceased trading with most of the big studios – so giving her the assignment was a bit like getting a navvy to dig holes and fill them in again. She still drove down to Beverly Hills every Wednesday to give Dorinda McGee her elocution lesson although it was increasingly doubtful that Rindy's new, much-improved English accent would be needed in the fight against the Martians.

Felix made a late entrance in a familiar-looking blazer of palest fawn slubbed silk, gleaming white flannels and shoes of blue buckskin. There was a glint of monogrammed gold as he reached for his cocktail (F for Felix; F for Foxton).

'How do you like the new shirt?' He shot his cuffs. 'Crêpe de Chine. Fox is bequeathing me his West Coast wardrobe. We're the exact same size – he just *smells* taller. Wait till you see me in the yellow silk suit. He won't need it in New York. This jacket would get you arrested on 42nd Street, or anywhere else pretty much. Except here. Why are you laughing?'

'Nothing really,' said Evelyn with a sad smile. 'It just occurred to me yesterday that Silas, my husband – my *late* husband, didn't have any coloured clothes. Even his pyjamas were grey. I bought him some orange ones for his birthday and I had to take them back.'

Evelyn thought again of the peculiar postscript to Deborah's last letter: 'the report we got was very vague'. What report? She had promised to explain in her next letter but that was nearly a fortnight ago.

She stroked the crêpe de Chine collar of Felix's shirt.

'My French mistress had a canary that colour.'

Felix changed the grip on his cigarette and waggled it in Marx Brothers mode. 'And *my* French mistress …'

He hugged hold of her arm and walked her towards the verandah.

'Nice place, isn't it? Fox's lease is paid up till the summer so I'm going to move in and take care of it for him. I don't think I can face another winter where I am; I'd run out of buckets.'

He tightened his hold on her arm and lowered his voice.

'I'm sorry we had to drag you into all that nonsense the other morning. I did think of calling McAllister but Connie is too fond of a good story. Hell, she'd probably put it in her next play –' a catty chuckle '– then nobody would ever hear about it. Poor Fox. But at least this way he's still got some kind of career, I guess. What am I saying? He can have a great career in legit. The crazy thing is that when you live in this place you forget there's a world outside and you start thinking that not making it here, leaving LA, would be the end of the world. And it isn't, is it?'

Evelyn leaned against the rail and looked out through the vines. Two tall, fashionably thin palm trees in the foreground were nodding together confidingly, as if admiring the blazing sunset beyond. A champagne cork popped in the room behind them.

'Isn't what?'

'The end of the world.'

'Isn't it?'

Chapter 14

There was no sign of Felix in the Writers' Block the following morning and no sign at all of Ted Monroe whose bookcase had been emptied and whose corner desk was now occupied by a comically slender young man in Prince of Wales checks and very thick spectacles struggling with the crossword in an old copy of the London *Times*. He looked up as Evelyn and Miss McAllister arrived, greeted them without getting out of his chair and wondered whether a spot of tea might be in order? Without a word, both women renewed their mutual non-aggression pact by turning on their heels and heading for the commissary.

'Is he for real? I think he's hot favourite for Man You Would Most Like to Dunk in a Sewer. Kiss did mention something about hiring some English guy – Hubert something? Or maybe Desmond something? – but that was months ago. He wrote *Crimson Lake* or *Burnt Sienna*, some name like that. It was a big hit with the longhairs, less so with the regular people, but Kiss said something about getting him to work up a treatment of *Tom Jones*. No one's holding their breath.'

Miss McAllister spooned more sugar into her cup.

'Did you hear Fox Meredith got arrested? He was in some dive on Sunset after the Games party and there was a homo raid and he ended up in the caboose so now it's back to Broadway for Mr Meredith. Publicity have been working overtime trying to get a lid on it but luckily for him it happened the same night Douglas Fairbanks Jr was seen descending the fire escape of the Marmont in white tie and tails at four in the morning. At least, they *think* it was Douglas Fairbanks. Might have been Dietrich in drag, I suppose ... but it kept the gossip columns busy. Meredith could have been on the lam with the crew of the Catalina ferry for all they cared. Somebody was sent down to the station to square the desk sergeant and no charges were brought but he's a lucky guy all the same. They could have invoked the morality clause in his contract but he's still getting six months' severance and back on Broadway next month like it never happened. If you saw a play that phoney you'd blow raspberries. Poor Fox. He was engaged for a while, believe it or not: Hildy Hammer – they both had bit parts in *Young Elizabeth*. He should have married her. Makes life a lot easier.'

'And what's happened to Mr Monroe?'

'*Theodore* finally got kicked upstairs. He's got an office on PZ's corridor, they doubled his salary and he'll never write another line worth a damn: the sable-lined, solid-gold coffin.'

Back in the office, Desmond Colley had taken off his suit jacket and was puzzling over an empty coffee percolator. Felix was still not at his desk.

'Is he not well?'

'Didn't you hear? His mother died so he's flown back east, caught the clipper this morning,' explained Connie. 'Funny him having a mother. He always *talked* about her but I thought he made her up like that invisible wife of his.'

*

233

Evelyn spent election night with Connie McAllister in a bar near the studio listening to the radio broadcast. As the result emerged, Miss McAllister ordered more daiquiris and an old German man at the counter began to cry and was then asked to leave when he started throwing peanuts at the wireless.

The following Saturday, on the morning of the Von Blick party, Felix rang to offer her a lift.

'And wear the white gown – or no ride.'

That evening, she sat at her dressing table, trying to make her face look a fraction more like her studio portrait. Pinned to the edge of the looking glass was a sheet of paper she had found on the floor of Stage Six. Written on it, in Von Blick's spidery German script, were the words 'Keep alive! No passivity in scenes!' The tyre-like tread of a technician's rubber sole was stamped across the paper. She put some more powder on her nose and looked at the effect, unconvinced. What would Jesus do? Jesus poked doubtfully at Alphonse's comb and risked another spot of lipstick.

She looked sensational, according to Felix. Felix looked sensational too – a new, improved, Technicolor Felix, bronzed by Foxton's sun-ray apparatus and taller somehow in Foxton's $100 tailcoat. He mixed two highballs and smiled.

'*L'chaim!*'

The suntan made his teeth look whiter and she noticed for the first time that the front ones were too perfect to be real. Silas could always tell when an actor's teeth were capped.

'You seem on good form ...' She realised too late that it sounded like a reproach. 'I was so sorry to hear about your mother.'

A furrow in the tanned forehead but he batted the thought away, keeping it light.

'I've been feeling a lot better, a *lot* better. Fox left a pack of his pep pills in the bathroom closet. They really help you concentrate – PZ practically lives on them, you can see why he gets so much done. I worked from home today. Got up at seven, I rewrote five scenes before lunch and this afternoon I finished the treatment of the story I sold them: *Foreign Entanglement*. It was published in one of the monthlies over a year ago and now all of a sudden my New York agent has PZ's office on the phone wanting to know where they can get hold of me.'

The original magazine story had been about a young pianist who helped a beautiful woman escape from an unnamed country overrun with jackbooted Esperanto speakers. The pair hide in a deserted mountain hotel, he serenades her ('Stardust' in A flat) and she frets about her family under the yoke back in Freedonia and they fall asleep in each other's arms while a Felix Bressart type (maybe even the real thing if MGM would release him) flaps around mixing *glühwein* and frying potatoes and talking about the evil new regime. Our hero wakes to find her gone, dashes to the railway station just in time for a parting embrace. Cue smoke, cue 'Stardust'.

PZ had skim-read a one-page precis of the original and immediately decided that the hero should be a member of a university ice-hockey squad who misses the team bus and wakes up with a three-day hangover in a Transylvanian beer cellar.

'Ty Hooper is in the frame for the lead, so they'd have to dub the vocals for "Stardust" ... I actually wrote it with Fox in mind but I guess you can't have everything. As a writer, I weep for my precious story but that cheque from Miracle sure buys a lot of handkerchiefs ...'

The kitten had jumped on to Felix's lap the instant he sat down and he had been tickling absently behind its ears but his technique wasn't to Happy's taste. He gave a sulky little miaow as he clambered down and headed off in search of fish, tail in the air. Felix laughed and lit a cigarette.

'Kiss been keeping you busy?'

'Up to a point.'

'I mean, I hate to pry, Mrs Murdoch, but what is it you actually do?'

'I was originally hired to assist Mr Peyton ...'

'Oh yeah? Like we don't have assistants in California? He didn't look like he needed a whole lot of help and, besides, nobody's seen him since Labor Day. You aren't invited to script meetings any more. You don't even type. And yet here you are: house, auto, model gowns. For what? You're not Kiss's mistress, are you? That's what Connie thinks. Or his long-lost daughter?'

Evelyn played for time.

'I think *War of the Worlds* is being put on hold for the moment,' she said, 'but Mr Kiss still wants me to keep up the voice coaching for Rindy in case they have a change of heart.'

'They shelved the air-force movie too. Nine of the guys in the squadron they had lined up didn't make it back to base and another four wouldn't screen test too well. I don't think the Senate Committee would have worn it anyhow. Kiss is already having to answer charges of incitement. I don't think anyone's going to let him near a war movie – not unless Hitler bombs Bel Air. *Then* we might be in business. Yes?'

Evelyn shrugged her shoulders.

'All right, Mrs Murdoch, if you want to be an international woman of mystery, that is fine by me.' He put her evening wrap around her and touched her neck with his lips. 'You certainly look the part.'

Otto Von Blick lived in a long, narrow house clad in aluminium-coated steel and surrounded by a very large, very shallow puddle of water that gave it the unnerving look of a U-boat surfacing from a loch. There was a large Ford headlight set into the sheer side wall facing the road, an architectural joke which gave the stark metallic house the air of a prison block (and gave its owner nightmares).

Felix had not been on Von Blick's guest list but his new, supercharged personality made short work of the butler and he stormed past him into the hallway. A chatty gang of latecomers were still kissing one another hello and Felix joined them with wife Bernice on his arm, leaving Evelyn a few paces behind. The invisible Mrs Kay was on particularly irritating form.

'Why do you do this to me, Bernice?' Felix's accent, sharpened by the time spent with his brother in Forest Hills, had risen to a querulous whine. 'Every time we go out you do this to me, Bernice. Every goddamn time. Yes, I know we always stand with a crowd of bums under the staircase. Yes, dear, I know that dress makes her look like a dolphin on a diet but that's no reason to say so. The woman can't help her looks, Bernice.'

In a darkened room at the far end of the hall a large cinema screen was showing the final cut of *Knights of Love*. The closing moments had Guinevere alone in her turret room waiting for her cruelly forgiving husband to climb the stairs. Magda Malo's expression was unreadable as she made love to her reflection in the camera-side looking glass but she registered a whole screen test of emotions thanks to a dozen violins and the unheard shouts and whispers of Von Blick ('No passivity in scenes!').

The lights came up and the movie screen glided away behind a wall of burnished copper. The guests drifted out to the main salon, congratulating their host en route. PZ's Miss Hansen probably dreamed of preview cards like this: *a triumph; one of your best; spell-binding; socko stuff, Otto baby*.

Otto baby made his escape into the hallway, lit a cigar and smiled a hello to Evelyn, putting an arm around her waist. His fingers lingered – was that why so many starlets wore satin and velvet? – and he steered her back to the main room which was empty apart from a few waiters collecting abandoned champagne glasses.

The walls were of palest grey with carpets the colour of ice cream. A trio of spotlights had been mounted at strategic points (fireplace, piano, sofa) waiting for faces. There were three, large, museum-worthy paintings. The largest canvas hung opposite the wall of glass doors that ran the length of the terrace and looked at first glance like another window: a Rousseau of tree ferns and lotus blossoms that mirrored the garden outside. The other two pictures had obviously been selected to match it: a Picasso in the correct shade of viridian and a large, bluish canvas showing a trio of nymphs surprised while bathing. *Still* surprised? You'd think they'd be used to it by now.

They weren't his favourite paintings, Von Blick confessed, but they were the only things that didn't look out of place in the new house. His two Renoirs had been relegated to the bedroom (and then only after the architect had signed off the building).

'But my favourite is through here.'

The study walls were lined with leather the colour of his cigar and the only painting was an Annunciation, portrayed by the artist with a Peeping Tom intensity. Mary was discovered in long shot as the mysterious winged messenger brought the news to her gold and crimson boudoir, the Holy Spirit shining down on her face like a follow spot. The shutters behind the Virgin were open and through the window shimmered the landscape beyond: an umbrella pine and a lapis-blue California sky: the reminder of a world elsewhere.

Von Blick thumbed a speck of dust from the frame.

'So. You want the full tour?'

On their way to the terrace he paused to slap a passing actor on the back.

'Bennett! Good to see you.' Then, more softly, 'Everything OK between you and Jeanette?'

'Sure …' The man hesitated. 'Sure it is. Why?'

'Glad to hear it.' The director held on to the actor's hand and bashed his biceps some more. 'You're like a son to me, Bennett baby.

'Gets 'em every time.' Von Blick chuckled and put his arm around Evelyn as they crossed the steel bridge over the moat-like swimming pool.

'So, Mrs Murdoch, how do you like my house?'

'I've – never seen anything quite like it.'

'Ah! A *diplomat*. I like that.'

The outbuildings, screened by a cypress hedge, included stabling for half a dozen horses and an entire separate annexe of kennels for his Afghan hounds. Their full-time veterinary nurse (they were all martyrs to mange) shared the servants' wing with a French chef, a pair of Filipina housemaids and the butler. The dogs' nurse had a crush on the butler but was barking up the wrong tree in Von Blick's considered opinion.

It had all been featured in the *House Beautifuls* that Evelyn had flicked through at the Chicago beauty parlour which said that despite the extensive staff quarters, a three-car garage, four sitting rooms and three bathrooms there was

239

only one bedroom. 'A bachelor's house', the magazine called it, but one might just as well say 'an orphan's house' or 'a misanthrope's house'. Even Evelyn's mother-in-law had a spare bedroom.

Mrs Murdoch's spare bedroom was a north-facing box with ugly yellow chintz curtains and ugly brown furniture. The top drawer of the tallboy was kept bare for the imaginary clothes of the imaginary guest but the rest were filled with a mad memory game of haphazard items: a manicure set, corn plasters, a tin opener, a pot of fish food, a patent enema and a cut-glass powder bowl with a swansdown puff whose porcelain handle was shaped like a ballerina's legs and feet as if a tipsy Markova had fallen in head first. A surprisingly frivolous and lovely thing for her mother-in-law to have bought. It was still in its cellophane box.

The bottom drawer of the tallboy housed a large collection of widowed gloves, far, far more than the always very particular and parsimonious Mrs Murdoch could ever personally have lost. It dawned on Evelyn that she must have found them in the street, in railway carriages, beneath pews, and had been stockpiling them in hopes of a usable pair. All but three were right hands.

Evelyn's reverie was interrupted by another friendly pinch.

'I like you, Mrs Englishlady. You know when not to talk: the perfect house guest – except I never have house guests.' He gave a bitter laugh. 'My flat in Berlin always had six *schnorrer* cousins saving on hotel bills. When we're doing the plans here I figure with one bedroom I stop them coming but my cousins won't be coming. Not ever. I could have all the bedrooms I want.'

Even twelve violins would have struggled to fill that silence. Evelyn kissed his damp cheek and the two of them walked back to the house where they were met by Paula Silverman, furs in hand.

'It's hello and goodbye, I'm afraid. I need to get back. Dad hasn't been well. They got a nurse but you know how Mamie likes to fuss.'

'Fuss?' Von Blick shook his head. 'If a man has a stroke I think his wife can fuss a little, no? *Fuss*. Tell Mamie I'll call.

'They say he won't last the week,' he murmured as they returned to the drawing room where Queen Guinevere was busy fascinating a silver-haired man with diamond shirt studs.

'I want to hear all about it,' she said, collapsing sideways on to a sofa, stage-managing her descent so that her gown fanned prettily around her. She draped a forearm across the back of the seat, flawless face troping to the kindly light, staring up at her prey, eyes on full power. The man took her hand in his, utterly mesmerised.

'You must promise me you'll give the stage another try: you're wasted out here. It isn't worthy of you. I'd love to see you play Hedda Gabler. Saint Joan maybe?'

'You read my mind.'

Felix was in the far corner of the room in the angle of an L-shaped couch amid a halo of laughing faces. He was offering to recite *Paul Revere's Ride*. What style did they want this time? A voice cried 'Cagney!' and Felix launched into a hilarious, pitch-perfect impersonation.

He spotted Evelyn as he finished and rose to greet her with a guilty smile.

'You all know the lovely Mrs Murdoch?' A black barathea arm curled around her and undecided fingers tickled her midriff. He pulled her round to face him and gave her a kiss on (or very near) the lips.

241

'I'm supposed to be your date and I'm neglecting you. You free for lunch tomorrow? Terrific. And I've got some tickets for a concert later if you like? Yes? I'll pick you up around two – give you a chance for some beauty sleep – not that you need it.'

'So you do own a lipstick.'

Rindy McGee was drinking pink lemonade from a champagne saucer. She was wearing ruffles.

'What happened to the *soignée* midnight blue?'

'Mother said I looked too old in it. She was right but it still sucks.'

She swapped her glass for Evelyn's champagne.

'I finally got around to reading that Martian book. No wonder PZ got cold feet ...'

Rindy had been trained to keep her face bright (a photograph could happen at any moment at this sort of gathering) but gave a genuine smile at the sight of someone behind Evelyn. Warm fingers were walking up the white satin buttons on the back of her dress.

'So, you finally found the zipper?' said a voice in her ear. 'And how's kitty? You got a name yet?'

Evelyn span round into her key light to answer him.

'Happy.'

She wished there was a mirror taped somewhere so that she could see what had made him look at her that way.

'Dance?'

His shirt front smelled of starch and cedarwood ('His cheeks are as a bed of spices, as sweet flowers: his lips like lilies, dropping sweet-smelling myrrh'). Von Blick's ingenious marquetry dance floor had been cut to look like the view from a skyscraper, the flat roofs of tall buildings looming vertiginously beneath their feet. They danced across the rooftops past Magda Malo who was now dancing with her Broadway producer. The actress moved with a dutiful, almost listless ease, like a rag doll nailed to his shoes. Monroe set a course for the open windows then rumba'd Evelyn into the lee of a yew hedge and took her breath away with a long passionate kiss, his body keeping the rhythm of the dance band. She put up a hand to stroke his just-razored cheek. As she arched her back she felt his arm tighten around her another notch.

'Let's get out of here,' he said – just like a movie.

It crossed her mind that she ought to let Felix drive her home but Felix had already motored off to join a bottle party with his new friends and so the two of them walked down the drive, climbed into Ted Monroe's big blue car and drove into the night.

It was gone twelve but the air was still warm in West Hollywood. A door opened and a woman in an art-silk kimono ran out from the porch of her bungalow.

'Heathcliff! Heathcliff, where are you, you bad, *bad* little man?'

A viciously clipped French poodle ran out from beneath an oleander bush and yapped past her into the hall.

'I guess that's Heathcliff,' said Monroe.

He led Evelyn giggling through an archway, along a cobbled path and up a winding staircase to a loft-like studio lit by the lanterns that hung from the trees outside. He switched on the radiogram – 'Stardust' in A flat – carried her to the bed, kissing her skin as he bared it, mapping her contours with his lips, whispering how he'd been waiting to take her in his arms since he first buttoned her into that sexy white dress. Then the kissing stopped. Relax baby; beautiful, beautiful baby.

The radio was still playing softly when she woke next morning: a dance tune this time.

'Morning, beautiful. Sweet dreams? You were smiling in your sleep.'

He was standing by the bed wrapped in a bath towel.

'You want breakfast?' He sat down beside her and pulled back the covers. 'Or maybe it's too early for breakfast ...'

More kisses, more shockwaves of pleasure. Another dance tune on the wireless to put them both back in an unmade movie, except that these were the scenes that the camera never showed. The director might take you as far as the altar, or even the bridal suite, but he relied on the idea that the audience knew or could imagine what followed and Evelyn didn't know and had never imagined. When Rhett Butler carried his prize upstairs, Evelyn knew there must be more for Scarlett O'Hara than a hard hand pinching her breast, an unshaven chin scouring her face, the jerking grunt that let her know it was over. There had to be and there was. Much more. 'Let him kiss me with the kisses of his mouth: for thy love is better than wine.'

She was woken by the brush of his lips on her neck. The music had stopped.

'OK, let's try again: eggs for Madame? Coffee? Orange juice?'

'Tea?'

He flicked her teasingly with the corner of the bath towel then wrapped himself in it and sauntered handsomely into the kitchenette to brew coffee and scramble eggs and grill bacon while Evelyn took a quick shower and wriggled nakedly back into her chilly satin gown. She stood at his side by the stove, unzipped and minus her underwear. How was a guy supposed to cook eggs with her standing there like Harlow in heat?

Only now, in the daylight, could she see the apartment properly. The vaulted wooden ceiling was like the interior of a galleon – or Mr Peggotty's upturned boat house. Looking out through the dormer window over his desk she could see a maze of winding paths and fantastical turrets and unexpected windows like an Oxford college built for munchkins. There were cats everywhere, camouflaged by the undergrowth like a puzzle picture in a children's comic (how many cats can you spot?).

The apartment was furnished like a set-dresser's idea of a writer's room. The bookshelves were bent under the weight of a hundred screenplays and the desk was sand-bagged with folders and reference books, every one thickly bookmarked with scribbled notes.

There were copies of his novels on the mantelpiece together with a set of baseball directories, a Bible and the manuscript of *The Magic Mink*.

'Rindy couldn't understand why you didn't publish it,' said Evelyn as he served her breakfast.

'Rindy liked it well enough but Bitsy had it sat on. I'm surprised she hasn't burned Rindy's copy by now. She took it *very* personally – you ever see that dame without her furs? It spooked her, the thought of them all watching her every move, how gauche she was, how lowbrow, how five and dime.'

He rubbed the back of his finger against the silk of her bodice.

'You could wear furs: white fox. You should always wear white.'

She pulled a face.

'And have you put me in a book? Besides, I'm hardly the type.'

'Phooey. You look like a goddess.'

Breakfast was cold by the time they ate it. He took the second pot of coffee over to his desk and began whittling pencils with his pocket knife. Evelyn looked at her watch; Felix was picking her up at two.

'I should go. Could you possibly give me a lift?'

'Nothing would give me greater pleasure but, sadly, Sunday is mending day.' He gestured to the pile of red folders. 'There's a cab number on the wall.'

'A cab? In this?'

She pulled at the creased white satin. Ted Monroe said she would find something in the closet. It was an unexpectedly tidy closet with shirts, jackets and suits ordered in rows on the long rail. Beside them at the far end hung a pair of shirtwaist dresses with white pilgrim collars. Evelyn suddenly felt very cold. Monroe was way ahead of her.

'My sister left them.'

It was far too small, she said. No it wasn't, he said, and zipped her into it with a far-too-practised hand. There were women's shoes on the closet floor.

'Your sister has very large feet.'

'Don't let's play games,' he crooked a finger under her chin, 'and no one's going to notice your feet – not with that figure.'

As she waited by the gate for the taxi she had ordered, a sleepy redhead in evening dress was parking her car. A ghastly glance of sisterhood at Evelyn's silver lamé slippers. Not notice? In this town? They could probably tell you the brand.

The cab sped through the sleepy Sunday streets and up on to Sunset Boulevard past limousines heading from brunch to lunch. The driver left her at the entrance to the main house (no, she didn't work here, it was her home,

246

and no, she wasn't free that evening). She tripped through the yew archway to the cinder path. Mr Hashimoto had been busy and the garden was very nearly shipshape. The grapevine had been clipped back and tied to its trellis with neat knots of green twine. The ground beneath it was carpeted with winter pansies. The dead hibiscus flowers had all been swept away and the fallen leaves had been cleared from the pond which was newly stocked with goldfish. As she rounded the hedge that screened the pool house she stopped short. Mr Hashimoto had cemented over all the cracks in the paving and the terrace was lined with pot after pot of flowering standard rose trees, half red, half white, exactly like the *Alice in Wonderland* bushes in front of PZ's office ('The wilderness and the solitary place shall be glad for them; and the desert shall rejoice and blossom as the rose').

Happy heard her approaching and walked up the path to meet her followed by Mr Hashimoto. Mr Hashimoto was now firm friends with the kitten, which followed him about the garden as he worked. The Bengal had defended its territory but the gardener had put an end to the rivalry by packing the older cat into a chicken basket and driving it home to Gardena as a surprise gift for his concubine.

'The pond looks much better,' she said. 'Very clean. Very nice job.'

'Kitty like,' he said. 'Pray with fish.'

Evelyn crouched down to stroke the kitten and it jumped on to her shoulder and rubbed its nose against hers. Mr Hashimoto smiled and bowed.

'Happy happy now.'

Chapter 15

EVELYN WAS IN THE DENTIST's chair and Silas, wearing his white coat with the side buttons, was coming towards her with a steel tray of very shiny porcelain teeth: a Nova Pilbeam smile.

She had fallen asleep in the sunshine after getting showered and dressed and was rescued from her nightmare by the arrival of her lunch date.

'I've never seen you look so lovely,' smiled Felix. 'All lit up inside.'

Felix himself was looking trim and expensive in a pigskin bush jacket worn over a cashmere shirt.

'I got you this.'

A slim, ribboned box from a Beverly Hills shop with a silk headscarf inside. Evelyn smiled sleepily at the pattern: a California sky of palms and oranges and bluebirds.

'It's gorgeous.'

'I thought we could take a drive after lunch and you could wear it as a wrap-around. Be a shame to muss up that hair.' A shy finger hooked a stray curl into place.

He could have kissed her if he'd wanted to – Ted Monroe would have kissed her – but instead he cut straight to the scene where he helped her into the passenger seat of Foxton Meredith's roadster and drove through the wide, sunny streets to a downtown diner with no waitress service and sawdust on the floors and where the chef piled fat notebooks of roasted meat and gravy between crispy logs of bread.

When Evelyn looked back on that long, happy luncheon she could remember laughing but could not remember the jokes themselves. It was the close-ups, the stills framed in the foyer, that lingered in her mind's eye: the wide smile of yellow mustard licking across his cheek; the steaming tray he brought back from the counter laden with all three flavours of pie.

'Your face! You look like you never seen dessert before.'

'It never really featured at home,' she had explained. '*Life is more than food, and the body more than clothing* – or so my mother-in-law always said.'

'Oh yeah? *Eat what is good and delight yourself in abundance.* If you want to play Bible games my big brother and I can keep this up for hours.'

'I didn't think you were the Scripture Studies type.'

'Hidden depths.'

His hand had reached across the linoleum-covered table and again she had raised her chin for the expected caress but he merely stole a piece of piecrust.

Had anyone shown her the ocean yet?

They took what he called the scenic route: west past the studio, north along Cahuenga Boulevard and then a scary, switchback ride along the crest of the hills, canyons falling away on either side of them like a process shot. The sprawling city shimmered implausibly beneath them, veiled in a mist of dust and petrol fumes, and the Pacific was just a grey blur on the horizon. The tyres of Felix's shiny new motor skidded very slightly on the unmade stretches of the road and there were burned rubber traces on the asphalted sections where drivers had played fast and loose with the hairpin bends. The car radio began broadcasting anxious strings and suddenly the romantic afternoon took a darker turn, as if the laughing lunch and the Technicolor scenery had merely been the build-up to a tragic climax: a car out of control; a scarf pulled tight around a soft neck; the muzzle of a gun pushed hard against a breast pocket.

It wasn't until the signs began promising Malibu that the air cleared and Evelyn had a heart-lifting glimpse of blue. She could only remember three visits to the seaside: Whitby, Worthing and Torquay. The seas she had seen smelled of seaweed and fried fish but the Pacific smelled only of salt. The music stopped as Felix pulled over on the coast road and they scrambled down a dune to the water's edge where they stood hand in hand gazing out at the unpaintable seascape, a formless composition rendered in swathes of colour: ochre; indigo; cerulean: sand; sea; sky.

When they reached Bolton Canyon the concert had already started. There was an unnatural yellow glow in the night sky, as if Martians were forging one of their deadly machines in the valley beyond. The unearthly mood was intensified by the eerie sounds wafting down the hill through the cottonwoods. Inside the auditorium, backed by a gigantic cup of white concrete, a Junoesque female was summoning Stravinsky's *Firebird* from the ether, flourishing her bare white arms in a spectral semaphore in front of what looked like some kind of giant crystal set. Her right hand mimicked the fluttering fingers of a cellist while the other batted gently at the air. Her doll's face was magnolia white and her dark brows permanently raised in surprise at the sounds her hands were making.

The audience, well-wrapped in furs and blankets, kept unusually still, fearing that any sudden movement of their own might break the spell, shatter the atmosphere and fill the air with wrong notes. Felix gave a happy sigh as the music ended and smiled up into the darkness.

250

'There ought to be fireflies. Back east we'd have had fireflies. They don't have them here. We'll have to get Cynthia Games to import some.'

The applause died away and the theremin player resumed her stance in front of the apparatus and proceeded to conjure the rest of her repertoire from the evening air, giving them Saint-Saëns's 'The Swan' for an encore. It had been a favourite of Silas's and, from force of habit, Evelyn looked along the row, half expecting to see his deceptively handsome profile. There was a rumble of distant thunder like a sound effect and she shivered, prompting Felix to pull their rug more closely around her knees, take shy hold of her hand and press it to his lips.

'My mother loved that number,' he said as they dashed to the car through the raindrops. 'She was always a push-over for strings. I wanted to have a gramophone at the funeral but the rabbi said no music allowed – can you believe that? Like he wanted a way to make it even worse. It was hell. All these people you only see when they're crying: weddings and funerals, always crying. And they're all talking about this woman I never met. What an angel, all her sacrifices.' He turned to Evelyn, his face wet. 'She wasn't an angel. She was a grand old lady but she was a pain in the ass. I'm sorry she died and I miss her but I can't cry the way they do. What good did grief ever do anybody? It won't bring her back, it doesn't prove anything. My brother is going to be sitting *shiva* for a week – he didn't even get out to vote – does that mean he loved her more?'

'Of course not.'

When they arrived back at Cedar Point he pulled her towards him and kissed her on the lips.

'Thank you for coming out with me today. I feel a lot better. We ought to make a date to hang all those pictures.'

251

He kept vague hold of her hand but there were no more kisses and he had not turned off the engine.

There was a studio envelope propped against the telephone in the kitchen and a bulging sack of oranges on the breakfast bar. She opened a can of fish for the mewling kitten, squeezed herself a glass of juice and sat down on one of the basket chairs in the sitting room to read her letter from Deborah. Happy, who had abandoned his supper after a few dubious mouthfuls, jumped into her lap and was kneading the cashmere of her cardigan into a suitable nesting place. There were three sheets of paper in the envelope but, in her hurry for the last collection, Deborah had not put them back in order.

…they wanted to know if we knew his blood group but his GP was over in New Malden, you may remember, and they were bombed out a few weeks ago – far more bombs in New Malden than Woking for some reason which has remained intact so far – perhaps the Nazis are saving it for themselves, like Paris and Belgrave Square. Anyway, someone's got to trek up north to the Scottish hospital and see whether it's poor Silas or not. A change is as good as a rest and Mrs M would try the patience of a saint which, as you know, I'm not.

Evelyn fell back in her chair which shrieked in sympathy making Happy jump clear. The letter hung by her side. She could almost hear the music swell, sense the lens moving in for a close-up as tears waited on the brink of her lower lids. Breathing hard, she mechanically put the pages of the letter in order and tried to concentrate on Deborah's narrative: a bearded amnesiac had been found in a Scottish military hospital. In his pocket was

252

the soft-backed, India paper Bible that Evelyn had given Silas when he left. There was a very good chance that her husband was alive after all.

If this had been a film someone would have poured her a glass of brandy – a giant-size glass that would make the hand that reached for it appear frail and childlike – or a kindly medic would emerge from her bedroom fumbling his stethoscope into his black bag: 'She's resting now. I've given her a sedative.' Evelyn felt her face drain of colour. She remembered reading once that the actress Eleanora Duse could blench or blush at will (how was never explained). She got up and poured some of the vodka into her orange juice.

Old Mr Buckingham next door was here when
the first telegram arrived and says he has a niece
in Dunbar and would we like him to nip up to
Edinburgh on our behalf which was very obliging I
will say. I tried talking this over with Mother but she
only said 'Who's Mr Buckingham?' so no joy there
and then Mr B has second thoughts and puts a note
through the door saying can we wait until the schools'
half-term exeat so he can spend a bit of time with his
great-nephew and I don't think we can really so I've
written to say I'll go. Sooner the better for everyone's
peace of mind quite frankly. The Bible's the only clue
they've got as they haven't heard back from the ship's
captain about Silas's identity tags and watch and
uniform and so on, none of which was in the parcel
sent home after the you-know-what. The Scots doctor
said not to get our hopes up but even he says the man
they've got fits the description I sent so I'm feeling
cautiously optimistic. I hope you've still got your
rabbit's foot. Will write as soon as I learn more.

Evelyn rinsed the empty glass in the kitchen sink, brushed her teeth, put on her nightgown and was about to get into bed when she crumpled to her knees by the side of it and felt her hand closing over her mouth to keep in the guilty prayer that sprang to her lips. Happy leapt up on to the quilt, his furry little body all *Tailor of Gloucester* against the sprigged calico squares. His baby-tiger face pushed against hers and a tiny tongue licked thirstily at a teardrop.

She lay awake into the small hours listening to the thunderstorm and wrestling with a choice of endings, except that she didn't have a choice. If poor Silas was alive then her place was by his side and she would walk up the front path, honeysuckle round the porch, a soaring, major-key melody in the air, and the door would open and he would fold her in his dry embrace and tell her how nice she looked. Hollywood would be in no doubt about what the happy ending consisted of even if it didn't make her happy. And if he were dead after all? What kind of happy ending was that?

Evelyn reached for the Bible on her bedside table and as she parted the pages and pointed a finger there was a crash of thunder overhead and a simultaneous flash of lightning: *God shall likewise destroy thee for ever, he shall take thee away, and pluck thee out of thy dwelling place, and root thee out of the land of the living.*

She was woken next morning by the telephone.

'I guess you've heard the bad news.'

'I ...'

She thought for a befuddled moment that Mamie Silverman knew about Silas, knew enough to know how bad the news was, and, before she could stop herself, she burst into noisy tears. Mamie, assuming, not unnaturally, that Evelyn was responding to her own news, found this enormously gratifying and began weeping herself.

'And you only knew him such a short time but Manny was like that, he had that gift, he *touched* people. We all knew his heart was bad but I guess I just thought he'd outlast me. The funeral's tomorrow. He'd have liked you to be there.'

Evelyn thought of Manny Silverman's bad temper at Nito's restaurant. Would he? Really?

She climbed gingerly out from under the bedclothes, taking care not to disturb Happy who had slotted his body into the crook of her knees, and went out to the kitchen. The clock said eight fifteen. It would be nearly noon in New York.

She dialled the exchange but Armistice Day was a public holiday and it was half an hour before the operator called back with Gregory Fenn on the line. She explained the situation as succinctly as she could.

'Are you at the house? Give me the number, I'll make some enquiries.'

It was nearly twenty minutes before her call was returned.

'Look here, I don't want to appear unsympathetic. Obviously in an ideal world you would be returned to sender ASAP but I've had a quick word with the only chap I could find – the office is pretty deserted today – and it's No Can Do for the moment, I'm afraid, unless you can persuade you-know-who to undertake such a transfer off his own bat and at his own expense which I wouldn't advise, quite frankly – he isn't flavour of the month with management. As you've probably gathered. he'll be undergoing, ahem, a *review* at the highest level regarding his unorthodox sales activities … I'm not saying that you've been cut adrift but, well, you've been cut adrift.

I mean if anything *major* occurs please feel free to get in touch but I'd be very surprised. I realise this will come as a disappointment but if there's anything we can do to speed things up at the Scottish end we will of course do all in our power ... ' He tailed off, as if fearing that HQ's powers would not stretch quite as far as the Clyde valley.

'I understand.'

'Jolly sporting of you. Let's hope you get some definite news either way in a day or so. Rotten for you.'

'Yes.'

Chapter 16

EVELYN HAD NOT been present at her mother's funeral which had been held the day after Von Richthofen was shot down. Various parishioners had been consulted and expressed the view that the occasion would prove too much for a small child but not seeing the casket lowered into the ground made it hard for the six-year-old Evelyn to come to terms with her mother's disappearance.

'Your mother is with the angels,' her father had explained.

'When will she be back?' Evelyn had asked.

She was initially sent to stay with cousins while her father struggled with his grief and took advice on suitable boarding schools. Meanwhile, little Evelyn began conducting elaborate obsequies for drowned kittens which she would shroud in old stockings, and lay tenderly in carbolic soap boxes together with bunches of catnip and cigarette cards from the Birds of Britain series. Her cousins thought her odd. They were very distant cousins, 'third cousins *twice* removed' as Cousin Timothy was fond of pointing out, even going so far as to draw a diagram in thick black pencil all over the nursery tablecloth which outlined the fecundity of their mutual great-grandmother (no jam in *his* rice pudding).

Silas had had no funeral, of course. They had had a few of the congregation home to tea at Mrs Murdoch's house after the Sunday service at which his passing was mentioned. Quite a few patients came and expressed their regrets then spent a fractious hour drinking weak Darjeeling and comparing notes on the various inferior dentists they had selected to replace him. A man called Russell had come out of retirement but he had qualified in the days when anaesthetics were for sissies and lacked Mr Murdoch's wonderful way with children.

Many of them had worn black as a mark of respect and Mrs Murdoch's ensemble was even sootier than usual for the occasion but she had discouraged any show of mourning by her daughters-in-law. It was an extravagance, she argued, and quoted Wesley (for a change) in her defence although Evelyn and Deborah both sensed that their mother-in-law desired a monopoly on all shows of grief. As a result, Evelyn had worn her trusty grey suit to the service. Did Hollywood wear black to funerals? In films they did: model hats with heavy veils; a scrap of Honiton lace glued to the glove's fingertips.

On Tuesday morning, the day of Manny Silverman's funeral, Evelyn ran her eye along the clothes in her closet which invisible Japanese hands had arranged in colour order like a box of crayons. The only items down at the dark end were crêpe (navy) and the old grey tailor-made. She slipped its jacket on over her nightdress and turned to look in the glass, tilting her chin and plunging her hands into the pockets: a Southern Railway ticket to Woking: third-class return. No place like home.

Navy would have to do, she decided, but her only hat was red so she went to the big, marble-lined department store on Wilshire Boulevard on her way to the cemetery where she played a short comic scene with a chasteningly smart saleslady who supplied her with what she called a 'navy felt Peter Pan' that seemed to fit the bill. She looked for Silas in the fitting-room mirror ('You've got hats') but he wasn't there.

Hats really were *day rigg-err* at the Silverman gathering which could be spotted from the parking lot beyond a model village of tombs. The kiosk-like houses of the dead slept twelve and had elegant, glazed front doors with potted plants either side of the entrance. Inside there were tiled floors and white marble vaults. One expected an English butler (or a French maid), a demilune table with its Sèvres bowl of calling cards and a pair of parcel-gilt *porte torchères*.

Beyond the gravelled avenues rose the newly built tomb of a silent movie actor who had died the previous year. The sepulchre, flanked by flaming maples and lapped by an emerald lawn, was presidential in scale. It was the kind of thing that one would expect to see as a centrepiece but the massive white slab had been shunted up against the perimeter wall of the cemetery (all the good plots having been sold in perpetuity to old California families). Manny Silverman, with his mania for real estate, had had greater foresight, acquiring a prime plot next to something called The Lake of Memories.

It was a highly respectable turnout but anyone who still had films to make was making a film ('business is business') and a few names were conspicuous by their absence. Otto Von Blick sent five hundred white roses, Helga Hart had sent a posy of wild flowers, the Raymond Gameses sent their empty limousine to join the cortège and Baines Frobisher merely sent a wreath and regrets. The dead man's son-in-law missed nothing.

'Ungrateful limey bums,' said PZ, making another mental note on his drop-dead list. 'They owed their lousy careers to Manny.'

It had said in that morning's *Los Angeles Times* that there would be twenty-two pallbearers. Evelyn had a mental image of twenty-two morning-coated mourners crammed under the coffin like a caterpillar with forty-four spongebag trouser legs but it turned out that the title was purely honorary and the actual lifting of the lead-lined flame-mahogany casket was undertaken by six professionals. Did they get much film work? she wondered.

The order of service in the chapel of rest began with Cedric Sedgwick who brought his round tones to Isaiah 35 ('then shall the lame man leap as a hart, and the tongue of the dumb sing'), followed by the dead man's favourite hymns: the first four (Christ-free) verses of 'The Battle Hymn of the Republic' and the whole of 'The Star-Spangled Banner'.

A veteran of Silverman's earliest two-reelers stood at the back of the chapel with a dark raincoat over the ruffled red frock of a Wild West saloon keeper and full Technicolor make-up (the charcoal-coloured hollows in her cheeks were especially startling). A studio driver was waiting in the yew avenue by the Garden of Eternal Love ready to whisk her round the block and back on to the lot where she was filming the preliminary scenes of *Duchess in the Dirt*. She slipped away the moment the rabbi had finished the Kaddish.

'What a trouper,' smiled Mamie. 'Manny would have loved that.'

The widow kissed Evelyn on both cheeks.

'You'll come back to the house, won't you, Evelyn? Sure you will. Our guest. Our friend.'

Paula and her sister had persuaded their stepmother to open up the Bel Air house for the funeral and so the jet necklace of rented black limousines slowed the Wilshire Boulevard traffic to a crawl. When they arrived Evelyn saw that Mr Hashimoto had hung a hatchment of white chrysanthemums around the front door and had painstakingly raked interlocking MS monograms into the gravel driveway: three hours' work heedlessly obliterated by the parking cars. A small butter-coloured horse box had been left alongside the Japanese bridge.

The house door was opened by an unseen hand and Mamie led the way into the doomy brown hallway and on into the doomy brown drawing room – as though the whole interior had been steeped in finest Ceylon. Mamie's lacquered claw gripped Evelyn's arm.

'The bitch is here! You see her? In her Lilly Daché hat and her sables Manny paid for. In this heat! Seventy-six degrees in November! And will you look at that veil?'

The first Mrs Silverman was swathed in black silk georgette that ran all the way to the hemline of her gown.

'Like *she's* the widow. I kind of thought we'd be too quick for her – he only died Sunday – but she got a seat on the Mercury. Landed at Glendale this morning.'

Mamie, tired and old after a week of watching by her husband's sudden sickbed, was at once offended and piqued by her predecessor's glamorous ensemble. She fiddled with the collar of her own dress so that her diamond necklace could be seen.

'Emily Post says jewellery isn't good taste with deep mourning but maybe *Emily Post* doesn't have a sixty-carat diamond rivière.'

She had raised her voice and one of the hired waiters glided across the room and paused at a side table nearby and began neatly restacking piles of neatly stacked plates.

'We could have had the open casket here in the room,' said Mamie, 'but the director guy opened it and I took a look and then we had it all sealed up again.'

She was on the verge of tears and sent the waiter for a glass of water as she rummaged in her black silk handbag.

261

'Mrs Post says excessive displays of grief are vulgar so Paula gave me some of those little pills she takes. I don't want to make a scene.' She took hold of Evelyn's left hand and began jiggling at her wedding ring. 'I guess it must have been worse for you, losing yours so young. If it hadn't been for that war you would have had him around for another fifty years.'

'Yes,' said Evelyn.

Mamie's glass of water hadn't materialised but a different waiter passed by with a tray of drinks and caviar toasts (even the canapés were in mourning).

'"Refreshments are never offered," Emily Post says; I looked it up: mean, East Coast bitch.'

From the far side of the room the voice of the first Mrs Silverman cut through the mournful mumblings like a dropped glass.

'*Cocktails? Such* bad taste.'

Mamie's sharp ears missed nothing. She turned to the nearest man.

'Get another martini for Mrs Silverman – Mrs Stadtler, I should say – and put a *black* olive in it.'

Mamie looked around her at the Stygian wood panelling.

'It's a good house for a funeral but how she ever persuaded Manny and those poor children to live here will always be a mystery to me.' She gave Evelyn's arm another squeeze. 'I want you to know you can stay in the pool house as long as you want. I'm not going to sell anything but I might not stay in Malibu. Maybe New York would be big enough …' A faint look of self-reproach at her ability to conceive of a future without her husband. She straightened her shoulders. 'I guess I ought to go talk to some people.'

Most of the grim gathering was composed of very old people in very young clothes: somebodies-turned-nobodies.

262

You knew before speaking a word to them that when you confessed that no, you hadn't actually heard of *Orchids in the Dust* or *Shanghai Caprice* or *Incontinence* or whatever had made their name, you would be chiselling another chunk off their crumbling self-regard, ruining their day, their week.

Zandor Kiss was on the far side of the room talking to Ted Monroe. Monroe was turning to leave and the producer made a bid to follow him without catching Evelyn's eye but she was too quick for him.

'Mrs Murdoch!'

Kiss-kisses on both cheeks.

'Very sad occasion but you look like a million dollars.'

'*Half a million*, Mr Von Blick says.'

The forgetful waiter who had been offering round the cheese puffs began restacking glasses on a tray. Evelyn could see him reflected in the looking glass above the gas-log fire as he stopped and scribbled something on his cuff.

Kiss's voice sank to a murmur. 'You did a nice job on that *Bermuda* translation' (a sudden tinkle of glasses as the waiter's tray gave a violent lurch). 'Very nice job and I got your notes about the Martian thing but to be perfectly *honest* –' and Kiss paused as if this were a rare occurrence '– from what Monroe said just now it doesn't look like the Wells project is going ahead any time soon. Not until after I go to Washington. I should never have brought you here. You should be back home fighting the good fight somewhere.'

'Isn't this a good fight?'

Kiss sighed, tired suddenly.

'Maybe, maybe. We'll see what those *farkuk* in Washington have to say for themselves.'

Evelyn moved closer and began speaking still more softly.

'Mr Kiss, I know you have a lot on your mind but I was wondering if you could help me with something? We thought that my husband was killed last Christmas but my family has had a telegram and it's possible there's been a mistake … Is there any chance that I might go back to London?'

'Back to London? Are you crazy? Do you know how many bombs fell last week?' He had turned to face her but his feet were angled for escape. 'That's great news about your husband, great news, *mazel tov*, but he wouldn't want you to go back there right now, the way things are. It'll be tough for you both but the war will end soon and then you'll have a happy reunion.'

He had the big finish all planned.

'But my job doesn't even exist. Mr Peyton is obviously busy elsewhere and there's nothing for me to do here.'

'Nonsense. Della's sending you another script to look over. Take all the time you need. Call me.'

He almost collided with Paula Silverman in his dash for the exit.

Paula looked very stylish in black, very *swan-yay*. Evelyn smiled a greeting and was surprised by yet another kiss on the cheek. The girl's lovely face turned, dead pan, to the scene playing out on the other side of the drawing room where the first Mrs Silverman was holding court with a trio of ancient actors all dressed in striped trousers, waistcoats and white slips: Wardrobe's idea of a family solicitor.

'Mother oughtn't to have come but I suppose she couldn't resist the Donna Lucia act. Poor Mamie. I thought Mother had more *savoir faire*, more *chain*, as old Grandma Silverman used to say. But then again maybe not – she picked out this house after all.' Paula gestured around her at the treacle-brown walls. 'Hideous, isn't it?

We lived here till they got divorced when I was seventeen. Dad couldn't get out of here fast enough.'

She scowled up at the coffered cedar ceiling.

'It's not a bad place for a funeral as it turns out, but can you imagine trying to throw a *real* party in a house like this? Making an entrance down that poky old staircase? Celeste and I always had all our big birthdays at the Marmont. And you know the really funny part? Mother's New York apartment is the exact opposite: ivory silk drapes; milk-white carpets; soft lights; big windows *and* she took all the best pictures: a Dufy; a Matisse; a Picasso. You couldn't hang them here – not if you wanted to look at them, anyway. People say it's very *English*. It's certainly dark enough. Sissy and I stayed with a friend of Mother's in England one time. Lovely old place … Sussex? Wessex? There was a fifteen-watt bulb in the bedroom. *Fif-teen* watts! Celeste – you haven't met Celeste, have you? – went right down to the village store and got another one.' Paula sighed and gestured around her. 'I guess it probably reminds you of home.'

A mouse darted out from behind the wainscoting, grabbed a fallen olive (black) and then whizzed back to its own panelled dining room.

'Yes. Yes I suppose it does.'

Except Woking wasn't home any more, Bel Air was. She thought of her bedroom down the hill in the bungalow, of the rose trees on the terrace, the picture windows, the Degas in her boudoir, Happy in the crook of her knees; thought of Mr Fenn and Mr Kiss insisting that an Atlantic crossing was out of the question until the opposing powers saw fit to arrange her happy ending.

Felix Kay had missed the funeral but had turned up at the house in time to shake the right hands.

'I'm up to my neck in the rewrites for *Duchess in the Dirt*. Are you OK? How's the garden? Have you been crying? You've been crying. Funerals get you that way?'

'I had a letter from home.'

'Bad news?'

What could one say? Yes, actually, the worst news in the world: there's a strong chance that the man I married is still alive and if he is I will have to leave Miracle, leave Hollywood, leave you, leave Ted Monroe, leave Happy, leave poor, cross Miss McAllister, and go back to life with a man whose idea of a romantic gesture was to spit on his hand first.

'Bad news?' she repeated, dazedly. 'Yes. No. Yes.'

Paula Silverman had slipped upstairs and swapped her black dress for her riding clothes.

'You will think me heartless but Columbine needs the exercise – as do I.'

'You should eat something.'

'You sound like my stepmother but you're right: I should eat something.'

She summoned one of the waiters and asked him to fix her a sandwich, any sandwich – anything but turkey, she said, because turkey would make her think of Dad and then she wouldn't be able to eat. So a ham sandwich. Or cheese. Cheese would be just fine. Any kind of cheese.

'Do you know the only time he ever let me and Sissy eat with them – at home anyways – was Christmas and Thanksgiving. And he always made me eat with the wrong hand. And he made us eat stuffing and cranberries and we used to be sick after.'

The girlish confidence was at once pitiful and pitiless.

'When he and Mother went on trips he used to arrange for the studio to make movies of us to send out to her in

New York or Paris or Cairo or wherever they were so she wouldn't miss us so much, so they could stay away longer. Mother always said the movies made her miss us even more. She still didn't come home, though.

'He wanted to give us both a screen test for a sixteenth birthday present. Mother thought not.' Paula jerked her head in the direction of a Chinese vase on the mantelpiece '*That* used to be one of a pair.'

She put a thumb under the diamond brooch on the collar of her jacket and tilted the stones to the light. It was shaped like a Greek alpha.

'He couldn't make my graduation.'

She gave Evelyn a goodbye kiss.

'So I guess I'm not sorry ...'

Funnily enough, it was that thought that made Paula Silverman start to cry. '*I'm not sorry,*' she repeated in a horrified whisper. 'He died and I'm not even sorry. Can you imagine that?'

'I think so.'

Chapter 17

I**T WAS GROWING DARK** by the time the last mourners had left – Mamie Silverman was beginning to think that Emily Post might have had a point. Evelyn helped the widow into her car and made her way back to the pool house across the Japanese bridge.

There was a glimmer of light at the far end of the path and the low, growling hum of machinery. She thought again of Martians at work. As she turned the corner by the yew hedge she saw something turquoise twinkling in the starlight through the screen of bamboo. The swimming pool had been filled and its underwater lights switched on. Steam was rising from the heated water. On the terrace beside it, ringed by a dozen rose bushes, Ted Monroe was stretched out on a steamer chair, popping macadamia nuts, Happy curled up on his chest.

'You took your time.' He passed her a fistful of kitten and got up from the chair to mix her a drink and light her a cigarette. Happy nuzzled against her cheek; his fur had the earthy, roguish smell of Cuban cigar.

'Your latchkey was under the mat. Have a nut. I found them in your kitchen – all the way from Hawaii: 2,500 miles – can you beat that?' He leaned down and blew a soft raspberry on the kitten's neck. 'We missed you. Your little Jap has been working overtime, he was only just finishing when I drove up. Can the English swim?'

The pool was the temperature of Woking bathwater and they floated up and down watched by a very wary kitten until Ted climbed out and reached down to pull her from the deep end then folded her in a towel and carried her bodily to the bedroom.

She was woken by Happy dancing on her chest to demand his breakfast. She opened a can then went out to the pool to clear the table. Her wedding band and engagement ring were nestling among the nutshells and she zipped them into the pocket of her handbag.

When she returned to the bedroom with a pot of coffee Ted Monroe was lying diagonally across the quilt, the muscles on his torso like the underside of a crab ('God has entrusted us with our bodies, those exquisitely wrought machines').

'You look very lovely this morning, Mrs Murdoch.'

Speaking her name seemed to jog his memory and he went out to the sitting room and pulled a studio document wallet from his briefcase.

'Della asked me to deliver this when I told her I was going to the funeral. You made me forget all about it.'

A magical hour later, after Ted had driven away, she sat down to read her post: a note from Kiss asking her to get to work translating *Puppy of the Baskervilles* into Spanish and a letter from Deborah with a Scottish postmark dated six days earlier. Deborah hadn't let the grass grow under her feet.

A man on the train said that Edinburgh was the Athens of the north, in which case God help the Greeks. What a dump. Dark, dirty buildings and I've yet to meet anyone with all ten front teeth. And as for the food? I know we used to joke about the school cabbage but it would make a nice change, I must say, to be offered a vegetable that had grown above ground.

Is it Silas, you ask? I wish I could give you a straight answer but to be perfectly honest it was very hard to tell and the beard is no help (they did try shaving him but said the screams distressed the other patients). It was all very difficult. He certainly seemed very pleased to see me but the matron says 'Patient D' is always like that (he's not the first case of amnesia they've had to deal with, obviously). He talks in a sort of music-hall Scots accent which was why they had him sent to Edinburgh in the first place before they'd got round to tracing you from the inscription in the Bible. He sounded pretty Harry Lauder to me and he must have sounded Scotch to the doctor from the hospital ship but of course now he's *here* the actual Scots all deny that any Scot ever actually *spook leek thot* but apparently the mind plays funny tricks when you've had shrapnel in it. The matron told me that she remembered a chap (I think this must have been the last war or possibly the Crimea or just conceivably Bannockburn), anyway a chap who had a bang on the head or gas or something who began speaking with a broad, bog-Irish brogue despite being born and bred in High Wycombe, so things could be a lot worse all things considered.

Matron did wonder where you were in all this. Which was a mite awkward, but I said Work of National Importance which worked like a charm. Is that even true? What do you do all day? You never send more than a postcard – careless talk, I suppose.

They finally got round to getting a photo taken so that his mother could have a look at him and she got very upset when she saw it (what with the beard and everything). 'Yes but is it Silas?' I ask. Silas didn't have a beard, she replies over and over, so no joy there. You can see her point about the beard. I drew one on a picture of Laurence Olivier in the paper and his mother wouldn't have known him either.

They asked me about distinguishing marks, and did he have a webbed toe or anything, and I said no thank you very much and they'd have to ask his wife or his mother. I did ask Mother when I got back and she said he cut his knee once when he was very small and she had kissed it better and then she started crying. Funny the things she remembers – so I don't think we're talking lifelong disfigurement. Was there anything? I was going to send you the snapshot they took but she has squirrelled it away somewhere.

I did show Beardie your photograph – that one at Runnymede – and he got quite excited although that may have been the bathing suit, I suppose (one of the straps is down, if you remember). We drew a blank on the blood group – even if the GP hadn't been bombed out I don't suppose he's seen him since measles and they don't exactly give you transfusions for that – so I'm pinning my hopes on the MO at the training place he went to who has yet to reply. I will get this off now and write again as and when.

PS. I found a *Picture Post* on the train home: 'A Plan for Britain', they called it: blocks of flats, plate glass all over, swings and roundabouts, injections, bottled orange juice, the New Jerusalem, all that. Post-war? They must know something we don't.

271

PPS. He insisted on kissing me goodbye and had a good old rummage if you know what I mean. Ring any bells?

Evelyn tore up half a dozen draft letters before deciding that a cable would be best: 'Please wire when man's identity confirmed. Good work. E.' She drove to the studio and gave the telegraph form to Miss Cavendish before walking over to Writers' Block.

'You OK, Toots?' asked Miss McAllister. 'You look like you'd seen a ghost.'

And Evelyn burst into tears again. Connie produced coffee and a compact and Felix said he had to dash off to a meeting with PZ but that he'd stand her lunch at the Brown Derby and why not try one of these? There was a dimpled white tablet in his hand and she swallowed it with a mouthful of coffee. *I've given her a sedative* … Only very much not a sedative. She was more than a third of the way through her Sherlock Holmes translation ('*Elemental, mi querido Watson*') when she noticed the time and drove to the restaurant in a sort of high-speed stupor.

Felix was enjoying his second cocktail at a window table, his chair turned around so that he could chat to the 'crazy Danish broad' who had made such a mess of Wally Grendon's soft furnishings, the sticking plaster across her nose imperfectly screened by the flocked black veil on her hat. He sprang to his feet and kissed Evelyn's hand before pulling out her chair.

'Did the rose trees arrive? I completely forgot to ask.'

She smiled her surprise.

'I saw the way you looked at the ones back at the studio so I fixed it with your gardener guy.'

'I bet Yuki had something to say about that. He's very territorial.'

272

'Who knows? He bowed a lot and said *"okama"* quite a bit. I guess we could look it up?'

'Probably best not. They're beautiful. Thank you.' He still had hold of her hand. 'So, how was your meeting?'

'Good. Pretty good. PZ says he loved the original story but that it was too depressing for a movie and he's right.' He let go of her hand and fumbled a cigarette from a new silver case. 'He's always right. It's still the same story – strange guy in a strange town – but we're changing the soundtrack, upping the tempo. Imagine Lubitsch let loose on *Anna Karenina* … On second thoughts: don't. We should order. The grills are good or we could have the Lobster Gumbo. PZ always has the Lobster Gumbo.'

'Is that really a dish? It sounds like the pen name of a hard-boiled novelist.'

And then she blushed. Perhaps no one was supposed to know about *The 29th Bather*? But Felix seemed surprisingly relaxed.

'Just as well I used an alias given the reviews it got. I'm sure Connie will have told you all about it. The *Atlantic* felt it lacked passion: "like a phallus made of marzipan".'

Evelyn hiccuped and took a sip of her cocktail.

'I quite like marzipan.'

It was Felix's turn to blush.

'I showed it to Von Blick when it was first published and he said he loved the homosexual angle so I said "What homosexual angle?" and he said "Ze two guys in ze apartment. Ferry interesting."' Felix shrugged. 'Hollywood. I need to wash my hands.'

The restaurant was very full and Evelyn had barely been able to hear Felix over the clatter and chatter but there was also an extraordinary whispering-gallery acoustic created

273

by the building's hat-shaped dome that made it seem as if distant diners were pouring their secrets into your ear.

'She has a telegram this morning sent.'

A familiar voice, a familiar German voice. Evelyn took her compact and located the speakers at the bar on the far side of the room: Joseph Weiss and chum.

'You thought she was just a decoy but it looks as if your pretty little English friend has penetrated your alias,' said Huber. 'She sent a telegram asking for your identity to be confirmed and one of the boys overheard her talking about "enemy post" at the Silverman funeral and she and Kiss were talking about Bermuda and she said something about a half-million banknote … It isn't clear how much she knows but you should head south and lie low for a month or two. Falsifying this new Alien Registration system is a federal offence. Get Guatemala to supply some new papers and you can start afresh. Your flight is from Glendale at seven in the morning. The necessary travel documents will be put in the usual luggage locker tonight.'

Evelyn put her compact away with trembling hands as Felix returned.

'You're looking brighter. Another cocktail?'

'Yes.' She was careful to speak very quietly. 'Do you think we might move over there? It's a bit draughty here by the window.'

If she could hear them, they could presumably hear her. Evelyn kept her back to the bar as she and Felix switched seats but the two Germans left as soon as they had finished their drinks.

'So. Are you going to tell me?'

'Tell you what?'

'What happened this morning?' He took her hand. 'I didn't have you down for the neurotic type.'

274

'I've had word from home. There's a man with amnesia in a hospital in Scotland. He had my husband's Bible in his pocket but nothing's been confirmed.'

'Really? What about dog tags? Fingerprints? Blood group?'

'They're looking into all that but it's very difficult. He was thought to have been killed at the River Plate and several of the bodies were quite badly burned so I suppose a mistake could have been made ... I doubt anyone will know his blood type. He was never ill. Deborah – his brother's wife – travelled up to Scotland but she didn't know Silas particularly well and the man had a beard ...'

'Jeez.'

Felix seemed depressed by Silas's feeble hold on identity.

'Surely his own sister-in-law would have recognised him? OK, so the guy had a beard and an accent but Spencer Tracy had a beard and spoka di Portuguese in *Captains Courageous* but we all still knew it was Spencer Tracy.'

'Yes, but you were looking at Spencer Tracy for whole scenes at a time. In close-up. Nobody inspects their brothers-in-law that minutely.'

'Whatever. She'd know. She's married to his brother, for God's sake. She'd know.' He kept tight hold of her hand. 'It must be tough.'

'It is. It is, you see, because –' her lips quivered and she felt silly suddenly, stagey '– it is because you see we weren't ... I wasn't terribly ... We hardly knew each other. We'd never ...'

And so she told him about Kowtow. She didn't have a key light on her face this time but she stuck to the same script and it worked the same magic. She had been afraid that he would hate her but the faint look of shock and discomfort turned to one of sympathy. He kissed her fingers.

'Don't cry. If he's dead he's dead. You grieved already.'

'And if he's alive?'

'So he's alive. *Mazel tov*. What's he going to do? Come and get you? Doesn't mean you have to go back. Why go back to a set-up that doesn't make you happy? Life's way too short. Get a different director.'

She gave a wobbly smile. If Lubitsch or Sturges or George Cukor or Otto Von Blick had had charge of her glum, rumba-less romance with Silas, someone else would have materialised by the sixth reel and given her a happy ending.

'Or get another soundtrack – or file for divorce – I know a lawyer – I know a couple of lawyers.' He still had hold of her hand and was buffing her ringless finger with his thumb. 'Get a divorce. You could get married again. People do it all the time. Marry me.' He pulled at his ear. 'Marry me. Fox always said I should settle down. He got engaged, did you hear that? He's only been gone ten days. The papers are calling it a whirlwind romance. She's his love interest in *The Lead Balloon*.'

Evelyn pulled her hand away.

'Please don't tease me.'

'I'm not teasing, Evie. Kiss cut you loose, didn't he? I heard Della Cavendish talking about it. Marry an American and you can stay, job or no job, Kiss or no Kiss. Think about it. We'd have a nice time.'

Nice.

'You'd die of shock if I said yes.'

'Try me. You're the writer and director on this story, Evie. It can end however you want.'

*

A familiar voice took the New York call.

'Is that Mr –?'

Jeremy Fitzmorton, HQ's man in Chicago, cut her off sharply.

'Such a jolly chinwag in the Maple Room, wasn't it? What can I do for you?'

'I thought I should let you know that our, er, competitor is going on a sales trip of some kind.'

She broke off. The silly salesman's banter didn't cover all eventualities and if Weiss could intercept telegrams – was Miss Cavendish to blame? – then there was no knowing who might be listening in. In despair she remembered Jeremy Fitzmorton's six months of Esperanto.

'Our man' – *nia viro* – 'has falsified his identity on his Alien Registration' – *registrio*. 'I believe he's planning to fly south tomorrow. He's to collect some papers' – *paperoj* – 'from left luggage at the airport before breakfast.'

She repeated her message in case Fitzmorton needed to jot it down phonetically and look it all up in a dictionary later but he signed off with a confident '*Bona laboro*'.

'I'm sorry we couldn't wangle your transfer. Tricky for you. Hope you get some good news.'

'I expect I'll manage.'

The main office was empty except for Desmond Colley who was seated at his typewriting table pecking out a memo to Miss Cavendish itemising his expenses.

'Are sunglasses chargeable?'

'I very much doubt it.'

'I was wondering – it's Evelyn, isn't it? – are you free this evening? I thought you might like to show me the sights?'

Mr Kiss had taken such pains to make Evelyn welcome but it was clear that his chivalry didn't extend to this spotty young novelist and nor had he sent Miss Cavendish shopping on his behalf – even the old, scruffy Felix would have drawn the line at those hairy tweeds. Evelyn felt slightly sorry for him but life was far too short to spend an evening in his company.

'I have a script to go through, I'm afraid, and I have plans. Another time?'

When she arrived home she saw a tiny stripy shape outlined on the windowsill. It jumped down and began rubbing against her ankles to make her smell more kitten-like. She fixed herself a tray of tea and went outside to sit by the swimming pool with Happy asleep in her lap and looked sadly across at the empty steamer chair beside her: *By night on my bed I sought him whom my soul loveth: I sought him but I found him not.*

The sun was already setting behind her as she drove across to West Hollywood. The mild night air of Hampton Avenue was heavy with heliotrope and late-flowering bergamot. She parked her car on the street outside a picture-book Arts and Crafts bungalow. There was no sign of life within but they had left the lights on and the curtains drawn back so that the interior was on display like a Dutch doll's house. The front sitting room glowed happy-ever-after and inviting: a Turkey carpet; Tiffany lamps like glacé fruit; a bowl of peaches on the table; a tabby waiting in the window. A canoe like the husk of a gigantic nut was resting comfortably against the side of the verandah behind a pair of slatted easy chairs (no fear of rain, or theft, or of being observed). The garden was a sea of blue agapanthus, and on the pavement out front a mound of yellow day lilies clustered around the trunk of a pepper tree like a starlet's bouquet.

The cats in the cobbled courtyard were gathered in a shrinking sunbeam and, down a crazy-paved path, some-one's pet rabbit was seated on top of a stone mushroom like a china ornament lit by the light from Ted Monroe's attic window.

She had the tiniest qualm as she turned into his doorway, thinking of the pilgrim-collared dresses in that orderly closet, but then she thought of his lips on her skin. One of the cats stretched to its feet and followed her into the narrow passageway and raced her up the staircase, nosing open the door at the top.

'You still hungry?' chuckled Monroe's voice as he crouched down to greet his furry friend. 'Sardines don't grow on trees, you know.'

'You sure about that?'

'Well look who the cat dragged in! Great dress! Is there a party I don't know about? Sit down, have some coffee.'

He shoved a pile of scripts to one side and made space for her at the end of his desk.

'I'm glad you came because Kiss handed me *that* on his way to the airport.' A small cream-coloured envelope was propped against the vodka bottle on the mantelpiece. 'He thought it might be important so he asked me to stop by your office on my way out but I forgot. Let me finish this and I'll be right with you.'

Deborah's note, marked 'Urgent and Confidential', was dated two days after her last letter and had been written in obvious haste.

You probably ought to sit down to read this. I wasn't sitting down when they telephoned and it gave me quite a turn. Anyway, you won't credit this but no one had thought to look at the man's teeth. If he'd been found in bits in a bamboo-banded trunk they probably would have but for some reason – pressure of work, who knows – they didn't bother until he developed an abscess at which point Mrs McMatron thinks 'funny'

279

and calls to ask about Silas's bridgework and we said
'What bridgework?' and then she said how well he
played the bugle and that put the tin hat on it rather.
It seems that our bearded friend was a musician in the
Royal Marines band on the *Exeter* and took a bang on
the head when the ship was hit. Lord knows where he
got poor Silas's Bible from. I wish in a way I hadn't
written before we knew for certain because now I will
have got your hopes up. I can't tell you how sorry I
am. I didn't write to Gilbert about it in the end so he
was spared all the worry. The Outlaw is upset, which
is natural, but the thought of the beard did bother her.
I still don't know what she did with the photograph.

It wasn't him. Shuddering with guilty relief, Evelyn
thought of all those monochrome movie heroines with
tragic telegrams crushed in their French manicured
fingers, hair rolled like skeins of pearl-grey wool, black
lips pulled into grimaces of pain, chalk-white faces dewy
with teardrops ready for their close-up: words delivered piecemeal like a dripping tap: So. He. Won't. Be.
Coming. Back. A hard act to follow. Who should direct?
Von Blick? ('a few feathers, some lights, a little smoke')
or Lubitsch? Could this all still pan out as a romantic
comedy? Without direction she was lost and she burst
into ugly tears of relief.

'Baby!' Ted's warm arms around her. 'Bad news?'

'No. Yes. No. Just a bad scare, that's all.'

'You need a drink. Then maybe we should go out some
place?'

Ted left the room and Evelyn refolded the paper and
tore it crossways into sixteen pieces and put the pieces
in the fireplace. The Bible was still on the mantelshelf
among the baseball guides. She teased it out and let it fall

open: '*Thou has turned for me my mourning into dancing: thou hast put off my sackcloth, and girded me with gladness.*'

'What are you doing?' Ted had returned. He was wearing a dinner jacket and had a glass in each hand.

'Asking advice.'

He switched on the radiogram and began knotting his bow tie in time to the dance music.

'I'm starving. Nito's? We could rumba?'

'You read my mind.'

Acknowledgements

These aren't real movie stars, these parties never happened and these films were never made. There was no Miracle Studios either but the British Security Coordination did briefly send an agent to Hollywood to help the British war effort and he really did have an assistant. That tantalising fact was the inspiration for this work of fiction.

HG Wells sold *War of the Worlds* to Paramount Pictures in 1926 but, although at least five scripts were kicked around, it wasn't filmed until 1953.

The US Senate's Foreign Relations Committee was due to investigate the Anglo-Hungarian film producer Alexander Korda on 12 December 1941 for alleged pro-British propaganda. The Japanese bombing of Pearl Harbour on 7 December meant that the scheduled meeting would never take place.

I should like to thank the staff of the British Library and the curators and docents of the galleries, houses and museums of Los Angeles. A generous grant from the Society of Authors made my research there possible.

My husband, Pete Mulvey, and dear friends Clement Crisp, Helen Garnons-Williams, Susannah Herbert and Kyran Joughin were kind enough to read and comment on early drafts of this book.

Thanks as always to Anna Webber of United Agents and to my editors Antonia Till and Alexa von Hirschberg and everyone at Bloomsbury Publishing.

A Note on the Author

Louise Levene is the author of *A Vision of Loveliness*, a BBC Book at Bedtime that was longlisted for the Desmond Elliott first novel prize, *Ghastly Business* and *The Following Girls*. She is a dance critic for the *Financial Times* and the *Spectator*. She has also been an advertising copywriter, a window dresser, a radio presenter, an office cleaner, a crossword editor, a university tutor, a college professor and a sales lady. Louise Levene lives in London with her husband and their two children.

A Note on the Type

The text of this book is set in Baskerville, a typeface named after John Baskerville of Birmingham (1706–1775). The original punches cut by him still survive. His widow sold them to Beaumarchais, from where they passed through several French foundries to Deberney & Peignot in Paris, before finding their way to Cambridge University Press.

Baskerville was the first of the 'transitional romans' between the softer and rounder calligraphic Old Face and the 'Modern' sharp-tooled Bodoni. It does not look very different to the Old Faces, but the thick and thin strokes are more crisply defined and the serifs on lower-case letters are closer to the horizontal with the stress nearer the vertical. The R in some sizes has the eighteenth-century curled tail, the lower case w has no middle serif and the lower case g has an open tail and a curled ear.